# BUTTERFLY
# BETRAYAL

# BUTTERFLY BETRAYAL

## A SENECA JAMES MYSTERY

## RUTH J HARTMAN

LEVEL
BEST BOOKS

Author Photo Credit: Iden Ford Photography

First edition

ISBN: 978-1-68512-497-7

Cover art by Level Best Designs

This book was professionally typeset on Reedsy.
Find out more at reedsy.com

*To all the farmers in my family, and the legacies they leave for us to enjoy.*

# Chapter One

Unless lying motionless in a puddle of blood was something my attorney routinely did, the poor man was probably dead. With care, trying not to step in the blood, I bent down and pressed my fingers to the side of his neck. No pulse. I wished it hadn't happened on my greenhouse floor. Once the initial jolt of finding my lawyer had worn off, I backed away, not wanting to be anywhere near the tragedy. Having discovered the man had been bad enough.

I yanked my phone from my apron pocket and dialed the sheriff. The sooner someone could get here, the better.

With a gasp, I jumped as something brushed against my bare ankle. "Winifred, you scared me to death."

My marmalade short-haired cat gazed at me with huge caramel eyes. She blinked, then locked her attention on Mr. Morton's still form.

"Oh, no, you don't." I scooped her up before she could saunter over to check him out. The thought of the poor man's blood on her white paws and whiskers made me ill. Finding a dead body, especially of someone I knew, seemed surreal. Part of me definitely saw him there, on my floor. The other part couldn't quite grasp it was real.

I patted my cat's wings. Not hers exactly, the ones on her butterfly costume. My crazy cat had a fit every morning if she didn't get to dress up. Since the monarch outfit was her favorite, it did wonders for publicity when people came to tour the butterfly farm or frequent my Painted Wings Café. My little furry advertisement.

I took her out of the greenhouse and into the bright sunlight. We both squinted. A few monarchs swirled around my face, one landing on Winifred's head. She let out a purr.

Winifred, not the butterfly.

Thankfully, my cat had never viewed them as live prey to hunt and maim. Or worse. Instead, she seemed to view the creatures as tiny friends.

A siren, shrill and long, sounded. Cody Bales, the town sheriff, would be here any second. I was so relieved it was still early in the day. The café wouldn't be open until noon, so at least there weren't customers milling around to see what all the fuss was about in the greenhouse.

As the vehicle zoomed up my long lane, Winifred pressed close to my chest, but she didn't claw at me to get down. She might be a tad skittish at loud noises, but it wouldn't stop her from sticking around to see what happened next.

Nosy cat. I could never get anything past her. Try as I might, I couldn't even eat a snack in my kitchen without her glaring at me until I shared. One time she'd even discovered me sitting behind the dryer while I wolfed down some chocolate chip cookies.

Not that I was hiding.

My lifelong friend, Cody, shut his car door and approached me with his loose-limbed amble. "Hey, Seneca. I think the dispatcher got the message mixed up when you called. Something about a dead body. I'm guessing something happened to your monarchs, instead?"

"Nope. The message was right. There's a body in my..." I vaguely gestured toward the greenhouse.

His eyes opened wide. "You're kidding."

"Not so much."

"Whoa." He shook his head like he had cleared out cobwebs. "Who—"

"Herman Morton."

Cody's mouth hung open for a second. He snapped it closed, then pointed toward the open greenhouse screen door. "Let's...have a look." But he didn't take a step. Just stood there for several seconds, blinking. Finally, he turned and headed that way.

I followed behind, but at a distance, not loving the idea of seeing all that blood again. "It ain't pretty in there," I said. I dreaded the thought of having to clean up the morbid mess. What had happened to the lawyer? And why in my greenhouse? I hadn't had an appointment with him today, so I couldn't imagine why he would have been here. Especially this early in the day. Had he fallen and cracked his head on the concrete floor?

Slowly, as if someone might jump out at Cody from one of the butterfly pens, he crept down the left aisle. Not wanting to, but making myself, I went too. I happened to know he'd never processed a possible murder before. In our town, the biggest event in the last few years had been Miss Philly Greenfield frolicking in the town square fountain wearing nothing but a hot pink thong.

Philly was ninety-two.

"Holy cow." Cody rubbed his hand along his clean-shaven chin as he stared at the crumpled, still body. "Who would have…. Why do you think….?"

I patted him on the shoulder. "That's why we have you, lucky man."

His Adam's apple rode up then down his throat as he swallowed hard. "Apparently." He reached into his pocket and removed a pair of disposable gloves. Snapping them on, he took a deep breath. As Cody carefully avoided the giant dark-red congealing pool, he pressed his fingers to Mr. Morton's neck. "No pulse, as expected."

"Right. I discovered that when I checked."

He peeked at me over his shoulder. "You touched the body?"

"Wasn't I supposed to? Make sure he was breathing or not?"

"Um, yeah."

"Plus, his body is cold." A shiver ran across my shoulders. "Didn't take that to be a good sign."

"Probably not," he said. "You found him how long ago?"

"Just now, right before I called."

Cody studied the door to the greenhouse. "Didn't see any sign of forced entry. But you lock it at night, right?"

I let out a sigh. Under normal circumstances, I wouldn't bother with the locks. The town was so small, and everyone knew everyone. But when your best friend was the sheriff and lectured you if things weren't secure, you tried to go the extra mile. "Of course."

"Aside from checking for a pulse, you didn't touch him, though?"

I grimaced. "No."

I must have squeezed Winifred without realizing. She let out a quick warning growl deep in her chest.

"Sorry," I said.

"Sorry for…." Cody frowned.

"Not you."

He eyed Mr. Morton, then me. "Seneca, why would you have to apologize to him?"

"No." I tilted my head toward my cat. "Her."

Cody's eyebrows rose for a second, then lowered. "Ah." There was no way he could understand what I meant, but he'd known me enough years to let it go while he had the chance.

I'd been told I tended to ramble when talking about my cat. Not that I thought that was true, and not that there was anything wrong with that.

After removing his gloves and turning them inside out, Cody stuffed them into a plastic evidence bag he'd had in another pocket. Investigating this death would let him use some tools and equipment he probably didn't often get to. But maybe that wasn't a good thing. Too bad we didn't have the luxury of a large staff of medical people to help do the job. In a town this small, there was no budget for additional assistance. Other than a part-time deputy, Cody was on his own.

Cody, of course, had been present at sites where town members had died of natural causes or farming accidents, but this was different. My friend's face had gone pale. Cody, six-foot-two with wide, muscular shoulders, had been the top wide receiver for our high school football team. I'd never seen him balk at doing anything. The guy was fearless. But this…maybe murder. Not a person's everyday task. Not even for a sheriff, at least not one from here.

Another trip to his car and he came back, this time with the sheriff department's camera. Then, picture after picture flashed, the light so bright Winifred growled and buried her face in my neck.

Next came some tweezers. Fascinated, I watched as Cody picked up various tiny pieces from the floor—grass, a thread, maybe a strand of hair—and placed them in individual baggies. My pride in him grew. Of course, he knew what he was doing while collecting evidence, having been trained and done the job for years, but Mr. Morton appeared to have been bludgeoned to death.

A whole new ballgame.

After stepping away, he headed out the doorway, then phoned the funeral director. Winifred and I followed. She might have wanted to stay and do her own investigation, but I needed some fresh air. Too bad the young monarch butterflies were stuck in there with a dead guy.

Cody slid his phone inside his shirt pocket. "He's on his way." Since the funeral home sat over the rise on the edge of town, Arnold would be here soon. Small towns operated differently than larger cities. There wasn't the same budget for personnel to attend death scenes. Here, our coroner was voted in and wasn't always a physician or even medical staff. Right now, it happened to be our funeral director.

I bumped my friend with my shoulder, something he and I had done to each other since we were kids. Although, when we were little, my shoulder and his had been more on the same level. Now, it was like an ant trying to knock over a tractor. "Thanks for coming," I said.

"It's my job."

"I know, but…. Well, this is something new for you."

"Yeah," said Cody. "Guess chasing Philly won't be the most outrageous thing to happen around here anymore."

"Guess not."

Cody reached out and patted Winifred on the head. "I see she opted for the monarch costume today."

"Yep. It's her favorite. Although, she does love the swallowtail outfit you gave her last Christmas. She likes to sleep in that one."

"Cat's pajamas."

I gave him a slight one-sided grin. "True."

Vehicle tires on gravel made us both turn.

Cody let out a long breath. "Here we go."

Arnold Wellings, the funeral director, drove at a snail's pace up the drive. But then, why would the man be in a hurry? It wasn't as if the person in the greenhouse was tapping his foot, impatient to get on with things. Wellings, a skinny, pale man in his mid-seventies with a crooked nose, appeared perpetually tired. His job wasn't a cheery one, though, so maybe there wasn't anything to get excited about.

Some people thought I was strange for being passionate about butterflies— I raised them to sell to zoos, museums, and schools and to be released at weddings and memorial services, plus they entertained customers at my café by flying around—but at least my clients were breathing. Still, I was glad someone in our town was willing to do his job. Gruesome but necessary.

Greeting us with nothing more than a curt head bob, Arnold ambled past and gazed at Mr. Morton. He squatted on his haunches, brown leather boat-sized shoes squeaking, and touched the deceased on the side of the neck. Arnold's hands were gloved. Funny, I hadn't seen him snap them into place. Did he go around town with them on, hoping to encounter someone who'd stopped breathing? It was the man's bread and butter, after all.

Bread. Butter. Dead bodies...

Repulsed at the idea of those together, I backed up a few steps, gasping when I hit a solid wall of chest. Whipping around, I stared at Cody. "Sorry."

His large hands steadied my shoulders. "Not the first time, is it?"

That much was true. Over the years, he'd been bumped into or had his feet stepped on multiple times. Graceful, I wasn't. Winifred squirmed for me to let her go, but that wasn't going to happen. No way did she need to get involved in what was going on.

The sound of arthritic knees popping had us both focusing again on Arnold. Now he stood a foot away from the body, writing something on a small form, the knobby knuckles of his hands appearing odd above such thin fingers. He handed the paper to Cody, then gave a sharp nod.

I frowned—couldn't help it. It was almost like Arnold had given Cody a receipt for Mr. Morton's stiff body. How morbid.

Cody re-gloved then helped the funeral director zip poor Mr. Morton into a black, shiny body bag and loaded him into the back of the hearse. During the whole time, Arnold hadn't uttered a syllable. Strange duck.

We squinted against the sun, watching the black hearse leave. With silent Arnold and not-breathing Mr. Morton, that would be one quiet ride.

"You okay, Seneca?" Cody stuffed the used gloves in a baggie.

I blinked, then focused on my friend. "What?"

"Are. You. Okay."

Right then, it hit me. Hard. A man, someone I knew, someone I'd done business with, was dead, had died on my floor. He'd left a stain of his life's blood right below one of my butterfly pens. I started to shake. My limbs went ice cold. Would I pass out?

"Here." Cody wrapped his arms around Winifred and me. "Shock has set in. Normal under the circumstances."

I nodded, my hair rasping against Cody's brown uniform shirt. He held me for a couple of minutes before I gently pulled away. His arms around me felt natural, though nothing more was read into it. He and I had been such close friends for so long, we'd often been mistaken for more. Somehow, we'd never been anything other than buddies. I'd hate to chance taking it further. If it didn't work out, I might lose the best friend I'd ever had.

"Feeling better?" he asked.

When his voice jolted me back to the unpleasant present, I bit my lower lip and nodded.

"How about I clean up this mess?" He thumbed behind us.

Eyeing the dark red puddle, I wanted nothing more than to have someone else make it go away, to take my hose and wash the bloody atrocity down my floor drain. But that wasn't how things worked, at least not for me. My life had changed drastically after my divorce. Now, things were up to me instead of being half of a couple. "No. You go on ahead. You have other things to take care of besides me."

His dark-blond eyebrows lowered over his brown eyes. "I don't mind. Honest. And as sheriff, I should do it anyway."

I shook my head. "I know. Go on, though. It's all good." I mentally cringed. Not good. I just didn't want to become too dependent on someone else.

Anyone else. As much as I loved Cody as a friend, I'd been independent for a couple of years now, doing things on my own, running the business, and taking care of most things alone.

Ever since my ex and I split.

Payne and I'd had a final argument so big, so loud, I was surprised it wasn't written up in the *Junction Gazette*. It didn't matter, though. Word of mouth got the message around in no time flat.

Cody eyed me, concern evident on his features. "Listen, I got some evidence from the body, but want a second look around. I'll block off the area temporarily, come back, and do another check for anything out of the ordinary. I need some time to think all of this through."

He rubbed the back of his sunburned neck.

I cradled the cat with one hand and grabbed Cody's arm with the other. I tugged him toward his truck. "Get moving, Sheriff. Do what you need to here, then—"

He halted so suddenly I nearly stumbled. "Seneca, we do need to talk about this."

Trying to appear tougher than I felt, I stood up straighter. "I'll be fine, Cody."

"You and I need to talk about what happened. There'll be an autopsy to see what he died of. Whether an accident or…" He obviously didn't want to say the word.

I sure didn't want to hear it. "Oh. That," I said.

"Yep. That. There must be some reason why he died here, on your property." When I didn't say anything, he sighed. "Okay. I won't push you to discuss this now. But we will. And soon."

I shrugged, knowing he was right but not wanting to admit it. I waited as he made another trip to his truck and returned with yellow crime scene tape to block off the area outside the greenhouse door.

Winifred, too interested in what Cody might be up to, growled when I repositioned her and held her tight. I grimaced at the image of her snooping around in the mess. White paws and red blood…not a good combination.

Once Cody had finished and left, I stepped around the taped-off area and took a minute to check on the newly hatched butterflies. They were fluttering nicely and seemed happy. I was glad the mayhem of having possibly witnessed a murder hadn't upset them.

Too bad they couldn't talk. Then we'd know what really happened.

Although, part of me was afraid to find out.

# Chapter Two

After Mr. Morton's tragedy, I needed to escape the confines of the greenhouse. I still couldn't believe what happened to my lawyer and that it'd happened here.

Several minutes later, I had all the windows raised and had even propped open the screen door to let in as much fresh air as possible. I tried not to picture the man's crumpled body, his blood splattered across the floor. For me, at least, the shock effect was delayed. After I'd found him and checked he wasn't breathing, I'd stared at him, as if I could make some sense of what I was seeing. When Cody had shown up, it still hadn't seemed real.

Until it did.

Was my experience with shock the same as others? Or was I simply slow on the uptake, as my grandma used to say? Either way, not enjoyable, and I wouldn't wish it on anyone.

Even my ex.

I exchanged my rubber boots for walking shoes, checked the butterflies one more time, then retrieved Winifred from the house where I'd temporarily stashed her, and took off. She followed me as I hiked toward the edge of my property, the side adjoining the land I desperately needed to purchase. I always kept a good eye on her. While milkweed ingested in large quantities could be harmful to cats, Winifred had never shown the slightest interest in eating it. If it wasn't tuna or kitty treats, she turned up her little pink nose at it.

Although she'd followed me there countless times, I guessed she never remembered what a long walk it was for short legs on furry paws. If she ever got lethargic and began to wilt, I picked her up and carried her like the royalty she was. Sometimes, I wondered if she thought she was part dog, trailing behind me like that. Most often, she only allowed me to be in her company on her own terms.

The hot sun beat down on my bare shoulders and face, ensuring a burn later. With all the commotion earlier, I'd gotten out of my daily routine, forgotten the sunscreen and my hat. It bothered me being out of my usual practice, not having everything in order. I was a creature of habit every bit as much as my monarchs, as if some instinct drove me to keep everything in line, in perfect rhythm with my world.

Surely, in a few days, everything would get back to normal. Dr. Reynolds, Arnold's cousin, would do an autopsy. They shared an office, but Dr. Reynolds served a large area, so was often out of town. Hopefully, he'd be available to do an autopsy soon. That might show Mr. Morton died of an accidental fall. It was possible, right?

Cody hadn't seemed to think so. In truth, I agreed with him. That meant the comfortable, safe existence on my farm, in the tiny town I loved, might not return as soon as I'd like, if at all.

Winifred trotted next to me, only falling behind every so often to sniff wildflowers or stalk a grasshopper. At least she didn't try to catch the butterflies. If she did, we'd have a heart-to-heart about not only that, but her habit of somehow sneaking into the greenhouse without me knowing. One of these days, I'd figure out how she did it.

The cat halted, flopped down, and rolled around in what appeared to be an ecstatic frenzy of happiness, making me laugh. She'd found my patch of catnip again.

"Yes, I know, kitty. All God's felines adore catnip, don't they?"

My cat glanced up and smiled, her eyes closed to slits as she jackknifed to the left, then to her tummy, then returned to her back. She pawed at the air toward something. Did catnip cause hallucinations? Maybe she batted at butterflies I couldn't see. When I continued my walk, she gave a loud mew of resignation and tromped along. Winifred's expressions often reminded me of a person's. I had a good idea she thought she was one of those, too.

Checking the milkweed as we passed, I nodded in approval. It was tall and healthy, with monarchs fluttering everywhere. Black and orange flying flowers—Gram's words. She was right. They were beauty in motion. My parents, who'd left our Indiana town and retired to Florida, had never been as fond of the little creatures.

I, however, had been smitten for as long as I could remember and had begged my parents to visit the farm more often than they would have liked. That was probably why Gram left the land to me. Mom and Dad hadn't been offended by that; in fact, they were thrilled that having it brought me joy.

The farther Winifred and I traveled, however, my good mood faded. Nearer my neighbor's property, the decline in butterflies was obvious. I'd checked them only a couple of days ago over here. How had things changed so quickly?

Then I had my answer.

My neighbor, Hal Atkins, stood a few yards ahead with a pressure washer attached to an extended hose from his barn. It took a few seconds for my mind to catch up to what I saw.

The man had his hose out and was spraying my monarchs. That would kill them.

"Hey!" I took off running, waving my arms. "Stop that!"

The noise of the water must have drowned out my voice. Either that or he ignored me. I ran faster, hoping to save as many of the butterflies from being chased off or destroyed as I could. Winifred kept up with me until we got close enough to the stream of water to get damp. She stopped, arched her back, and hissed.

Closer now, I grabbed Hal's arm, trying to deflect the spray in the other direction. What did he think he was doing?

He frowned, like I was the one trespassing, breaking the law. "Get off."

My mouth dropped open. "What—" Stunned, I let my hand slide from his arm. Why was he being so mean, so hateful? It was bad enough he'd defaulted on our agreed-upon sales contract for his land, but why was he intentionally trying to destroy my monarchs? "Have you gone crazy?" I grabbed for the hose again but touched only air. A third try, and my foot slid across the muddy dirt. My knees hit the ground. Finally finding a foothold on a few rocks, I got back up.

Hal moved closer to the milkweed. The monarchs batted their wings furiously as they attempted to stay perched on the stalks. A harsh, fast bolt of water drove them away. A couple were floundering on the ground. They would die.

"No! Don't!" I leapt forward to scoop them up, hustling them away a few feet to a dry area. Hopefully, they'd be okay. With anger I was sure showed on my face, I glared at Hal as I marched back toward him. Whether it was my expression, or Hal had snapped out of his temporary insanity, I didn't know, but he angled the spray away from the milkweed.

Finally, he turned a knob on the hose, and the water died down like a balloon losing its helium. With an exaggerated sigh, he said, "Just had to get in the way, didn't ya?"

Shaking my head, I stared at him. "I don't know what possessed you to do this or begin to know why you've made such a turnaround from how you used to be. Have you lost your mind?"

His eyes narrowed. "Things would turn out much better for you if you'd just leave it be."

Leave it be? My hands landed hard on my hips. "Now, hold on. I'm not gonna stand by and let you destroy my property and my livelihood because you've got a screw loose. I hate to say it, Hal, but you need to get off my property. Now." I pointed, as if he wouldn't know where my land ended and his began.

"You don't know what you're messing with, Seneca." He didn't budge.

At least he remembered my name. For a minute, I'd been afraid he'd lost his marbles. Still, something bad was up. "What are you talking about? It makes no sense why you're trying to get out of our contract. That's bad enough. But attempting to get rid of my monarchs? What did they ever do to you?"

He didn't answer. Instead, he grabbed the hose and began to coil it into circles from his shoulder to his elbow and back, the rubber of the hose squeaking with each turn. Thank goodness he was putting his hose away.

That still didn't explain why he'd been spraying the milkweed in the first place. No matter how I tried to figure it out, there was no sensible reason why my neighbor was trying to harm the monarchs. Was it some type of mental glitch? He was in his eighties. Maybe he'd had a stroke or something. If I tried to talk some sense into him, would he listen?

I touched his arm to get his attention, but he pulled away. With something akin to Winifred's growl, Hal kept coiling the hose. The shorter it became, the more steps he took toward his property.

Hal never said another word, didn't even glance my way again. What had happened to change him? This was someone who'd always had my back as my neighbor and had assured me for years that as soon I was ready to buy, he'd sell. He'd said he wouldn't sell to anyone else because he understood how much his land, full of milkweed for the monarchs, would mean to me.

With the precious monarchs now headed closer toward extinction, it was more important than ever that their habitat stay intact. I hated to even think about a world where the black and orange beauties wouldn't exist. I'd confided that, as the swarm grew, we'd outgrow the milkweed I had available. And over time, we'd require the vast amount of it on his land. The only way for me to stay ahead of things financially was to increase my monarch numbers. And the sole way to do that was to acquire Hal's land.

My neighbor had been so supportive. He even helped me out a few times on the farm when I'd first taken over from Gram. He hadn't known much about the butterflies and their habits, but he'd assisted me with fixing broken machinery and repainting my barn. The sole reason he kept the milkweed growing on his land, instead of plowing it under, was out of respect for Gram and what she'd started here. Up until now, he'd shown me the same courtesy.

Had someone else, for whatever reason, convinced him not to sell to me?

But why? What reason would be so secret he couldn't tell me?

Fuming, I watched him head back to his own barn. I grabbed my cell phone from my jeans pocket and dialed Cody.

After the first ring, he answered. "What's up, Seneca?"

It was then I realized I should have called the sheriff's line, not his personal

14

one. They recorded calls for all crimes reported. Too late now.

"Hey, Cody, have a situation here."

A sound, like a small gasp, came from the phone. "Not another body?"

"No, thank goodness. But you know my neighbor, Hal?"

"Sure. Nice guy."

"That's what I thought," I said.

"What do you mean?"

"He…." I was still so angry I was shaking. "I caught him using a pressure washer on my butterflies."

"Why?"

"For whatever insane reason, he was trying to kill them."

Silence.

I watched as my neighbor left his barn and went toward his house.

"So…what should I do?" I asked Cody.

He let out a loud breath. "You're right. It does sound weird. Listen, I'm in the middle of a lengthy meeting with the mayor, so if this isn't life or death, I'll be with you later today. You okay till then?"

"Yeah. Thanks." I ended the call and glanced around. It actually might be life or death for my butterflies, but nothing Cody could fix if he came right away or a little later. Hal was now nowhere to be seen, so at least the confrontation was over.

The pressure hose had done some damage. An entire row of milkweed sat in a sodden lump on the ground. The good news was the butterflies seemed to be calming a little. Gone was the frantic fluttering, instead replaced by their normal, gentle flapping of wings. I would have to check later to see the full extent of the damage, searching deeper into the milkweed patch. That wasn't something to look forward to.

Remembering the two butterflies I'd moved, I hurried to check on them. One was sitting in place, its wings slowly moving up and down. The other one, though…

It wasn't moving. Not a wing. Or an antenna. A tear rolled down my cheek as I gently scooped the little guy up, watching him lie lifeless on my palm. "I'm sorry, little one. Sorry I wasn't here to protect you." How many more would I find once I checked more closely? Seeing the tiny broken body sent pain straight to my heart.

Why had Hal done this? And how was I to prevent it from happening again?

After catching my neighbor in his crime, and his default on our agreed contract to buy part of his land, I needed an attorney more than ever. I bit the bullet and dialed my ex-husband's number. Normally, I did whatever I could to avoid Payne. Now I had no choice. If I didn't settle matters with my neighbor and soon, my monarchs wouldn't last the season.

"This is Payne James."

Clutching the phone tighter, I said, "It's me."

I could almost hear his lips curve into the smirky grin he wore a lot. "Seneca. Have you changed your mind? Miss me?"

On the tip of my tongue was, not in this lifetime or any other, but unfortunately, I needed him. "Listen, this is a business call."

Something shuffled. "What business?"

"I need an attorney, Payne."

"Thought you used that other guy."

"Mr. Morton is, was...uh—" I stammered.

"Did he refuse to work with you anymore?" He laughed so loud, I pulled my cell away from my ear for a second.

"No, Payne. He's dead." There, I'd gone and done it. My ex-husband couldn't keep a secret. Not the best quality in a lawyer, but I had to tell him why. If I didn't, he'd just goad me and make up his own reasons until I fessed up.

"You don't say." More laughter.

Too bad Payne was the only legal choice now in Maple Junction. I waited until his mirth subsided, which took longer than it should have. Finally, he'd calmed down to an occasional chuckle.

Irritated, I tapped my finger against the side of the phone. "Yeah, he died today. Or last night… Either way, he was working on a case for me. So now I—"

"Now you need me. This is awesome."

I dug my fingernails into the plastic phone case, not caring if it left permanent indentations. Hating to say the words, I blurted out, "Yes, I need you. Can you take my case?"

Knowing him as I did, his mind was twisting all possible outcomes into something that would benefit only him. He didn't disappoint. "I'll do it, if—"

*Here it comes.*

"—you give a flattering testimony to everyone in town about my law practice. Morton stole a lot of my clients over the years. Though, I guess he won't be doing that now, will he? Still, another lawyer could always take over his office, so I need all the help I can get."

I let out a breath. Part of me had been so afraid he'd ask for us to get back together. Telling people Payne did his job well? No sweat—even if I had to fib a little to do it. "Deal."

"All right." A scraping sound came through the phone. Had he pulled up a chair to his desk? "What's the case?"

"It's about the monarchs. They—"

He groaned. "Not that again."

Unfortunately, it had been an ongoing argument while we were married. He thought the butterfly farm was a hobby. Couldn't understand why anyone would get so worked up about them. But to me, it was more of a calling. My grandmother had left me the farm. She'd always loved monarchs and instilled that love in me. When she died, we released several dozens of them. As the orange and black beauties fluttered upward, I sensed my grandmother's spirit ascending with them, finally free from pain, at peace at last.

"Listen, Payne, it shouldn't matter to you what the case is. You agreed to take it, and we have a deal. You do this for me, win this case, I'll even take out ads in the *Gazette* about your astounding law practice." Saying those words nearly gagged me, but I forced them out.

"Fine. So, give me the details."

I paced back and forth, ready to dive into the particulars, seriously wishing it wasn't necessary. "Okay. The property next to me, Hal Atkins—"

"Yeah, I remember," he said. "Go on."

This was going to be extremely annoying if he kept tossing in that he already knew everything about me. Unfortunately, he pretty much did.

"Anyway," I went on, "I need that land for the milkweed."

"For the *butterflies*." He said the last word like it had caught his tongue on fire, and he couldn't wait to spit it out. He'd always hated them, probably because they were so important to me.

"Yes, the butterflies. I don't have enough land to plant more milkweed for them to lay their eggs on or for the caterpillars to eat. They'll all die out if I'm unsuccessful in getting more land."

"These insects are really that important to you, Seneca?" He already knew the answer and was probably hoping to annoy me further.

"Very important."

Payne sighed into the phone. "Continue."

"Mr. Atkins had told me for years I could buy that extra acreage from him whenever I wanted. That he wasn't in a hurry to sell, that it would be there when I was ready."

"And..." Was he circling his hand in the hurry-up motion? It was one of his favorite things he did when he was impatient, which was often.

"He reneged. I approached him about it, all ready to pay him, and reminded him of our signed contracts, and he informed me something better had come along. I told him I'd have my lawyer speak to him, but he wouldn't budge. Now Mr. Morton is no longer with us..."

"You want me to take care of this." Payne's voice held a definite note of satisfaction.

"Yes. He won't listen to me. I need the milkweed on that property. That's the job. When can you start?" So far, the conversation hadn't gone nearly as awful as I'd imagined.

"I'll start...right after you have dinner with me."

I huffed out a breath, hating this, but somehow not surprised. The last thing I wanted was to spend time with him. He always liked to be in control. That was one reason I couldn't stay with him. I'd felt like I was choking, drowning, when we were together. Was I so desperate to work with him? Yes, unfortunately. "Fine. One dinner."

"We'll see." He laughed. "Wednesday night. Teddy's Bar. I'll pick you up at seven."

"No. I'll meet you there at seven." I ended the call before he could argue.

# Chapter Three

I stopped by my café, Painted Wings, a half hour after my cousin, Evie, opened it for the day. She and I were born on the same day and had always lived in the same town, so we were more like sisters than cousins. I needed to speak to Evie, in private, to tell her about all that had been going on. It wasn't something I wanted to text her or tell her over the phone. No, one family member finding out another had discovered a corpse in her greenhouse was definitely face-to-face news.

She was standing close to the entrance beside the open door. Giving me the thumbs-up, she continued her conversation with Mable Kane, one of our town's treasured octogenarians, who still volunteered at the local library. Actually, Evie wasn't talking, just listening. Obviously, she wouldn't have time to slip away for a conversation with me. I'd have to catch her later.

I liked to check to make sure things were running smoothly, but also, it was a great way to find out the scuttlebutt happening around Maple Junction. If anything had happened, or was going to, at least one of my fellow citizens would know. Mainly, I wanted to see if word had somehow leaked out about poor Mr. Morton.

For Painted Wings, I'd also been lucky to have found Murray Grimes, a cook who could perform miracles with sandwiches, sides, and appetizers. In his fifties, he had one of those mustaches like some I'd seen pictures of from the Old West—long, white, and fluffy. The man was surly and gruff, kind of like a walrus in a perpetual bad mood, but underneath, the guy was a softie. I'd seen him talk encouragingly to butterflies who happened to wander into the cooking area, gently shooing them back out onto the patio portion of the building so they wouldn't come in harm's way from the hot grill.

Most townspeople, though, only saw the grumbly side of Murray, brushing aside his often sarcastic comments. However, it all worked. Citizens of Maple Junction were used to him, and visitors to the café often commented on the quaint butterfly theme of the eatery and the quirky man who fixed amazing meals. Anything to bring in customers was all right with me.

Murray's bushy eyebrows lowered as he peered at me from across the room. "Finally decided to grace us with your presence, Seneca?"

I gave him a mock glare. "Now, you know how busy my days are. I can't stand here doing nothing, watching the world go by."

He waved me away with his hand. "Well, you're not the only one with work to do." He walked away, back to the kitchen, to create his masterpieces of culinary delight.

I stepped into the bar area, glad to see several of the tall stools at the front counter filled with customers. As I glanced around, my heart warmed as I could count each person there as a friend. "Hey, all." I gave a wave.

"Hey, Seneca," said Mike Larsh, a twentysomething convenience store employee. He'd glanced up from his paperback book, the cover sporting a man dressed in colonial garb. Mike was super sweet, but odd for his age. None of his peers seemed interested in actual books, just their phones.

I smiled at Mike, then headed back to the counter where Murray waited for me. Without a "hello," "having a good day?" or even "how's your mama?" the cook handed me a diet pop with strawberry flavoring added. No having to ask for what I wanted, no waiting in line. Being the owner definitely had its perks.

Three ladies who often met here for lunch were perched on the farthest right stools. All the women were somewhere in the range of mid-thirties and had a couple of kids each.

Betty Rollings ran the local flower shop. Sitting next to Betty was Linda Princeton, who owned a quaint bookstore on Autumn Street. Though the shop was small, Linda made sure to always have a good supply of new releases and best sellers in stock. Plus, she was quick to order anything for a customer she didn't already have. On Linda's other side was Millie King.

Millie had worked at the local parks and recreation office for as long as I could remember. Really nice ladies, all of them.

Between the three of them, they frequently knew the lay of the land—well, at least in our little town. If they'd heard anything about Mr. Morton, I was sure they wouldn't be shy but instead would come out and tell me about it.

Moving closer, I leaned against the counter to Betty's left. "How're you all doing?" Trying to appear nonchalant, I took a long sip of my drink.

Linda leaned forward to see me better. "Hey, Seneca. We're fine. Just talking about the latest."

I stirred the straw around in my drink as I waited for more. "Oh, what's that?"

Millie eyed the other two. "Well, I have a new boss. There's a new forest ranger."

Relieved the big news wasn't anything more than that, I let out a breath. "Really? I didn't realize Ranger Nelson was leaving."

"Neither did I. Or anyone else."

"A surprise, then?" I asked.

"Very much so. The new guy is very nice. We get along well, and he's excited to be in Maple Junction. He just isn't Ranger Nelson. Even though my former employer could be too serious at times, I'd worked for him for so long. I'll miss him."

I nodded. The park ranger had been there since I was a kid. "Is he still in the area?"

Millie shook her head. "No one knows."

That seemed odd. "Didn't he say where he was going on his last day?"

Millie frowned. "That's just it. I didn't see him. Or talk to him. He left a note on his desk, typed out but signed. That's how he always wrote notes. His handwriting was nearly indecipherable. I found it when I went in the other day. I'm sure he talked it over with someone at the State Department level, but it stings a little that he said nothing to me."

Linda tilted her head. "Maybe he was ill or just ready to move on."

"Yeah. Maybe." Millie shrugged her shoulders but didn't look convinced.

At the very least, word of the dead lawyer, just fifty yards from where we stood hadn't gotten out yet. It would. I knew that. But the longer it stayed quiet, the better. Once that hit the fan, it would be all anyone would talk about, at least until the next newsworthy story took its place. Although, I couldn't imagine much topping the news of one of Maple Junction's own being murdered.

Two monarch butterflies picked that moment to float in through the open doorway, twirling around each other in a lovely, choreographed dance of orange and black wings. I grinned. Though I spent every day with the painted beauties, I was nevertheless impressed every time I saw one.

All the ladies looked down and smiled. Was there another butterfly on the floor? I'd need to move it, so it didn't get stepped on.

Glancing in that direction, my grin grew wider. My cat had decided to join us. "Winifred," I said, "hello, dear."

After setting my drink on the counter, I picked her up. Her butterfly costume shimmered in the bright rays of sunshine that poured in from the skylights.

Betty held out her hand and wiggled her fingers. "Hey there, Winnie."

I stroked the cat's silky fur a few moments longer, until she gave me a low growl. Time to put her down. She liked being petted, but when she was done, she was done. After lowering her gently to the floor, I watched as my cat haughtily strolled, tail pointed straight up, toward the open doorway and out into the sunny day.

Since it seemed nothing of real note had happened, it was time for me to get back to work. Butterflies needed lots of daily care, checking the larvae in the cages, walking out to my field to make sure the adults were flourishing and were getting enough room on my current supply of milkweed to eat and lay eggs, making sure the area around the milkweed was free of weeds so the milkweed could grow healthy and strong. But standing here in my café wouldn't get it done. With a final wave at the ladies, I turned toward the door.

Johnny Overmeyer, a retired insurance salesman, sat near the entrance. I headed that way. "Hi, Johnny."

"Hey, there." Johnny gave me a saucy wink, a daily occurrence. Though he was in his eighties, he liked to flirt with every female around. All harmless. And with his bright blue eyes and thick white hair, the effect was adorable.

Ready to walk on by and get back to the greenhouse, I stopped short when Johnny held up his hand.

He swallowed a bite of his grilled cheese and tomato, then said, "Heard you had a little trouble 'round here."

*Here it comes.* "Oh? What did you hear?"

"'Bout that man."

Trying not to get too overworked so I wouldn't get visibly upset in front of customers, I blinked and forced my voice to remain calm. "Which man?"

He pointed his thumb over his shoulder. "That neighbor. Hal Atkins."

My shoulders slumped as I relaxed. "Oh. Hal." I hadn't remembered seeing anyone else around my milkweed. How had Johnny heard about it? Had Hal been mouthing off to whoever would listen, somehow placing the blame on me?

"Heard he was spraying your butterflies?" he said. "Something crazy like that."

I frowned, hating what Hal had done, but not wanting to provide more grist for the rumor mill when word of Mr. Morton's demise would add to it soon enough. How could I downplay the event while still being truthful?

Glancing past me, the man's eyes widened. "Well, what do you know? There he is now."

Whipping around, I faced the entrance. My gaze locked with my neighbor's.

Perfect. Now what? Did I say hello? Ignore the fact he was here? I didn't want to have a war with someone who lived right next door, a man I'd considered a friend. But honestly, I couldn't fathom why he thought destroying my property, as well as something he knew I loved, was a good idea.

Hal froze in his steps, like he was shocked to see me. I did own the place, after all. Did he think we wouldn't run into each other? Then, as if he hadn't noticed me, he walked past me down the aisle, which separated groupings of small tables surrounded by chairs.

24

What? He was going to ignore me? I should have allowed him to pass, to get what he came for and leave, but the memory of him purposefully trying to kill my monarchs was still fresh in my mind. "Hey...Hal?"

The man spun around, his face suddenly red. "Now look, Seneca. I don't want any trouble from you."

Silence. Every eye was turned my way. Even Murray, standing at the order counter, had halted, his hand holding a plate out to Lorna Watkins, the napkin underneath the sandwich still swaying gently from the movement, like a butterfly lazily flapping its wings in the evening breeze.

Great. Now I'd done it. Every single person here would leave and immediately tell at least one other person what happened. And that was how rumors got started. Why had I let my temper get the best of me here where there were lots of witnesses? First, I needed to speak to Hal and diffuse a possible negative situation. Then, hopefully, I could address the others in the café and convince them everything would be okay. Whatever way this encounter turned out with Hal might determine what people said about it later on.

I blew out a slow breath, trying to stay calm. "I don't want any trouble either. At least not more than there already has been." Though I wanted to keep my voice and expression neutral, I still wanted the guy to know how much what he'd done had hurt. Maybe emphasizing it now, but calling him out without specifically saying the words, would make him not do anything like it in the future.

He gave a glance toward the front counter. "I only came in here for a cup of coffee. Like I do nearly every day. Can't a man do that? Buy something without getting harassed? Why does it seem like everyone wants something from a person?"

My mouth dropped open. "Me, harass you?" From the corner of my eye, someone moved. I wasn't helping matters by engaging with him, but somehow, my brain and my mouth didn't quite communicate. "I can't believe you'd say that, Hal, after what you did."

Intense whispering came from the ladies at the counter as they leaned close together. Linda pointed in my direction.

Hal eyed the counter again, gritted his teeth together, and headed toward Murray. My cook stood there, a cup in his hand. He would have known what Hal wanted, since my neighbor was indeed in here nearly every day for the same thing.

Wait. When had Murray handed the order to Lorna? And where was the woman now? Had I been so focused on Hal I hadn't noticed her slipping by me to leave?

My heart sank. With Lorna already out the door, the rumors would start any time. The lady was notorious for loving a juicy new story and being the first to spread it around.

I only had myself to blame for that.

Maybe I was to blame—for that—but Hal was the one who did the deed in the first place. The sad thing was, I still couldn't fathom why.

When I glanced toward the entrance, Evie stood there, mouth open, staring at me. Well, now I wouldn't have to fill her in on all the problems with Hal, though, after hearing our exchange in Painted Wings, my cousin would have several questions of her own. I needed to tell her about Mr. Morton before she heard some other way.

Evie took a step toward me, but Mable Kane grabbed onto her wrist, keeping her there, apparently not finished talking about whatever was so important to her. The older woman did have a hearing impairment. It was possible she hadn't even heard the harsh words between Hal and me.

When my cousin glanced at the other woman's fingers wrapped around her wrist, she looked back at me and shrugged. I got it. If she tugged away, she might upset Mable. And no one wanted that. She was a sweet lady, just a little confused at times.

Without another recourse, I waved, mouthed, 'I'll talk to you later,' and slipped out past them into the bright sunlight.

# Chapter Four

Needing to get back to the caterpillars, I headed to the greenhouse. Winifred was already in there. She'd done that several times lately. I'm not sure how she was getting inside since I always shut the door.

She greeted me with a shrill, scolding meow, like I'd stuck her in there and gone off and left her, even though I'd cuddled her only a little while earlier. Picking her up, I held her, so we were eye to eye. "Listen, kitty, I don't know how you're getting in here, but it needs to stop. It's not that I'm trying to be mean, but it's my job to protect you. Certain things in here are not for you to play with. Or sleep on. Or eat."

My cat thrashed her tail back and forth like a broom until it brushed against my hand. Did she think it would injure me? I wouldn't tell her that her fluffy tail was as soft as feathers that tickled so bad, I nearly dropped her.

The sound of more tires on the drive had me peeking out the screen door. I frowned. It wasn't Cody. And it wasn't my ex., though I wouldn't have put it past him to race right over as soon as I'd hung up on him. He only lived a few blocks away, unfortunately, and would be giddy at the prospect of having me under his thumb.

No, I'd never seen this truck before. It was a large blue Ford, dusty and dinged around the front fenders. I wasn't in the mood to show anyone around the farm today, considering this afternoon's excitement. Still, I'd need all the good publicity I could get once word got around about Hal and the fact that Mr. Morton had died on the premises.

A man pulled into my small parking area a few yards away and got out. He was short and thin. Maybe fifty? He glanced around the farm, then smiled when he spotted me. As he walked, I noticed he had a bad limp, nearly dragging his left foot.

I set Winifred down. She smacked my shoe with her paw and darted under a caterpillar pen. Sighing, I headed out to speak to him. As I walked, gravel dust floated up from beneath my shoes. "Hello. Can I help you?"

When he was close, an angry red burn was visible on his left cheek. The same side as his limp. Maybe from an auto accident? "Jesse Vance," he said. "Nice place you have here."

I glanced down, making sure my hands were somewhat clean of cat fur, and shook his hand. "Thank you. I'm Seneca James." We stood there for a second while I waited for him to say something more.

"I had a question," he said. "Figured this was the place to ask it." As he spoke, it struck me that he didn't make direct eye contact, as if shy.

"Okay." Many times, strangers noticed it was a farm and wanted to buy fresh produce, like maybe I ran a fruit market. Apparently, the large painted butterfly next to my sign that said, "Majestic Monarchs," didn't get the point across. I had so much to do and no time to waste on mindless inquiries. It wouldn't be the first time someone happened to wander up here, wanting to look around because they needed to use up an hour or so. Maybe it never occurred to them that I might not have time to waste trying to keep them entertained.

"You see," said Jesse, "I'm the new ranger for Pines Park."

Though our town was small, we were fortunate to be situated beside a large recreational area. People came from all over to visit. He pointed behind him, like I might not know that one side of the property butted up to my farm.

Trying hard not to tap my toe, I waited. Aside from the fiasco of Hal and the milkweed, the unpleasant business of Mr. Morton had put me behind in my work. I needed to make up for it right now. Hoping he didn't plan on staying too long, I nevertheless kept my voice pleasant and said, "Nice to meet you."

"I was pleasantly surprised when I heard of the opening here for a park ranger. This size park and surrounding town are exactly what I'd hope to find."

Millie was right. The new ranger did seem like a nice guy, but I still didn't have time today for chit-chat.

He glanced down toward his feet instead of at me, then said, "The monarchs at the park don't seem to be doing well. I don't want to lose them completely. Was hoping you might have some suggestions."

That snapped me out of my irritation. Anything to do with the welfare of the little winged creatures was the top priority. I indicated a bench nearby that resided in the shade of a large maple tree just outside the greenhouse. "What's the problem with them?" We sat down. Self-consciously, I reached up to my hair, trying to tame some of my curls so they weren't flapping in the breeze, but that only made them bounce back like coiled springs. One piece even smacked me in the eye.

The corners of his mouth lowered. "I've checked the records from the previous ranger for monarch numbers. From what I can tell, they've declined quite a bit, so I'm worried for their welfare."

"Oh, no. That's terrible."

Jesse glanced toward the driveway, then back to his feet. "I asked around, and everyone told me you were the expert in monarchs."

"No, not an expert," I said.

He pointed to the greenhouse. "With your farm here, you obviously know a lot about them. I think they're in grave danger. Could you possibly help me?"

"Of course." What other choice was there? I'd do just about anything to keep butterflies alive. The more, the better, as far as I was concerned, even if they weren't the ones directly associated with my property.

"Thank you." He let out a breath, like he'd been afraid I might have said no. "And I've also been concerned about—"

Someone else was headed our way. I glanced over my shoulder. This time, it was Cody. I watched, waiting until he got out of his car and reached us.

Cody stopped abruptly when he saw I wasn't alone. "Sorry, I thought—"

I stood, then introduced the two men. I knew Cody would want to discuss Hal's actions and Mr. Morton too, but wouldn't do it in front of a stranger, wouldn't in front of anyone else until we knew more about what was going on.

Cody widened his eyes, obviously wanting to speak to me alone. I gave a smile as I said, "Jesse had some questions. For me. About butterflies. Monarchs. He's the new ranger. From the park." Why did I stammer when around someone new? Maybe because most of my conversations were with people I'd known since I was old enough to form words. After a while, friends and neighbors tended to adopt a sort of shortcut when talking about common topics. Plus, maybe Jesse's apparent shyness was rubbing off.

"Oh." Cody rubbed the back of his neck. "I should come back later."

"Would you mind hanging around, Cody?" I asked. "I'm sure this won't take long." I glanced at Jesse, hoping what I'd said was true.

"Right," Jesse said. "Won't take long at all."

"Okay." Cody pointed toward my cat, who was on her hind legs, peering at us from the greenhouse screen, whiskers twitching with curiosity. "I'll go see Winifred."

"Thanks," I said, though I hated to ask him to wait. I had called him, after all, and he was a busy man. "Now," I turned to the ranger. "About the butterflies."

"Anything you can tell me to help would be great."

With a nod, I said, "First, do you have adequate milkweed?"

His eyebrows lowered. "Honestly, the park I ran before had barely any monarch population at all. I don't have much experience with them. The only reason I took notice of these and began to monitor them was the former ranger kept such meticulous records."

That was true. According to what I'd heard, Ranger Nelson had been a stickler for everything to do with the welfare of all the creatures in the area. At least, he had in the past. Maybe as he'd gotten older, the job didn't hold the same appeal. If so, had he neglected the care of the monarchs? "Maybe it would help me to see the records. Would you be all right with that?"

"Yes. I have no problem showing the records to you. I could bring them here or..." He shrugged.

Much as I didn't want to take the time away from my own butterflies, I said, "It might be better if I could see them, see the milkweed too." Simply checking figures in records wouldn't tell me if the milkweed was adequate, the butterflies thriving, or the caterpillars healthy.

"That'd be great. I appreciate it." He checked his watch. "When might be good for you?"

I tried to appear upbeat. No use burdening the new guy in town with my problems concerning destruction of property and murder. Besides, he seemed to have enough problems of his own. "Tomorrow? Say, one o'clock?" That would give me time to do my morning chores, my assessment in the greenhouse, and do a quick pop-in at the café.

"Can't thank you enough." He stood, then headed to his truck.

As he drove away, the greenhouse door screeched, and Cody came back out.

I waited for him, knowing we had a lot to discuss. "Thanks for coming, Cody. Sorry about the wait."

"No problem." He shaded his eyes against an errant ray of sunshine. "That's news to me Ranger Nelson had left. So, everything okay?" He pointed to Jesse's retreating truck.

"Sure. He's having problems with the monarch numbers in the park."

He nodded. "Oh, okay. So, about Hal... Tell me again what he did."

I shrugged. "It's like I said. When I walked to that edge of my property, Hal had dragged over a pressure hose from his barn and was spraying down the milkweed and monarchs."

Cody shook his head. "Whatever for?"

"Wish I knew. I think maybe he's losing it or something."

He took his pen and pad from his shirt pocket. "Did you say anything to him?"

I crossed my arms over my chest. "Well, yeah. I was yelling like crazy, asking what he was doing, trying to tug the hose away."

"All right," said Cody. "And did he say anything back?"

My brow scrunched as I thought about it. "That I didn't know what I was in the middle of. That I shouldn't have gotten in the way."

Cody's eyes widened. "Like a threat? Did you take it that way?"

"At the time, I was so mad, I'm not sure it registered. Going back, yes. I do think it was a threat. Then later, he actually came into the café and got his usual order. There were a few words between us, but the worst part was all the other people who heard us."

He jotted everything down. After glancing over what he'd written, he touched my shoulder. "I'll go talk to him. You'll stay here?" He raised one eyebrow, like he didn't trust me not to tag along.

I laughed. "Believe me, I have no desire to see him again right now. That's why I called you. And Payne."

His body stiffened, and his jaw clenched. He hadn't cared for Payne in high school. Had liked him even less after I'd married him. "For what?"

I thumbed behind us to the greenhouse. "Lawyer. Dead. Need a new one?"

"Yeah, okay." He gave a reluctant nod. "Too bad there isn't another attorney close by you could call."

"Preachin' to the choir, mister. If there was anyone else, I'd be all over it," I said.

"I'll go see Hal, then let you know how it went, okay?"

"Yeah, thanks, Cody."

"I wish this hadn't happened to you, Seneca."

"Me too."

He gave a small smile, then turned and walked to his car.

With a deep sigh, I returned to the greenhouse. When I entered, Winifred was napping on top of the nearest pen. She opened one eye but didn't bother to lift her head.

"Hard day, dear? I'm sure me feuding with a neighbor and finding my lawyer's body in my greenhouse can't compare to the atrocities you've suffered." I ruffled the fur on her head. "Like your food dish being only half full."

At the word food, the cat's eyes opened wide. She climbed to her feet and squalled.

With a laugh, I petted her some more. "Yeah, Mama stepped right into that one, didn't she? Well, come on, then." I waved my hand toward the corner where I kept a food dish. "Let's get starving kitties something to eat."

I left her alone, knowing she didn't like to be interrupted while gorging on her meal, as if I would try to steal it away when I'd been the one to give it to her.

As I checked on the caterpillars, I tried not to stare at the spot where I'd found Mr. Morton. But it was difficult. Though all visible remnants were gone, I could still envision him sprawled in an unnatural position—one leg thrust forward, as if he tried to take a step or run away, and his chin tucked so low on his chest as to appear uncomfortable.

*Uncomfortable? Seneca, you idiot. The man was murdered. It doesn't get worse than that.*

# Chapter Five

The next morning, my part-time assistant, Annie Hastings, showed up at eight am. She came twice a week to help me in the greenhouse with the butterflies, working around her classes from a community college she commuted to an hour away. I hadn't known her well beforehand since she was quite a few years younger than me, but knew her mom, Dana, who worked for Cody. I figured if I couldn't trust the offspring of a sheriff's employee, who could I trust?

Annie was tall, skinny, and geeky, with crazy red hair and tiny wire-rimmed glasses. I'd had my doubts about her ability to lift the butterfly pens and heavy supplies, but she'd proven me wrong. Kid was strong as an ox. If she just wasn't so weird. Not being mean when I said that. I did like her. But sometimes, things she blurted out were, let's say, unexpected.

When I entered the greenhouse, she was there, sweeping the floor, the stiff bristles of the broom scratching against the concrete. Even though the police tape had been removed, my eyes were drawn to the spot. I couldn't look away. The image of him crumpled there would stay with me forever.

"Seneca?"

"Hmmm?" I couldn't stop staring. Remembering. The expression of surprise frozen on his face. The giant pool of crimson crawling across the floor in an ever-widening circle.

"Uh, are you having a stroke?"

Startled by her question, I snapped out of my trance. "No. I'm not having a stroke."

"Heart attack?"

"What? No. Of course not."

"Oh, dementia." She shook her head sadly.

I rolled my eyes. "I'm fine."

She stared at me, wide-eyed, like I was out of my gourd for thinking myself to be healthy when, in fact, I might expire any second where I stood, and she'd have to call the funeral director to come get my lifeless corpse. "If you say so."

Annie was taking lots of science classes. She wanted to be a doctor and was always trying to diagnose everyone she talked to. I'd had to discourage her from doing that to people who toured the farm or frequented the café. One poor man had left here after talking to Annie, sure that the tiny mole on his chin was a portal to a humongous brain tumor that would kill him within the week. I shook my head. Maybe Annie's mom would try to convince her to lower her standards a little from wanting to be a physician. I wasn't sure future patients would survive her lack of a bedside manner.

I hadn't told Annie what happened to Mr. Morton. She'd find out soon enough. It wouldn't surprise me in the least if she wanted to attend the autopsy and offer her opinion on what he'd died of.

Strange as she was, the girl was good with butterflies and caterpillars. At least if she tried to offer them a diagnosis, they wouldn't listen. Winifred was afraid of her, but I think it was because of Annie's clown-like hair.

Leaving her to check the pens, I headed off to make sure Hal hadn't destroyed any more of my milkweed. Anger inched up my spine again, thinking of the poor little monarch he'd killed. There might be more, and I hadn't found them yet. Or predators had already made off with them. What had come over the man?

A few yards from my greenhouse, I heard a vehicle door shut, and I stopped. Winifred, who'd followed me, growled. As I picked her up, I whispered, "It's okay. Just Cody."

"Hey," he said as he reached us. "Where're you two girls off to?"

Grinning, I handed him Winifred. "I'm off to check the milkweed. The girl you're holding is too nosy to stay behind."

"Can I be nosy too?"

I tilted my head toward the field. "Sure. Come on."

He tucked the cat beneath his chin as he cuddled her. "What kind of butterfly costume is she wearing today?"

"Painted lady."

"Very nice."

We walked on, me trying to keep up with his long-legged pace. "I'm guessing you didn't stop by just to compliment my cat's attire."

When he rubbed Winifred's chin, she purred. "I'm afraid not."

"Give me the news, which I assume isn't good."

"I did talk to Hal," said Cody. "It took me a few hours to find him, as he'd been away from home for a while."

"And...."

Cody paused to set the cat gently on the ground. She glared at him and swished her tail. Cody raised his shoulders in a shrug. "Seneca, I'm not sure how to tell you."

"Just say it, okay?" What could be worse than what had already happened?

"All right." He ran his hand through his short hair, one of his nervous gestures.

We continued walking, him—a frown on his face—me—with cousins of my winged clients fluttering in my stomach.

Cody let out a deep sigh. "When I spoke to Hal, he seemed genuinely surprised at your accusations. Said he hadn't seen you for over a week."

An involuntary gasp popped out. "That's a lie!"

He grabbed my hand and gave it a gentle squeeze. "I know."

"Sorry. Go on," I said.

"When I told him how upset you were at what you'd witnessed, he was more concerned about your welfare than what you'd said he did."

"What's he doing?" I asked. "Why would he make this up?"

"He said *you* must have made it up, Seneca."

Stunned, I stopped walking. Cody did the same. "I didn't. You have to believe me."

"Of course I do. Never thought otherwise." He glanced down at Winifred, who was rolling in a patch of catnip again. "Don't suppose you have a picture of Hal destroying your milkweed, or better yet, got a video with your phone?"

I balled my fist in frustration. "No. Wish I had, but I'd been so shocked and mad that—"

He touched my shoulder. "It's okay. Just wondered."

I continued toward the milkweed, and the man and cat followed. "So basically, Hal's saying I invented the whole scenario."

"Afraid so," said Cody.

I shook my head slowly. "I don't understand."

Cody touched my shoulder. "Seneca, maybe he—"

Close to the property line now, the very man in question stood outside of his barn. Hal was on his phone, his back to us.

Cody put his finger to his lips to quiet me, and I nodded. When we reached the milkweed, relief washed over me as I gave it a quick perusal. No further damage showed in this section, at least. I crouched down to briefly inspect beneath the plants. At least, as far as I could tell from here, there weren't any more tiny orange carcasses. Though some wasp might have already taken off with them.

I kept my voice low as I said, "I'll need to get my trailer out here to clean up the mess Hal made yesterday."

"That reminds me." Cody took out his phone and quickly snapped a few shots of the damage. "Doesn't prove he did it, but will at least show something happened."

"What am I gonna to do about what he said. I can't just—"

*"Hello?"*

Shocked, I turned around at Hal's voice. "He's actually coming over," I whispered. "The nerve."

Cody gave me an encouraging smile as we faced my neighbor.

Hal reached us, his expression uncertain. "Hi, Seneca. Uh…not sure what's up, but—"

I took a step toward him. "How could you do this?"

"I didn't—"

"Destroy my property—" I waved my hand toward the milkweed on the ground "—and then lie to the sheriff about it?"

37

My neighbor shook his head sadly. "I'm really sorry for whatever you're going through. But I didn't do what you're accusing me of. You know that."

"No. What I know is you took a pressure hose and—"

He glanced at Cody and back at me. "I didn't want to say this, but now that you've confronted me with the sheriff in tow, I have no choice. I tried to protect you when I, uh, fibbed to the sheriff earlier."

"What are you talking about?" I shrieked.

"You were the one," said Hal.

"One, what?"

He blinked, like he couldn't figure me out. "When I walked over here yesterday, you had my hose. You were dousing your own plants, your own butter—"

"That's not true!" My voice screeched so loud, Winifred dove into the milkweed.

Hal sighed. "Maybe you need to get help. There's a therapist over in—"

I held up my hand. "Stop it. I don't wanna hear more of your lies."

With a shrug at Cody, Hal said, "Sheriff, I'm not sure what else to tell you. I wasn't even going to say anything about what Seneca did. That is, until she forced the issue and sent you to talk to me."

I eyed Cody as I pointed to Hal. "But he—"

"Listen," said Hal. "I would have let it drop, Seneca. But since you insist on dragging me through whatever you've got going on, I can play it that way."

"What are you saying?"

Pointing to his barn, he said, "Technically, I guess you stole my property."

"I never—"

Hal went on. "You went to my barn, got my hose, and were using it over here." He crossed his arms.

"You can't be serious." There wasn't any reason I could think of for him acting this way. Lying about what happened. It made no sense. None.

"Oh, but I am," he said. "I've always liked you. You've been a good neighbor. But I won't have people accusing me of things I didn't do. Something like that could ruin a person's reputation." He narrowed his eyes at Cody. "What'cha gonna do about this, Sheriff?"

Cody's face darkened. Was he embarrassed, or angry? "Now, Hal…"

Hal's hand shot out, finger pointing right at Cody's chest. "Either do your job, or I'll find someone who will. I know she's your friend and all, but you've got a responsibility to the people of this community."

Cody glanced down, then back over at me.

My jaw went slack. No, he couldn't. He wouldn't.

"Seneca," said Cody, "he's given me no choice."

"You're arresting me?" My voice came out all high-pitched and squeaky. If Winifred had thought about coming out, she wouldn't now.

Cody waved his hand in a dismissive gesture. "Of course not. But I do have to at least file a report."

Through my clenched teeth, I said, "Then you can put it in the same folder as the one I'm filing against him."

A hint of a smile appeared on Cody's lips, but quickly disappeared. "That could be arranged."

My neighbor let out a harrumph. "See that you take care of this. Do something about her." Turning on his heel, he stomped to his own property.

Cody took my hand and tugged me away from the milkweed. "Let's head back to the greenhouse, okay?"

Unable to speak after hearing Hal's lies, I nodded. What had come over my neighbor to make him destroy my property, try to ruin my livelihood, then fib about it? Would I ever find out? Did I want to? Maybe the reason behind the lie was worse than the falsehood itself.

As I checked over my shoulder, I spotted Winifred trotting behind us. From her frown, she was unmistakably miffed. First, Cody hadn't carried her as long as she would have liked. Then, I'd yelled at Hal and frightened her, making her take refuge in the patch. Because of that, she now had tiny pieces of milkweed plants stuck like burrs in her fur. She tried to run away from the repulsive, unwanted things hanging on her. When that didn't work, she'd stop and twitch all over like an electrocuted dust mop.

Cody gave my hand a squeeze, then released it. "I'm really sorry that I have to file that report."

"It's okay. I know you have no choice."

He slid me a sideways glance. "Of course, there isn't anything that says where I have to file it."

"Huh?"

"It's funny," he said, "every now and then, a file gets misplaced. Behind the filing cabinet. In the bottom of a seldom used desk drawer. One time, a piece of paper even found its way into the trash."

I narrowed my eyes, trying to figure him out. "Found its way...."

His eyes were wide, all innocence. "Yes, ma'am. Don't know how it could have happened. Such a terrible miscarriage of justice."

With a grin, I said, "I knew I kept you around for some reason."

He laughed. But just as quickly sobered. "I don't expect the thing with Hal to be a problem. The issue with Mr. Morton, however...."

"Yeah, I know. How long until we know what he died of?"

"A routine autopsy usually takes a few hours to perform. The results can take days or weeks, depending on what they're searching for. If the death is deemed accidental, we do nothing."

I swallowed hard. "And if it's..."

"We'll worry about that then, all right?"

I crossed my arms over my chest. "Easy for you to say. It didn't happen in your greenhouse."

"Are you afraid?" asked Cody. "I mean, do you think you might need protection for a while? Since we don't know who did it or why."

"Ah, protection, meaning you, I take it."

"Or Bud." Cody's deputy, Bud Olsen, was nice enough, but naive. If you told him a flock of pterodactyls was flying over, he'd run out into the street without even checking for oncoming traffic.

"I'll pass on Bud," I said.

"Okay." Cody stopped and faced me. "How about me?"

It would be so much easier to sleep at night knowing Cody was around. I'd feel safer, protected, and calmer. But that wasn't going to happen. No way was I going to fall into the trap of depending on a man for everything again. No matter who he was. I'd learned that lesson the hard way with Payne. "I'll be fine."

"Seneca." His eyebrows had lowered until his eyes were half-hidden.

"I mean it. Besides, with a watch-cat like Winifred, what could happen to me?" I glanced over at my cat, who had rolled onto her back, trying to dislodge a twig from her belly fur with her teeth. She looked like a deranged land otter.

Cody smirked. "Yeah, she's a real menace to society, that one."

"Nevertheless, we'll be fine."

Too bad I doubted my own words.

# Chapter Six

Evie had texted me, letting me know we were out of ketchup for the café. After texting back with the thumbs-up emoji, I headed to the grocery. We usually ordered most supplies wholesale, but when it came to immediate needs, I doubted our customers would want to wait for the postal delivery.

When I returned to the café, I nodded at several customers who were gathered at tables, eating, and talking. As I walked past, Mr. Morton's name floated up more than once. Apparently, at least some information had gotten out. I hoped it didn't include the fact that he'd been murdered. My steps faltered, and I glanced to my right.

Angel Bales – Cody's cousin—and Connie Sellers were sharing a table. They co-owned the local quilting/knitting shop downtown. "Well," said Connie, "I heard Morton was struck by lightning."

"Wait. I thought he died inside the greenhouse," said Angel. "So how could that happen and not burn the whole place down? We would have heard fire engines. And smelled smoke. My dog goes crazy and starts barking at both of those things. You've heard him when we even light our outdoor grill. He goes ballistic."

Connie shrugged. "Don't know. Just what I heard."

When Angel noticed me standing nearby, she set her drink down on the table, her cheeks turning red. Connie's mouth opened, then closed. She pulled her hands from the table where they'd been wrapped around her cup and set them on her lap.

I could tell by their sheepish expressions when we'd made eye contact that they hadn't meant me any malice. Instead, their expressions were of concern on my behalf. Giving them a one-sided smile, I wanted them to know I understood. Both ladies sighed, seeming relieved I wasn't upset.

A few tables down, Sid Fairchild sat with Norman Gates. They were old buddies, both widowers, who ended up doing a lot of things together. Their nicknames were curmudgeon and curmudgeonier. Not that anyone would say that to their faces.

Sid motioned Norman closer like he was going to whisper, but the man didn't possess the ability to speak quietly. Instead, he nearly shouted, "Hey, that Morton guy?"

Norman bobbed his head. "Yeah?"

"I have a theory about how he died. Wanna hear?"

"Do I have a choice?" asked Norman.

"What I'm thinking is, he was in the greenhouse, and all the bugs in there—"

"The butterflies?"

"Yeah, those. They all ganged up on him at once, beat him to the ground with those fast-moving wings, and he hit his head or something and died."

Norman smirked. "Really? That's all you've got?"

"Well, Mr. Smarty-pants, what do you think happened?"

"Here's a more likely scenario. It wasn't a bunch of insects, but something bigger. With claws."

"Claws?" asked Sid, "like a bear? When's the last time you saw a bear around here?" Sid waved his hand around the room.

"Yeah, okay, then what?"

"It was that scary orange feral cat who hangs around here."

Norman frowned. "The one that wears clothes?"

"That's the one."

"I'm not sure a feral animal would allow someone to dress them in—"

Sid glared. "Anyway, I think that bunch of fluff scratched him to death. He bled out. End of story."

Norman bit his lip. "All right. I guess it's worth consideration. Gotta watch those sneaky cats. Never know what they're up to."

Both men stared warily at the floor. Were they looking for Winifred? I half expected them to pull their feet up on their chairs to stay out of her kill zone.

Instead of looking ashamed that I'd caught them talking about my butterflies and my cat, they both openly gaped at me. Neither one of them spoke, but the second I walked past, I heard gruff-sounding whispers about me always getting into trouble these days.

I did my best to ignore them. They were regular customers, after all. If I tossed out everyone who'd ever rubbed me the wrong way, Murray and Evie would only have me and Winifred to serve the café specials to.

As I moved on, a flash of orange caught my eye. Speaking of Winifred, she sat on a stool like a queen, ready to hand out some severe royal sentence, her eyes squinted halfway closed, her tail lashing. I reached over and gave her a one-handed pat, which seemed to appease her for the moment. I had half a mind to carry her over to Sid and Norman. Just to say hello.

When I looked closer, I could see a butterfly perched on Winifred's tail. Ah, that must be the reason for her tail thrashing around. The monarch took the hint and slowly rose in the air, fluttering its wings in lazy flaps, barely stirring the air around it. Then, the painted beauty landed on a high wooden ceiling beam and perched, seeming to survey her kingdom.

Just like Winifred.

I carried the grocery sack to the counter. Evie wasn't there waiting for me, but Murray was. Handing him the bag, I said, "Evie texted me to bring this. Is she here?"

"No. Cut her hand with a serving knife. Went to the doc for stitches."

"What? Oh no! Is she okay, does she need—"

He shook his head. "She'll live. Said she'd be in later. Nothing major."

I let out a breath. "Well, that's good, at least. But if you knew she would be out, you should have texted me, too. I can help you out today."

He set down the bag, then waved me off. "I don't need any help. Never have. You have enough going on with your monarchs. Especially lately. Why didn't you tell me about what Hal had done? I had to hear about it here at Painted Wings."

"I didn't want to worry you. It's…nothing." At least, I hoped so. If Murray was this upset about Hal, wait until he learned of Mr. Morton's death in the greenhouse. But he needed to know. "Listen, there's something else I need to tell you."

His eyebrows lowered, the expression menacing. If I didn't know him so well, I'd think he was ready to yell, or growl. For some reason, he had a soft spot for me, which made working with his gruffness that much easier. "What's that?" he asked.

I glanced around, making sure everyone was otherwise occupied with their food and company, so we wouldn't be disturbed. Motioning him to follow me, I stepped behind the counter and around a corner to the food prep area.

"Seneca, what's going on?" His muscular, tattooed arms crossed over his broad chest. Another person might have been intimidated by his size and demeanor, but I knew that deep down, he was full of fluff.

"Um, something happened. Something awful," I said.

"I'm guessing this has nothing to do with a customer complaining about not liking their spicy pierogi."

"No," I said. "It doesn't."

"Go on."

Swallowing hard, not wanting to even think about what I'd walked in on in the greenhouse, I forced myself to continue. "Have you heard anything about Mr. Morton?"

"You mean lately? No. Why?"

I forced out the words, "He's...dead."

Murray shook his head. "No. I hadn't heard a thing. No one has mentioned it. Kind of surprising with the way things get around in this town. Sorry to hear that. I know he was your attorney and all, even though most people didn't like him."

That was an understatement. And my cook, especially, hadn't cared for the lawyer. At all. Apparently, a long time before I'd met Murray, he'd had a bad experience with Mr. Morton. Something about getting way overcharged for legal services.

Murray shrugged. "The guy was old. A heart attack or something?"

"Or something."

"Seneca. Just spit it out. I do have customers to serve, you know."

I knew his apparent irritation was a cover for something more. Concern for me. Yes, he could be gruff, but somehow, he'd always looked out for me ever since we'd begun working together. "Yeah, okay," I said. "Um, when I'd gone into my greenhouse to check the butterflies, there was something strange in there and...."

He lowered his eyebrows.

Looking him directly in the eyes, I said, "When I got there, Mr. Morton was lying on the ground."

"You mean he died in the greenhouse? What was he doing in there?"

"We're still not sure," I said.

"Who's we?"

"Cody and me."

"Cody? As your friend? Or as the sheriff? What's really the story here?" He glanced around the corner toward the order counter, then back.

Once I said the words, the story would be out. Not that he would intentionally spew forth the details to everyone, but it was human nature when you saw so many folks daily for something to accidentally slip out. But there was no choice. Everyone would hear about it soon enough. "What's really going on, Murray, is this. Mr. Morton died on my greenhouse floor. And not by natural causes. He was probably murdered."

The cook's eyes opened wide, as did his mouth. "Murdered?"

His voice had risen. I pressed my hand to his arm, hoping he'd be quieter. Hoping even more that no one else had heard the word. Nothing like unnatural demise to get everyone's attention. "Yes, well, we think so."

"Seneca, this is serious. You could be in danger."

I refrained from rolling my eyes. Keeping Cody at bay for wanting to continually protect me was enough. Though I appreciated Murray's concern, I didn't need someone else fretting about me. Why was it, just when I'd been feeling more empowered to be my own person, to not have to depend on the men in my life, something happened to make them hover like mother hens?

46

But then, it wasn't about me, was it? Or my wants or needs. It was about the guy who'd been alive when he'd entered my greenhouse and, for whatever reason, or by whoever's hand, had exited my property in a body bag. "Thanks for your concern, Murray. Really. Cody has already scolded me about being more careful."

"Good."

"But until we can figure out who did this, keep an eye out for anyone strange hanging around the café," I said.

Murray's eyebrows rose.

"Yeah, okay," I said. "A lot of the customers are strange. But you know what I mean."

"Yes." He cracked a seldom-used smile. "I know what you mean. Believe me, I'll be watching everyone. It could be someone we know. Did you think of that?"

A shiver ran across my shoulders. "That would be even worse than a stranger, wouldn't it?"

"Guess it doesn't matter either way to Mr. Morton."

"No, I guess it doesn't."

A shuffling noise came from out front. Murray frowned. "Better get back to it. You okay, then?"

"Yes, I'm fine. Thanks." I followed him around the corner and back to the counter.

Lorna Watkins was there. She tapped her fingernails on the countertop, the grating sound making me squirm. "Guess it's too much to ask for condiments for my hamburger? I am on my lunch hour, you know. And would like to enjoy the sandwich I paid for before I have to head back to work."

Oops. Ketchup.

"Sorry, Lorna." I grabbed the bag where Murray had stashed it under the counter when he and I had left to talk. Reaching in, I handed her several packets, more than I'd usually supply a person. "Is that enough?"

Giving an unladylike sniff, she said, "I guess it will have to do. Boy, the service in this place isn't what it used to be."

I let out a sigh, thinking she'd head back to her table. But then, she stopped and stared first at me, then over my shoulder. Whipping around, I wondered if she was now looking at Murray, but he wasn't there. Must be working on someone's order in the back. So, what had Lorna been staring at behind me? Or was it the fact that neither Murray nor I had been available when she'd wanted something.

When I focused again on her, I nearly took a step back. Her expression was downright hateful. Was the lady this upset about ketchup? She was one of our pickier customers, but even with that, it seemed a little over the top.

A terrible thought hit me. What if she'd overheard us talking about Mr. Morton? And how he'd been murdered fifty yards away in my greenhouse and had not simply died by natural causes. Or by Winifred?

Everything in me wanted to ask her, to find out what she knew. But I couldn't. Because if she had heard us, she might not admit it. And if she hadn't, I would have then spilled the very beans I was hoping to contain. At least for a while.

As Lorna stomped away, Murray leaned close. "That lady might be worth keeping an eye on."

"You mean because of our conversation about strange customers hanging around?"

"No," he said. "Because of her past history with the guy who was just murdered."

# Chapter Seven

When Murray had thrown Lorna under the bus for a past with Mr. Morton, I'd been dying to know what it was. But a busload of hungry customers that had flooded in right then ended that conversation. I needed to talk to Murray again. And soon.

But today, I needed to meet Jesse at the park. It took me no time at all to drive there. I'd been there before, of course, but couldn't remember the last time. Taking care of the monarchs took a huge chunk of time. Not that I was complaining. I loved it.

The ranger's building was near the middle of the park, a small structure made of pine boards with a shingled roof. The colors blended in nicely with the surrounding trees and plants. The pines were so thick on both sides of the dirt drive, the building wasn't even visible until I was nearly at the front door. It was like some magic fairy garden.

There wasn't a vehicle parked out front. Maybe he was out in the park somewhere. I wouldn't know where to look. Should I wait?

A screen door on the cabin screeched open. "Seneca?" Jesse stepped out onto the small cement porch, his boots squeaking when he angled around to shut the door. "Thanks for coming."

"Oh. Of course."

He looked at my shoulder when he said, "Why don't I show you what we've got."

"Sure," I said.

We rounded the building and hopped into his truck, parked out of sight. The seats and floor were spotless. How did that happen when he was constantly driving around the park, climbing in and out of his vehicle? Maybe he was a clean freak.

The windows were down on the truck. Several larks sang from somewhere to my right and above, though I couldn't see them. The path back down the drive had grown sunnier in the short time since I'd arrived due to the nearness of midday. A sudden breeze caught at tree branches, causing them to sway to some melody only they could hear. The park was beautiful. I'd forgotten just how much I enjoyed it.

I couldn't think of any small talk on the way to the milkweed, but I guess he couldn't come up with anything, either. A very quiet ride. Thankfully short. As awful as I was at trying to fill a quiet void, I usually tried anyway. Like something terrible would happen if more than a couple of minutes went by without inane conversation.

When we reached the milkweed patch, Jesse stopped the truck, and we got out. Once I had a chance to take in the whole patch, my eyes opened so wide I wondered if it would be permanent. I couldn't believe the vast amount of it the park had. And butterflies were everywhere. Though his flock seemed healthy, my heart sank. If I was unsuccessful in getting Hal's land for more milkweed, my monarchs would never reach this capacity. They might not survive very long at all.

"Are you all right?" His glance met mine for a millisecond, then darted away.

Somehow, I forced myself to blink, then turned to Jesse. "I'm fine."

His eyebrows lowered. "You appeared to be a little, I don't know, shocked?"

With a laugh, I said, "Only because the milkweed patch is so huge, and monarchs are in abundance."

"That's good?"

"Very good," I said.

"Okay, not sure why there seem to be fewer monarchs than what the previous ranger listed. But, like I said, this isn't my area of expertise. Maybe I just don't know what to look for."

"Why don't we examine your records and check it out?" I asked.

"All right." We got back in the truck. He grabbed a notebook from the console between us. "This is what I came across in the ranger's station." Jesse handed me the book.

I ran my finger down the page, taking note of each entry, again feeling envious that I didn't have those kinds of numbers on my farm. Would I ever? "Actually, from checking out your swarm—"

"Swarm?"

"A group of monarchs," I said.

"Ah." He nodded.

"And your army—"

"Army?"

I tapped the notebook with my finger. "Your group of caterpillars."

"Why am I picturing millions of tiny marching boots on their feet?" he asked.

I smiled. I'd often thought the same thing. At least he seemed to have a sense of humor.

"Guess I have a lot to learn about them," he said.

If he'd never worked at a location that dealt with significant numbers of monarchs, it was understandable he wouldn't have much knowledge of them. "I think the numbers are okay. They're always changing from one form to another. Egg, larvae, caterpillar, and butterfly. It's hard to tell who's who when you check on them during the transition."

Jesse's face reddened. "I feel a little foolish now. Maybe I mistook the situation, that there really isn't a problem?"

"Don't feel bad." I gave a small wave of my hand. "You said you're not used to dealing with butterflies. Their numbers can be deceiving when they're pupating, and you're not sure what you're looking for."

He lifted his shoulders in a shrug. "Listen, I feel bad about having you out here when it's apparent there really wasn't a problem. I know you must have taken time from your work to come here."

He was right, but I didn't want him to feel worse than he already did. "It's okay."

"No, it isn't. You're a busy business owner whose time is valuable."

"Honestly, I don't mind," I said.

"Still... I should have told you when I went to your farm."

"Told me what?" I asked.

"How much I admire what you've done."

I blinked. "Oh. Thank you." Though I shied away from personal attention, when someone wanted to talk about the monarchs, I was all over it.

"No, really," said Jesse. "You have an amazing operation out there. Driving up to your farm, I could see a lot of your land. The way it's tended, cared for. It's obvious you have a passion for what you do."

Passion. He'd found the right word, exactly. Because that's how I felt about the monarchs. Their beauty. Their amazing life cycles. The way they brought joy to not only me, but everyone who ever visited the farm to learn more about them. I tried to think of any time, just once, when my ex had complimented the farm or even acknowledged my passion for butterflies. There weren't any instances I could think of. Grateful to have it now, I glanced away, not knowing what to say. After a few seconds, I grinned. "Thanks."

"Makes me wish I had worked with monarchs before," he said. "Glad I get the chance now. Just from listening to you, I can tell they must be amazing creatures."

"They are. So amazing." I placed my hands on my lap, wondering if I should talk about them some more. Or would that be too much? Maybe he was just being polite in complimenting my farm.

He tapped his finger on the steering wheel in a nervous gesture. "Maybe later on, you could teach me a little more about them. I know now that they're doing well, that the numbers are good, and the swarm is thriving, but now I find I'd like to know more. I'd like to see that they continue to thrive."

"Of course. Any time." My heart swelled with pride that I'd affected another person in a positive way about something I cared so deeply for. Aside from those closest to me, not many people knew enough about the creatures to talk about them at length.

"Also..." he glanced out the window "...if you had the time, and only if..." He gave me a brief glance then looked away. "I'd love to start something at the park about the monarchs. To help visitors learn more about them. Or have something connecting the park to your farm? I think people would really like that."

How exciting. And why hadn't I ever thought of it before, approaching the former ranger about a collaboration? The possibilities were endless. "That's a great idea."

"You think so?"

I nodded, and my grin must have come across as kind of goofy. Couldn't be helped. Any time someone seemed as excited about butterflies as I was, the joy was contagious. The momentum of my thoughts for future joint efforts spun through my mind.

Jesse checked his watch. "Sorry to cut this short, but I have a meeting to get to soon."

"Oh, no worries. None at all. Thanks for giving me the chance to check out your swarm."

After he'd dropped me off back at my vehicle and had left, I texted Evie about meeting up at the covered bridge at the park to talk. She got an hour each afternoon for a break, so I was hoping she could get away. Within seconds, she answered.

Evie got there only a few minutes after I did since my property adjoined the back of the park. Walking toward the bridge from her car, she waved. "Hey. What's up? I'm guessing this has to do with whatever Hal was mad about in the café?"

I nodded, then motioned her to follow me. I walked up into the bridge and stopped near the middle of the waist-high stone wall, leaning my forearms against the top. Evie did the same. I glanced out at the river that ran beneath the bridge, listening for a few seconds as the water trickled and splashed over smooth rocks. "First of all, how's your hand? Are you okay?"

She held it up, sporting a small bandage on her right thumb. "I'm fine. It really wasn't all that bad, but Murray insisted I get it checked out."

I grinned. "I'm glad you're all right. And yeah, Murray tries to come off all gruff and everything, but we know the truth, don't we?"

Evie smiled. "Yes, we do. Now, about Hal?"

"It's partly about Hal, but there's more."

Her eyebrows rose. "That looked pretty intense when you were talking to him in the café. I'd wanted to come to you, but Mable had her talons wrapped around my wrist. So, you're telling me it gets worse than what Hal did in there?"

Letting out a breath, I said, "Unfortunately."

"Go on. What happened?" she asked.

"First of all, with Hal. I was out getting ready to check my milkweed. When I got close, Hal was there."

"You mean out by his barn?" she asked.

I shook my head. "No. At my milkweed."

"Okay…weird, but not the first time, right? I mean, his property is right next to yours."

Something down below in the water splashed, catching my attention. Turning back toward Evie, I said, "Right. He used to help me out a lot, remember?"

"Sure, when you first took over the farm. I've always liked Hal. Was shocked when he was yelling at you at Painted Wings."

"I wasn't shocked."

Evie touched my arm. "What? Why?"

"Well, I wasn't shocked at the café because when he'd been at my milkweed, he'd… he had out his power washer and…"

Her eyes widened. "What for?"

"Evie, he was spraying my monarchs."

My cousin gasped. "But…why?"

"That's what I'd like to know."

"That's awful. And makes no sense," she said.

"I know."

Her eyebrows lowered. "Oh no. How are the monarchs? Are they okay?"

I shook my head. "Still don't know the extent. And honestly, I'm kind of afraid to find out."

Evie wrapped her arm around my shoulders and gave me a brief side hug. "Well, what did Cody say?"

"How do you know I told Cody already?"

She raised one eyebrow. "Come on. It's Cody."

I gave a one-shouldered shrug. "Yeah, you're right. And yes, I did. He checked it out, but said Hal put the blame on me."

"But that makes no sense. How could he blame you for something he did?"

"In essence, Hal lied about me to Cody."

"But Cody didn't believe him," said Evie.

"No," I said. Deep down, I'd known Cody would have believed me, but it had been comforting, just the same, when he'd said it out loud.

"That's good. Then, when Hal came at you at the café, it was because of all that?"

"Right."

"Wow, that's terrible," said Evie. "I'm so sorry you had to go through that. But why didn't you tell me when it happened? I could have helped, or—" She placed both hands on her hips.

"It's not something I wanted to talk about over the phone or put in a text."

Evie brushed her bangs from her face as a strong breeze blew through the inside of the bridge. "Yeah, okay. I get it. Thanks for telling me. Let me know if I can do anything to help. And I mean anything."

"Thanks, I will." I bit my lip. Now on to the hard part.

Evie lowered her eyebrows. "What? Oh. You'd said there was more?"

"Yeah."

"Might as well tell me now." She checked her watch. "I will need to get back soon if I want to eat something before my break is over. Can you tell me fast? I've been so busy, I barely have time to talk to anybody, even the customers."

"Okay. Here's fast. I'd gone into my greenhouse the other morning. Mr. Morton was there. He was dead. And it wasn't an accident."

Evie's eyes widened, and she pressed her hand to her stomach. "Never mind about me getting back to eat. Suddenly, I've lost my appetite."

# Chapter Eight

After Hal's stunt with his pressure hose, it was time to take a careful inventory of the damage. I needed to wait until everything dried out to assess it properly. I'd done an initial walk-through shortly after the fact and found some butterfly carcasses, but part of me was afraid to see exactly how bad it was.

I put on my boots and got in my truck. Driving back to the milkweed, I nearly stopped to turn around and go back home. Did I really want to see how awful it might be? What would I do if it was worse than I'd originally thought?

If something terrible happened and I couldn't keep running the butterfly farm, I'm not sure I'd recover. Not only would I feel like a failure, letting myself down and Gram's legacy, but I had no earthly idea what I'd do with my life instead. There'd never been anything else that grabbed my attention and warmed my heart as working with the monarchs.

When I got to the field, I slowed and stopped, gazing across the stalks through the windshield. But I didn't get out right away. After telling myself to stop being a chicken and just go find out, I hopped out of the truck.

The milkweed Hal hadn't destroyed was doing fine. Healthy and mostly unharmed. Though if I hadn't caught him when I did, it could have been so much worse. He could have wiped it out completely, leaving me with nothing for the monarchs' survival and much of my livelihood gone.

Had that been Hal's intention? To put me out of business? What other reason would he have?

Either way, I was thankful I'd come out here that day when I had. Glancing around, I forced myself to do the hard part. Scrutinize the numbers of remaining monarchs closely and see how much damage my neighbor had managed to inflict.

Down on my hands and knees, I crawled along the perimeter of the rows, using a hand-held clicker to count off the remaining viable monarchs. It was all I could do not to scream every time I saw a tiny body hidden deep in the stalks, wings motionless and torn, the orange and black colors fading and brittle. Tears burned my eyes, but I wiped them away with the back of my hand. Why did it feel like Hal had killed a part of me along with the monarchs?

*Get this part over with, then you can move on. Rebuild your swarm.*

But what would keep Hal from doing the same thing again? And again? Until I was wiped out? Was it time to get some kind of alarm or security system? The idea seemed absurd, living in tiny, friendly Maple Junction. But who would have guessed this would happen? Or that my attorney would end up mangled on my floor? Sometimes, it seemed like a nightmare I couldn't wake up from.

Forcing myself to continue, I finished my appraisal and stood, stretching the knots out of my back. According to the numbers, if my count was anywhere near correct, Hal had robbed me of at least ten percent of my swarm.

Ten percent. I let out a groan. It had taken so long to get the number of butterflies I'd had, and now...

*Get a grip. Yes, ten percent.* But it could have been so much worse. I'd have to order more caterpillars to increase what I'd lost, though of course that wouldn't happen overnight. It would set me back in time and money. Not to mention, I needed to replace the milkweed that had been destroyed as well.

I went to my truck, grabbed my notebook, and jotted down the results of my findings. The numbers appeared even worse when I saw them in writing. Like I'd somehow failed.

But then I scolded myself. I hadn't caused this, after all. If Hal had done what he'd said, upheld the promise of selling me the land, none of this would have happened. At the very least, he should have come and spoken to me about it calmly, as two adults should. Instead, I'd been forced to have my lawyer contact him about the contract, and it had gone downhill from there. I needed to fill Cody in on the latest. With everything going on, I was keeping him busy lately in his official capacity.

Ready to get back to the caterpillars in the greenhouse, I headed toward the truck. I still needed to get rid of the ruined milkweed stalks but that could wait. It would be a busy enough day as it was. Halfway into the cab to head back and regroup—feel sorry for myself—I heard voices.

They were coming from the direction of Hal's barn.

Lately, nothing that happened over there was good news. At least not for me. I quietly shut the vehicle door and edged around the side of the nearest milkweed row. Though my back was still cramped from crawling around, I crouched down again, not wanting to be seen.

One voice was Hal's. I'd heard it from over there for so many years, I'd know it anywhere. Like part of my childhood. I used to anticipate seeing him, go over to visit him, or follow him around when he'd come to Gram's.

Not anymore.

How sad that someone I'd liked forever was now a person that I'd never be able to trust again.

The voices rose. Shouting. They were talking over each other, so it was hard to make out what they were saying or who the other person was. Under normal circumstances, if a neighbor was arguing with someone in his own barn, I'd butt out and mind my own business.

These, however, were not normal circumstances. I sat very still, hoping to make out who the other person might be. But the voices rose and fell, tumbled over one another in the argument, that I still couldn't tell if the other person was someone I knew or not.

My neighbor must have been more agitated than the second person, because his voice got louder, the words more pronounced, while whoever the other one was kept his—I was sure it was a man now—voice lower.

Hal shouted. "Don't you see? He's gone. Dead."

Dead? Were they talking about Mr. Morton?

The other man replied. Something about blame.

"Who cares who takes the blame? For all I care, that girl next door can fry for it. Would serve her right for all she's put me through."

My mouth dropped open, and I gasped so loud I smacked my hand over my mouth to keep quiet. How dare he? Wanting me to be charged with a murder I didn't commit went much deeper than destroying my monarchs. The man must have lost his mind.

Then the second man, his voice still somehow muffled, like maybe he had his hand near his mouth, said, "…. lawyer…. could have gotten in the way of… killed and…"

I wished I could hear more of what he said. Then maybe I'd know who it was.

"Just be glad he's dead," said Hal. "You of all people should realize that if he was still alive, we'd be in a world of hurt right now. As it is, now Payne James is sticking his nose in, checking things out."

They had to be discussing Mr. Morton, since they talked about a male who was dead, and had lumped in me and Payne as well. But why was Hal so concerned about the murder, obviously glad Morton was dead?

Unless he was the one who'd killed him. Or knew who did.

I watched a couple of monarchs flitter around my left shoulder, their antics joyful, as if nothing bad had happened, and some of their fellow butterflies hadn't been murdered by my neighbor.

Murder.

Maybe Hal had it in him to kill more than monarchs. I never would have guessed he'd been capable of either, especially not to kill another human being. How had I so misjudged him all this time? Had he been that good of an actor, so deceitful that even my grandmother had trusted him as a friend? She'd always been a great judge of character. It seemed unfathomable that she wouldn't have seen through him. If that was the case, what had happened to cause Hal to do what he'd done to me?

Mr. Morton had stood in the way of Hal possibly not getting out of his contract with me, but was that worth murdering someone for? I shook my head, slowly, hoping that somehow, the motion would knock something loose in my brain, help me sort out the craziness that had become my life.

Give me some answers to all the questions.

Hal, having lived next door for so many years and having been over here countless times, knew a lot about the farm and the way it was run. He knew my habits, where I kept a spare key hidden beneath a leg of an outside bench, what time I normally did certain duties, and when there might be additional people here, such as Annie. Or... when it would be easier to slip over from his property and cause some trouble with the butterflies.

Or murder my lawyer.

A few days ago, I never would have considered Hal capable of anything like this. But then, a few days ago, Mr. Morton was still breathing. And my life, aside from the contract dispute, had been moving along like always. Calm, sure, and quiet.

The memory of watching Cody finally remove the crime scene tape, then me hosing down the concrete in the greenhouse crossed my mind, as I witnessed the blood and who knew what else slide across the floor at the mercy of the hose, circle the drain before disappearing below the floor. My stomach flipped. Time to stop thinking about it.

I realized the voices had stopped. How long had I stayed here beside the truck?

Something rustled, like branches being shoved out of the way. In shock, I watched as Hal emerged from my milkweed. He must have entered from the other side, closer to his barn.

Rushing forward, fists clenched at my sides, I shouted, "What do you think you're doing?"

Startled, he jumped. His face reddened as he stared at me, hands held in front of him, ready to take on an attacker. After a few seconds, he lowered his arms. "What do you want?"

"What do I want? If you hadn't noticed, you're on my property. You've developed the bad habit lately of doing that."

He stepped closer, slowly, stealthily. Like he was stalking me.

My heart hammered hard. My every inclination was to back up, jump in the truck, and hurry away. But I couldn't. This man had already cost me money, time, and work. Not to mention, he might be guilty of murder.

Though my legs trembled, I stayed put.

With his finger pointed right at my face, he said, "You need to mind your own business."

"This is my business. My land."

His face darkened even more as a large vein pulsed visibly in the side of his neck. "This goes much deeper."

"What happened to you, Hal? You used to be such a nice man. Gram trusted you."

"Things change. People do, too."

I shook my head. "Not like that."

"You don't understand. You never could."

"Then help me to. Surely, there's a way to work this out between us. Get rid of the lawyers." I hadn't meant it that way, in light of what happened to Mr. Morton. I brushed aside the thought. "Just you and I sit down and work out the details. You know I need your property, and you know why. Can't we just—"

"No!" It came out as a shout. "It's too late for that. It's gone too far."

"There has to be something." I reached out to touch his hand, something that came naturally from our past, when we'd been friends.

Hal smacked my hand away, the sound like a gun firing. The skin on my hand burned, but I tried to ignore it. Wouldn't let him know he'd hurt me.

"Now," he said, "why don't you get back in your truck, head to your greenhouse, and do whatever it is you spend your days doing with those silly bugs."

Indignation ran hot through my veins. He knew, had always known, how important the monarchs were to me. Had been to Gram, too. "Those silly bugs are my livelihood. Without them, I'd lose the farm."

"Maybe that's what should happen."

Shaking my head, I glared at him. And for the first time, I wondered what he'd been doing coming through my milkweed just now. The way he'd been startled, he'd had no idea I was even here. It hadn't been to talk to—or argue—with me, so what was his reason? I pointed behind him. "Come over here to do some more damage? Didn't bring your hose this time, I see."

"There are more ways than water to destroy what's in my way," said Hal as he stalked back to his own property.

My mouth dropped open. Was he talking about the milkweed? Or what had happened to Mr. Morton?

Maybe something worse he might do to me?

# Chapter Nine

I regretted agreeing to meet Payne for dinner. But my ex hadn't left me a choice. Wavering on what to wear, I had no desire to dress up on his account, yet didn't want to be a hobo either. People saw me like that too often when they came to the farm. Instead, I settled on comfortable but dull. Jeans and a tank top with a summer sweater over it.

My stomach fluttered with some of my tiny, winged friends. Ever since we'd split, I'd gone out of my way not to see him, hear him, or hear about him. Occasionally, I'd spot him in the grocery store or something, but I always tried to get away without speaking. This meeting would end all that, at least as long as I needed him to be my attorney.

But I was glad about one thing. Teddy's Bar was the type of place where you didn't feel like you were on a date. Which we most definitely were not. It was loud with rock music and laughter, not quiet with candlelight. Fine by me.

As I made my way up the sidewalk to the restaurant, I spotted Lorna Watkins sitting on a park bench with her cell phone pressed to her ear. Hopefully, she wouldn't see me. For one reason, I wanted to get my dinner with Payne over quickly. And for another, Lorna was rude, snippy, and more than a little scary at times.

As I neared her bench, her voice floated across the sidewalk. "Listen," she said. "I don't care what you believe or not. Herman Morton was a terrible person!"

My steps faltered. I wanted to stay and listen to her conversation, but knew I didn't have the luxury of extra time. Instead, I slowed my gait, hoping to hear more.

"He's where he should be," Lorna screeched. "Dead! Thank goodness he can't hurt me anymore." Lorna ended her call and shoved her phone into her purse.

I rushed past her, glad that she seemed interested in whatever it was she rummaged for in her purse. I'd fill Cody in on what I heard later. But for now, I had something very unpleasant of my own to deal with.

When I stepped inside the restaurant, Payne was already there. He was standing by a table near the back. I'd kind of forgotten how handsome he was. Something that had gotten me in trouble in the first place. I'd known him since high school. His bad boy image had seemed so exciting. My parents hadn't wanted me to date him, but of course, I snuck out and did it anyway. Too bad I didn't listen. Might have saved me wasted time and a severely broken heart.

"Hey, Seneca." He leaned toward me, like he was going to give me a kiss.

"Uh. No." I pulled away just in time.

"Gonna be like that, huh?" His eyebrows went so low I could barely see the top part of his eyes.

"We're divorced, Payne."

"Not my choice." The man actually pouted. Ah yes, something else I'd nearly forgotten. Nope, didn't miss that, not even a little.

Sitting down at the booth, I waited for him to do the same. No use giving the townspeople an item for local gossip. It was enough that he and I were together in a public place. Tongues would wag. Gossip would have us married again by breakfast tomorrow.

With a long, audible sigh, Payne took the other side of the table.

I set my purse on the bench beside me. "So, about my case."

"Wow. Harsh, Seneca." His fake expression of injury was almost comical. "What?"

"Not even a hello?"

"Hello." I said it with a scowl. That was the nicest I could manage.

Payne lifted his hands palms up, as if to say, guess that didn't work. "Okay, then. Fine. Go ahead and tell me about it."

Irritated, I gave the tabletop one sharp rap with my fist. "We went over this on the phone."

"Refresh my memory."

Aggravation reared its head as I glared at him. The man had the sharpest mind of anyone I knew. There was no way he'd forgotten anything I'd said. He only wanted to listen to me say it again just because he could. When he continued to watch me, that annoying smirk on his face, I knew I wouldn't get anywhere until I complied.

"Okay." It came out sounding like a sigh. "My neighbor Hal and I had already signed contracts for him to sell his land to me. Then, he reneged. I need that land for the milkweed for my monarchs. For their swarm to grow."

I'll give Payne credit. He didn't comment on how much he hated the butterflies. However, his expression of distaste rivaled that of a little kid who's told there's nothing for supper but an enormous plate of raw rhubarb.

He tapped his fingers on the tabletop. "So—"

A waitress stopped at our table, her smile way too cheery for what he and I were about to discuss. "What can I get you folks?"

Payne ordered a steak sandwich and a beer. I got a salad and water.

After she'd walked away, Payne leaned forward. "Gosh, Seneca. Drinking water? Living on the wild side, aren't you?" His tone was pure mockery. But I'd come to expect nothing else.

Ignoring his jab, I crossed my arms over my chest. "Can we get back to the reason we're here?"

He rolled his eyes. "Whatever."

That had been one of his go-to responses when he didn't like what I said. Hearing it now caused an actual shiver to run down my back. It was hard to get my words out since I was clenching my teeth so hard. "What I need from you, is to speak to Hal. He can't be allowed to get away with this. Make him see reason. Since we already have a signed contract."

"What if he doesn't? See reason, I mean. How far are you willing to go with this?"

With a shrug, I said, "Take him to court, I guess." Everything in me wanted anything but that. However, if I didn't get the land, the monarchs, which had been reproducing quite nicely, would die out. Milkweed was essential to their livelihood. If there wasn't enough to go around, not all the butterflies would make it.

Plus the fact I needed to grow the swarm to increase revenue, along with profits from Painted Wings Café. Though my grandmother had given me the farm, there were still tons of bills to pay. I was determined to make it on my own. And not depend on anyone else. Especially a man.

Especially this man.

"We can do that." He rubbed his hands together, like he salivated to drag someone to court by their hair, bouncing them up the steps to the town's small courthouse. "First, though, I'll need to stop by to see him. Do you have your contract handy?"

Right before I'd left the house, I'd remembered to stuff it in my purse. I dug it out. "Here."

He unfolded it and spread it on the table. After he perused it to the end, he said, "Well, your one-hundred-year-old attorney did the minimum he could have with the wording, but it'll get the job done."

"Seriously? You're talking bad about a man who was just—" I stopped myself just short of the word.

"Was just… what? You never did say what he died of."

I glanced around, wishing the waitress had brought our drinks, wanting something to occupy my fidgety hands.

"Seneca?" He leaned forward. "What aren't you saying?"

That's the bad thing about having been married to someone. They know you too well. I huffed out a breath. Payne was resourceful and never missed a trick. He'd hear about Mr. Morton's murder soon enough. Somehow, he knew things before most people in Maple Junction. I sighed and leaned forward. Keeping my voice low, I said, "Murder."

For the first time I could remember, Payne was stunned. His eyes bugged out, and his mouth gaped open. When he finally closed it, he shook his head slowly. If the subject wasn't so macabre, it might have been fun to know something before he did. Finally, he said, "Wow."

"Yep." I nodded.

Suddenly, he sat up straight and gave me the eye. The one he used on clients who weren't telling him everything. "Wait."

Uh-oh.

"How do you know this? I haven't heard anything from my sources," he asked. Over the time we were married, he'd mentioned those sources time and again but never who they were. I'd always figured he'd done it to try to impress me. I knew for a fact there were times when he made things up to try to sound good. He blinked slowly, assessing me. "Unless you—"

"Of course not!" My words had come out so loud, even with the music blaring, several customers turned to stare. I swallowed hard and whispered, "I didn't kill anyone."

"Then...." He moved his hand in a circle.

"Well, you see..." I grabbed a napkin from the table dispenser and wadded it into a ball. "I found him."

For the second time, I'd caught him off guard. Interesting. "Tell me more about that," he said.

"Eewww. No. I don't want to talk about that. That's not why we're here." Shoving aside thoughts of all the congealing blood, I glared at him, hoping he'd give it up and move on.

"Still, I'd like to know."

"Forget it," I said.

"But—"

The waitress brought our food and drinks. "Hey, Seneca," she said. "Heard that lawyer guy died in your greenhouse. Is it true his inner essence was taken by aliens, and they only left his body behind?"

My mouth dropped open. I quickly recovered and shook my head. "Um, no. There weren't aliens involved."

Her face fell. "Darn. I had aliens in the local pool about how he checked out." She shrugged. "Oh, well. Enjoy your meal."

I watched her walk away. What other crackpot theories would people come up with that I hadn't already heard? I swallowed hard. The reminder of finding Mr. Morton nearly spoiled my appetite. I stuck my fork in the salad and acted like I was interested in the croutons. Maybe Payne would drop the subject of my dead lawyer.

Probably not.

He grabbed his sandwich and took a humongous bite, then, talking around the food spewing from his mouth, said, "So who did it?"

Grossed out at the discussion subject and the disgusting, slobbering atrocity across the table, I set down my fork. "We don't know."

"Who's we?"

"Cody."

His barked-out laugh sprayed his side of the table with bits of his sandwich. "Should have known."

"He is the sheriff," I said.

"Yeah, but I bet you would have called him even if he wasn't."

Well, he had me there.

Payne glared at me. "I always thought, and still think, you two were way too close while you and I were married."

Indignation caused my hand to clench, tight. "Not true."

"Wherever you went, he was there. And what about now? You can't tell me, with all the time you two seem to be together, you haven't gone past the friends' stage."

"N—" I'd started to say no but changed my mind. "None of your business."

He pointed his finger right in my face. I wanted to bite it. "See, I knew it."

Let him think what he wanted. Perverse of me, I know, but it was nice for him to not be right about everything. I took a drink and set it down with a thunk. What if Payne spread it around, and it got back to Cody? What would he say?

Probably laugh it off. It wouldn't be the first time somebody assumed that about him and me.

After eating a few bites of salad, I asked the waitress for a to-go box. Watching Payne noisily inhale his sandwich made my stomach queasy. Finally done imitating a famished warthog, he wiped his mouth with his napkin, tossing it on top of his empty plate. "I assume I can hold on to this contract for now."

"Yes." Since I didn't trust him, I'd made a copy first. Guess I'd learned a few things by being married to a lawyer.

"There is something else." He leaned toward me.

I closed my eyes for a second, frustrated. "What would that be?"

"You said you'd found Morton."

"Didn't you hear me say I didn't want to discuss that?" But I knew the more I protested, the more he'd gleefully pursue the subject.

"Not about how he looked or anything. But have you considered the fact that you might be a suspect? The police usually check out the person who found a body."

A suspect. The realization that he was right, hit me in the gut. I gasped in air, afraid there'd be a shortage. Like I wouldn't get enough.

He glanced around before saying, "If that's the case, you're gonna need me."

"I don't require a guy's shoulder to cry on, Payne." Especially not his. Never again.

"What I meant was, me being a lawyer," he said.

Another direct hit to my midsection. If it came to that, it would be necessary to use Payne for more than just getting Hal's land. That might mean the difference between me being free or....

Anxiety clutched my heart. Would I be convicted? Go to prison? And as a cat-mom, my next thought was Winifred. Who would take care of her if that happened? My face must have lost all color because Payne reached over to grab my hand across the table.

"Hey," he said, "I didn't say that to scare you. Just being practical."

I glanced down at our joined hands. Why was Payne being nice? Unless this was all about a possible murder trial where he could strut around in a courtroom with a really big case.

Just being practical.

Frowning, I slid my hand from his. I grabbed my purse, to-go box, then stood. Digging in my purse for money, I tried to avoid Payne's eyes. Didn't want to think about murder. Prison. Winifred being homeless.

With a wave of his hand, he said, "Keep your money. You'll need it for my fee."

Wanting to be anywhere but here, I stuffed my cash back into my bag, turned, and left.

# Chapter Ten

My pickup bumped along the dry grass as I hauled the trailer toward the edge of my property. Rage still simmered just below the surface at what Hal had done. How dare he? Even if he was going through something, a late-life crisis or whatever, he didn't have the right to take it out on me. On my milkweed. Renewed anger burned in my chest at how many monarchs were now gone.

I climbed out of the cab, then peered back into the open window. "Winifred, you can either stay here and nap or come outside. Your choice."

After ignoring me for a few seconds, she swished her tail back and forth, dislodging specks of dust that danced in the stream of sunlight filtering through the window. She bent her head and licked at a spot on her chest. Finally, she settled down on the passenger seat, her chin on her front paws, like that had been her plan all along. And to make me wait while she got there.

Okay, then.

I tugged on my work gloves, then grabbed my decrepit rake from the truck bed. Before I started my work, I gave a quick glance toward Hal's. Didn't see him. Good. Because if I did, and he dared to come onto my land again, he might just get smacked in the head with my gardening tool. I sighed. Better forget that. If it happened, Cody would have to arrest me, and Payne would have something else to represent me for and....

Wait.

Nothing good could come from panicking, assuming the worst, even though that's where my mind traveled ever since finding Mr. Morton. Time to get to work and fix the damage. There must be some way for me to obtain Hal's land. Otherwise, my swarm wouldn't grow. And with the mayhem he'd caused with his pressure washer, I was worse off than before.

With resolve, I started clearing out broken milkweed at the end of my patch, farthest away from Hal's place. Maybe by the time I got closer to his barn, I'd have cooled off enough to not want to do him bodily harm.

Fat chance.

Bending at the waist, I inserted the narrow rake between the milkweed that stood intact. I had to go slow, making sure I didn't further damage the stalks that hadn't suffered from the pressure hose. A few nearby butterflies flitted away when I invaded their territory. "Sorry, guys. I'll make it all better for you soon. I promise."

If I hadn't come up on Hal when I had, would he have destroyed it all? I was still flummoxed as to why. He'd been nothing but kind and considerate all the years I'd known him. What would make a person completely change like that? Maybe he had some illness. A brain tumor?

Great, now I sounded like Annie, handing out diagnoses like coupons at the grocery.

I worked steadily for several minutes until I'd formed a large, damp pile. Abandoning the rake against the side of the truck, I scooped up an armful of ruined stalks and tossed them onto the trailer. Another armful followed. And again, until that pile was gone.

It took me quite a while to accomplish my task, but that might have been good. Maybe I got rid of some of my irritation while I burned calories.

A quick check into the cab showed Winifred asleep and dreaming. Flipped on her back, paws batting at some invisible foe. Maybe she was battling Hal. Maybe she'd put claw marks from his eyebrow to his chin. I smiled slightly. Not a nice thought, but let's face it—I was so mad at him. But that line of thinking wasn't helping me get the job done. I went back to work.

Once the trailer was full, I'd take it to the back of my property and burn the milkweed. I stopped in my tracks. Why hadn't Hal simply set fire to it instead of dragging over his pressure washer? It would have been quicker and gotten rid of the whole patch in no time. Had he been afraid someone would come to investigate the smoke right away, but wouldn't hear or see him with the hose?

*Joke's on you, Hal, since I caught you.*

My smugness died. *No, Seneca. Joke's on you.*

With a sigh, I kept at it. A few monarchs fluttered near my head. I held still as one lit on my shoulder. "Hey there. Glad you're still with us. No thanks to our evil neighbor."

The female orange and black beauty slowly flapped her wings down, then up, pressing them together. The movement was so slow, so measured as to be hypnotic. When I was a little kid, I'd follow Gram around when she'd check the butterflies. If it took longer than expected, sometimes I'd find a corner and take a nap. Often, there'd be a few monarchs perched on me when I woke.

One of my favorite pictures was one Gram had taken of me like that. Sound asleep on an old plaid blanket in the corner, a monarch perched on my head, and two more on my arm. Why couldn't life be that easy now? Everyone getting along. Sticking to their word if they said they'd do something?

I forced myself to keep working, making piles of soggy milkweed debris and loading them onto the trailer until it was full. Setting down my rake, I walked to the end of the row to see how much I'd have left for an additional trailer haul.

Not too much. Maybe I could just—

Shuffling—maybe footsteps? —stopped me cold. Was Hal coming over here again? I reached down into my pocket to make sure I had my phone. If he dared commit another crime on my land, this time, I'd get proof on video.

Crouching down, I did a half-crawl-half-walk to the edge of the milkweed row. I peered around the end stalk and got a surprise.

It wasn't Hal.

As I watched, the man—fifty-ish, heavyset, with short gray hair, partly bald, wearing dress slacks and a button-down shirt—was setting up a tripod.

On my land.

When he turned, I realized it was Lonny Gibbs, a local surveyor. I'd seen him around but had never officially met him. His phone was now in his hand, held up in front of his face. He moved his thumb to a button on the front. Was he taking photos? From what I could tell, he was getting ready to survey Hal's property, but he stood over the line on mine.

Not gonna happen.

I stood and brushed clumps of milkweed from my clothes. Then, I took a deep breath and let it out. Making my voice loud enough so he couldn't help but hear me, I said, "Excuse me. Can I help you with something?"

Startled, he nearly dropped his phone. He fumbled but caught it. "Um... hello."

Walking—more like marching—I hurried toward him. A few feet away, I stopped. Anger, hot and fierce, overtook me. What Hal had done was terrible. But this was beyond the pale. How dare he allow someone to come in and take over when he has a contract already signed with me? "What do you think you're doing?"

"I'm..." He glanced toward Hal's barn. Was he expecting someone to come and rescue him?

Crossing my arms over my chest, I waited, half wondering if Hal would come out to join him. After putting his phone in his shirt pocket, Lonny approached me. Everything in me wanted to either kick him or run away, but I forced myself to stay put. Something about him was off-putting. Was it the way he studied me with narrowed, hawk-like eyes, or the nearly imperceptible way he curled one hand slowly into a fist at his side?

My heart raced. Fear ignited a slow burn inside my stomach and traveled to my throat.

An insincere smile appeared on his face. "I'm Lonny Gibbs."

I glanced down at his outstretched hand. There was no way I was touching it.

He lowered it to his side, and his fake pleasant countenance disappeared. "Might I ask who you are? Miss..."

Too bad Cody wasn't here this time. I'd feel so much better with him beside me. Whatever it was that bothered me about Lonny wasn't good. I just couldn't pinpoint what it was. "I'm the person who owns the land you're standing on. The land you've got your equipment set up on." With a tilt of my head, I indicated the three-legged intruder.

His eyes widened. "Oh. I... didn't know."

Yeah right. "What are you doing, anyway?"

He blinked but didn't answer.

Peering around him at the tripod, I said, "Are you surveying Hal Atkins' land?"

"Why... yes." Tiny beads of sweat popped up on his forehead. Was he nervous? Lying?

"Listen, Mr. Gibbs. You need to remove that —" I pointed to the tripod "— from my land."

He narrowed his eyes. "Fine."

"I have a signed contract with Hal. That land should come to me. I need it." Even though Hal was acting crazy, had reneged on our contract, I refused to believe we couldn't work it out somehow. Even if it meant going to court. I hated the thought, but what else could I do?

He rose to his full height, which was a couple inches above mine. "Miss, whoever you are, I assure you that I need the land."

"Why can't you go buy someplace else? Anyplace else? There're tons of empty lots and farmland for sale around here. What are you planning to use it for anyway?"

I knew I was treading deep waters here. It was none of my business what he'd planned for the property. But the fact that he wanted to take the very acreage I had to have really stuck in my craw.

"If you must know—"

"Oh, I must." I tapped my foot on the dirt.

"—there are plans to build a trendy upscale shopping mall."

I nearly choked on a laugh. "Here? In little Maple Junction?"

"That's right."

"Whatever for?" The most glamorous thing anyone I knew shopped for was new kitchen curtains after their annual spring cleaning. Our rural town was plain and simple. And so were the residents. No way I could envision anyone making regular purchases at a place that sold expensive do-dads that had no real purpose.

He watched me, sizing me up, making fear slither across my shoulders again. "Maybe if you had something to attract attention like the mall we will build, Maple Junction wouldn't be so little." He turned quickly away and grabbed the equipment. There were now three small holes in the dirt.

Mr. Gibbs lugged the tripod closer to Hal's barn. Once there, he gave me a glare over his shoulder before getting his phone out again. His voice was harsh and raised to whoever it was he spoke. Too bad I couldn't make out the words.

Then again, did I really want to know?

The trailer needed to be unloaded at my fire pit, but I didn't want to leave while Mr. Gibbs was still around. Would he simply come back over the property line once I left? To stall, I went to my truck to check on Winifred. She was still snoozing, though not twitching like she was before.

Opening the door quietly, I climbed in and sat beside her. I ruffled her fluffy head, then smoothed out the fabric of her monarch costume. Watching her lying there in her little outfit at least made me smile. Not easily done since I'd found Mr. Morton and had to deal with all of Hal's craziness.

My cat purred in her sleep, her own smile curving beneath her rounded, chubby cheeks. I petted her a while longer, then slipped back out of the truck.

When I rounded the edge of the milkweed again, Mr. Gibbs wasn't alone. Hal had joined him. They stood close together, whispering, both sets of hands flailing in excitement. Or desperation.

Hal glanced my way. My first inclination was to dive into the stalks like Winifred had done previously. But I was on my property. He was in the wrong. Why should I run and hide?

Suddenly, both men stopped talking and turned to face me.

Their expressions weren't friendly.

# Chapter Eleven

I couldn't get the image of Lonny Gibbs and his surveying equipment out of my head. Was he serious about building a shopping mall right next door? It didn't make sense. But then, the way he'd sneered at me and had been so condescending, he might have been lying anyway. The fact that Hal seemed to be in cahoots with him on top of the way he'd tried to destroy my milkweed and then lied about me to Cody, had me itching to do something. Something to get an advantage on Lonny. Right now, Hal was acting so crazy, I wondered if I should just keep my distance for a while. But Lonny…maybe I could find something out about him.

There were lots of gossips in Maple Junction and a bunch of people who always seemed to know what was going on with everyone else. But the one who was at the top of my list, who always, somehow, had the latest news on whatever was most interesting, was Karen Blain.

Karen was the main bank teller at the smaller of the two banks in town. And the woman loved to talk, mostly about other people. I also happened to know she was a sucker for Murray's cheesy fries, because she was one of my regular customers. She came in and ordered them at least twice a month, and usually finished off a large order all by herself. Not that I was judging. Murray's fries were seriously amazing.

Time to make a special delivery to the bank.

After grabbing a large helping of the fries from the rack beside the fryer, trying to ignore Murray's frown as I did so, I placed them inside a red and white checked cloth napkin and then in a small wicker basket with a handle. Might as well go all out in trying to bribe Karen by making my offering look pretty. The aroma of the fries would get me in the door, but the whole package would hopefully help seal the deal of getting needed information.

I hurried to my truck, placed the basket on the passenger side floor for safekeeping, and hightailed it to the bank. I knew the business hours of most places in town since I frequented them so often and remembered that Karen would only have twenty minutes or so until her lunch break.

Maybe the fact that I was bringing food when she was certain to be extra hungry would help my cause.

In the bank parking lot, I parked next to another car. It didn't look like Karen's. But hopefully, if it was another customer, they'd be wrapping up their business in short order. I'd bet Karen was talking their leg off right about now. Maybe they'd even be glad when I went in and interrupted them so they could escape.

As I stepped inside, it took a few seconds for my eyes to adjust to the dimness of the room. The interior of the bank was downright gloomy. Wouldn't it make more sense to have a cheery atmosphere? It was where people went to get money, after all. And didn't money usually make people happy?

Karen was indeed yakking, loudly, without taking a breath. A young woman with a feisty toddler on her hip was impatiently tapping her foot. Karen wouldn't be able to see it over her counter, but it was obvious the customer was more than ready to flee.

Holding up my basket, I got Karen's attention. "Hey, thought I'd bring you a surprise. From the café."

The teller's eyebrows rose along with the sides of her lips.

*Ah, yes. This might work.*

With a huge grin, Karen waved me closer. As I stepped past the younger woman, she gave me a relieved smile, then promptly scurried to the door.

I didn't blame her. I'd be the same way, having been on the receiving end of Karen's talkativeness more than I'd care to admit.

"Seneca! You brought me a surprise? What's the occasion?" Her words were aimed at me, but her eyes never left the basket in my hands.

"Oh, just…I know how much you like the fries Murray makes. Thought

I'd bring you some." All right, that sounded lame.

She clutched her hands to her chest and smiled. "Oh, how wonderful." If I'd presented her with diamonds, I'm not sure her reaction would have been any more gleeful. Glancing at the clock, then back at me, she winked. "And wouldn't you know, I was just about to close up for the lunch hour."

I tried to form an innocent expression. Of course, I knew. That was my diabolical plan, after all. "Well, that worked out great, then."

She reached down, locked her money drawer, then walked to the half-door at the end of the counter to exit the teller area.

When she reached me, I held out the basket. Taking it, she peered beneath the cloth napkin.

"What a treat. Thank you so much."

Then, I waited. I'd filled the basket with more fries than probably four people could eat in one sitting. Maybe she'd take the hint.

"My goodness, Seneca. There's so much here. Maybe you'd like to join me?"

*I would indeed.*

"What a great idea," I said. "Thanks. I think I will. I happen to love Murray's cheesy fries, too." I followed her out a side door where there were a few picnic tables for the employees to take their breaks or eat lunch on nice days.

We sat down at the farthest one from the street, located in the most shade.

Along with the fries, I'd placed a bunch of disposable napkins and a plastic fork. Karen took a couple napkins out, spread them on the tabletop, and scooped out some fries with the fork. Once I'd done the same, we spent a couple minutes enjoying the food and the sunny day. When a good portion of the fries were gone, I wiped my hands on a napkin and placed my forearms on the table.

Karen finished what was on her napkin, looked longingly at what was still in the basket, then, with a sigh, closed the napkin over the remainder. Did she think I'd take away what was left?

Pointing toward the fries, I said, "Take those home with you. For later."

Her shoulders slumped with relief. "Great. Thank you. I'll return the basket next time I'm in the café."

"No, you keep that. Part of the gift."

Karen winked. "Too bad. I was hoping for free refills."

We both laughed.

Time to get to business. Trying to act as if I really didn't care all that much, I said, "So, anything interesting happen lately?"

As she wadded up her paper napkins and set them to the side, she shrugged. "I guess nothing earth-shattering." She blinked. "Oh wait, I did hear about Mr. Morton."

"Um, what did you hear?"

"Not sure if this is accurate or not… but I heard he got some terrible disease?"

"Oh, really?" I asked.

Karen nodded. "Yeah. Jonas down at the post office told me that Morton had recently received a postcard from Costa Rica."

"Okay…"

"Well, according to the scuttlebutt, that postcard was laced with the disease. And Morton contracted it. And died. Poor Jonas was so scared that he'd contracted it from the postcard too that he camped out on his doctor's doorstep until he examined him and called the all-clear on Jonas' health."

How in the world did Jonas come up with that crazy theory? I tried to keep a straight face as I said, "Uh, it's true Mr. Morton is dead. But I hadn't heard about the postcard angle. Pretty sure it wasn't that."

"Shoot." She snapped her fingers. "And I had postcard-laced-with-horrible-disease in the betting pool."

I waited, knowing how she'd respond to my earlier question about having heard any news lately.

She tilted her head. "What about you? Anything going on with you?"

Her question also gave me the opening I'd hoped for. "Now that you mention it. Something did happen. Just today."

All ears now, Karen leaned forward. "What? Tell me."

"I was at my farm. You know that back edge that sits next to Hal's property?"

Her head bobbed up, then down.

"There was someone else there. Someone who shouldn't have been."

Her eyes widened. "Go on."

"Well, it was Lonny Gibbs. Do you know him?"

Waving her hand, she said, "Oh, sure. He's a customer here. As a matter of fact, he was in here just recently."

I'd discovered in the past that Karen didn't like silence and wanted to fill it up with words. Her words. Even when it went past appropriate boundaries for talking about bank business and customers. So, I kept quiet and waited.

Karen looked toward the street—did she think someone was spying on us? —then back to me. "That man is in a world of hurt."

"Is that so?"

"Let me tell you—"

*That's why I'm here.*

"—he's gotten himself into a boatload of financial woes," she said.

I sat up straighter. I'd come here hoping to find something out about Lonny but knew it might not come to anything. Maybe Karen really did know something that could help me.

Karen tapped the tabletop with her fingernail. "Lonny Gibbs came in here wanting a loan. Begged our loan officer. To tell the truth, he actually wept because he needed money so bad."

"So, what happened?"

"The loan officer tried to help him. He really did. But Lonny's finances were in such bad shape it didn't look like he'd be a good risk for the bank to take when it came time to pay back the loan."

"Wow, so he got nothing?" I asked.

"Nothing."

I toyed with the crumpled napkin still in front of me on the table. "Did Lonny say anything else? Like... what he might do next?"

Karen nodded. "Oh yes. Well, first, he spewed all kinds of venomous threats to the loan person, saying he'd be sorry, the bank would be sorry. The whole town. You get the drift."

"Sure." I wanted to move my hand in the hurry up and continue motion but didn't dare.

"Lonny lamented that his sister wasn't going to bail him out this time. And since the bank had turned him down too, he had to do something drastic."

"Lonny's sister? I don't think I know her."

"I bet you do," she said.

"Really?"

"His twin. Lorna."

My eyes widened. "Not Lorna Watkins."

"Yep, that's the one."

Was Lorna somehow in on what was going on with Lonny, even though, according to him, she wouldn't bail him out? I'd been curious about Murray's comment before, that Lorna had a past with Mr. Morton. But now that I knew the connection between her and Lonny, I was even more interested.

Karen leaned closer. "Then, Lonny —and let me tell you he wasn't keeping his voice down even though other customers could hear him —said he was going to get the money some way. Even if he had to steal to do it. Can you imagine?"

I was beginning to do that very thing. Maybe Lonny, along with Hal, were in on something together. And that something, whatever it was, wouldn't do me or my farm any good. At all.

# Chapter Twelve

Since Lonny and Hal hadn't left yet when I'd been ready to go unload my trailer, I'd put off the task. Besides, I had more important chores, like taking care of the monarchs. And it benefited me to let the soggy milkweed dry out more anyway.

Annie was waiting beside the greenhouse when I got there. Winifred, at my heels, saw my assistant, skittered in place with her paws, then turned and ran back toward the house. I shook my head at my weird cat, mentally prepared myself to spend the day with my weirder assistant, and headed that way.

"Hi, Annie."

"Hey, boss." She pushed her thick hair behind her ears, but it immediately sprang back into her face. With a sigh, she reached into her jeans pocket, grabbed a hair band, and forced her curls into reluctant submission.

I did like her. Honest. She was hard-working and gentle with the butterflies. It was people she had trouble connecting with that was sometimes an issue. She'd talk to them, but the things that popped out of her mouth were often ludicrous.

When I had the door unlocked, I let Annie step in ahead of me. I switched on the main lights, smiling as Annie made a beeline for the caterpillar pens. When she bent down and asked them if they had a good night's sleep, I smiled.

She and I worked steadily for an hour or so, caring for the caterpillars, checking on the newly hatched monarchs, cataloging their progress, and tidying up. Every time I had to walk over the spot where I'd found Mr.

Morton, I found myself edging around the area. Almost like I'd step on the poor man if I didn't.

Would I ever stop the habit? Get to the point where I didn't think about him every single day? Hopefully, the memory would fade soon as time moved on.

A noise came from outside.

"Someone's here." Annie, with her long-legged stride, rushed to the closed screen door, peering through. "A van. Several people getting out. All older." When she glanced at me over her shoulder, eyes large behind the ovals of her glasses, her expression was one of horror. "Seneca, I think it's a bus tour." Her fear couldn't have been more apparent had she uttered the words, axe-wielding fiend.

Though I wasn't in as much distress as Annie seemed to be, I did unconsciously hunch my shoulders. With so much to do, a lot to catch up on from being otherwise detained the past couple of days, it wasn't the best day for visitors.

But what could I do? March out and demand they turn back around and leave? No. The farm needed good word of mouth to keep bringing in potential customers. To do anything to drive anyone away, even if I didn't have the time to spare for them, would be ill-advised.

I stepped toward the door, smiled at Annie until she got the hint and moved aside, then walked out into the cloudy, humid day to greet our guests. "Good morning." I waved and headed toward them.

My assistant had said it was a van, but it was the largest one I'd ever seen without calling it a bus. Annie's fears were realized when person after person made it down the steps and to the gravel drive. They were, indeed, all past retirement age. Not that I minded. Not a bit. People who'd been around longer than me always had interesting stories. Experiences I'd never had. But sometimes, the older visitors took longer to move around, tended to stay longer, looking for something to occupy their day.

Stifling a sigh, I stuck out my hand to a man who appeared not to be a member of the tour, but in charge. He was a forty-something skinny man with a floppy hat, knee-length khaki shorts, and black socks with snow-white tennis shoes.

Like an over-exuberant kids' summer camp counselor.

"Hello!" His enthusiasm was a little much for this early in the morning, but maybe he'd had a lot of caffeine to keep his charges moving and in order. Not that they appeared rowdy or anything. More like they'd find a warm corner and take a nap like Winifred. "I'm Richard Brockman. Director of Where Would You Like to Go Today Tours."

Did the poor man have to say that whole thing every time he introduced himself?

"Nice to meet you. I'm Seneca James. Welcome to Majestic Monarchs."

An eighty-something woman, blue hair—no, really, bright blue—came closer. "Fabulous place." Her orange caftan swirled around her mint green flip-flops. Her rectangle red plastic glasses frames sparkled in the dim sunlight whenever she moved her head, a kaleidoscope surrounding her eyes. It was oddly mesmerizing.

"Thank you." I bit my lip against a laugh. Though today wasn't the best day for a tour, these folks might be interesting, to say the least. Maybe they'd take my mind off my troubles for a bit. "I'm happy to show you all around the grounds, though the café won't be open until noon."

A second woman, had to be six feet tall, joined the first. Her shoulder-length silver hair was stick straight, hanging down over a neck scarf of mud brown. Her black, tattered army boots squeaked on the ground as she pivoted. "Oh, hey. An actual greenhouse. I've never been this close to one before." She'd said it as if my building was a rare albino rhinoceros found unexpectedly in the wild.

Richard cupped his hands around his mouth and shouted, "Come on out, folks. Don't be shy." Several more people alighted from the van, mouths agape, staring every which way, as if they'd landed on planet Saturn.

After a glance at the side of the van, my suspicions were confirmed. The tour had originated in New York City. If they lived in that huge city and this was their first tour to rural Indiana, maybe it did all seem like another planet.

Of course, having never been there, I might feel the same about their hometown.

Once Richard seemed confident all his little chickens were accounted for, he swirled around on the heels of his shoes and faced me with a grin. "Everyone, this is Seneca James. She runs this beautiful establishment." After they murmured to each other and took pictures of every tree, bush, clod of dirt, and even some of the gravel on the drive, Richard said to me, "Now, we're ready."

"Great." I made myself smile, though all the while, I'd waited for them to get off the bus, stand in a line to count off for Richard, and make sure they all had their cameras, purses, fanny packs, bottles of water, snacks, bug repellent—did they think they were going to be stuck in the jungle for a few days?—I'd mentally made a list of all the chores I should have already completed by now. At least they'd brought their own food, so maybe no one would be too put out if they couldn't buy any at the café yet.

Hoping Annie had gotten a good start on some of those jobs, I glanced toward the greenhouse door.

No such luck. Her pale face was pressed to the screen, hard enough that her nose was flattened against it. Her eyes were wide, like she was watching some rare herd of blue-haired wildebeests frolicking on the prairie.

With a small shake of my head, I waved my hand in the direction of the greenhouse. "If everyone would like to step this way, we'll start the tour inside."

Anxious whispers came from behind. One woman shrieked. Was she afraid the butterflies might attack her? The most they might do was flutter someone to death.

*Stop thinking about death.*

"All right now," said Richard, his hands out, palms pushing down. "Stay calm, everyone. Don't get overexcited."

If something as sedate as cocooning caterpillars got them worked up, what would happen if they came across a rock concert somewhere?

I opened the screen door. Annie, still gawking at the older folks, hadn't seemed to notice the door was no longer closed. Finally noticing me standing there, she scurried down a side aisle and perched on a stool in the corner to watch.

"Okay, everyone. Come on in." I held the door open as they filed past. Remembering how Winifred had avoided spending time with Annie, I was suddenly glad my cat hadn't followed me in here. Not only would she have freaked out at all the strangers here at once, but some of the visitors, in awe of the trees and greenhouse, might have gone off the deep end at seeing the resident wildlife in her yellow swallowtail butterfly costume. Fur would have flown.

Not necessarily Winifred's.

After waiting until their excited whispers ceased, I pointed to the first pen. "These are monarch caterpillars. You'll notice their outer coverings."

One woman edged closer. "They actually live inside those little sleeping bags?"

"Temporarily, yes. Those are called cocoons."

"Cocoons." The word echoed around the confines of the room. These poor people needed to get out of the city more often.

I patted the top of the pen. "Their life cycle goes from egg to larvae, to caterpillar, and finally to butterfly."

Heads nodded, and cameras flashed. I wondered if, when they got their pictures developed, they'd even remember why they'd taken photos of small, hanging body bags.

Body bags. I shuddered. *Don't think about dead people, not now.*

Something touched my arm, startling me. I glance down to see Richard's fingers lightly pressed on my sleeve. "Miss James. Are you all right?"

Suddenly, Annie bolted forward, fear of blue-haired people forgotten, parting the crowd to make her way toward me. "Wait! Let me have a look at her."

"Oh no." I swallowed hard. "I'm fine, honest. Nothing to worry ab—"

Before I could finish, Annie was at my side, her fingers pressed to my wrist. Was she taking my pulse?

"Are you a doctor, dear?" asked a man with glasses so thick his eyes were magnified, resembling large blue quarters.

Annie nodded.

What was she doing? "Um, Annie?" I waved my hand at her, trying to get her to stop.

She winked at me, like she and I had some special secret she was now ready to reveal to the world. "I'm going to medical school."

The way she said it made it sound like she was already attending, not simply hopeful of one day going.

Several of the tour members crowded closer. The questions began, people interrupted each other, trying to get the doctor's attention. No good could come of this.

"Can you check this mole on my arm?"

"My sister has the lazy eye. Any advice for treatment?"

"I'm afraid my sciatica is acting up, and I've forgotten my meds. Could you write me a prescription?"

Annie's face glowed with joy.

Prescription? Advice was bad enough. This was getting out of hand. "Uh…" I tried to get my assistant's attention to draw her away from her fans and have a little chat about her not being a real doctor. But she only had eyes and ears for her new adoring patients.

Oh boy. This was going to be a long morning.

Richard, not appearing in the least surprised or upset about the turn of events—maybe this happened often when they sensed the presence of medical personnel—leaned closer. "I wonder if I might ask you something. Over there?" He tilted his head toward the far corner, away from the throng of people now asking for individual prescriptions and treatment.

"But…" I pointed toward Annie, "I need to make sure she doesn't—"

"That can wait." The sudden pressure of his hand on my upper arm got my attention.

What was going on? Seeing I wasn't going to get Annie's attention for a while and guessing there was no harm in the people asking for prescriptions Annie couldn't give them, I acquiesced and went with the strange little man a few yards away.

With a last glance at my assistant, I finally gave my attention to Richard.

He raised one eyebrow and said, "When I was asking around about your butterfly farm at another local establishment, I heard some interesting news."

"Really?" I crossed my arms, waiting.

"Well, according to a young woman at the checkout counter, while I bought snacks for my tour members, an extraordinary event took place recently. She told me an interesting tidbit."

I sighed. Couldn't help it. I should have guessed this would happen, though I hadn't expected it quite so soon. "And what was that?"

"The girl was saying that a man was murdered. Right here in this very greenhouse." His eyes had gone wide in anticipation.

Perfect. If his people were excited about worms in sleeping bags, how would they handle the knowledge that they stood only feet away from a recent murder? Denying it wouldn't do any good, since it wasn't a secret. "Yes, that's true."

He gasped and clasped his hands together in delight. "Excellent. I'll get that award for sure."

"I beg your pardon?" I asked.

"Every year, a tour guide within the company is awarded with the Where Do You Want to Go Today Most Interesting Tour Stop Award. No one in the history of tour stops has ever been in the location of an actual murder. It is because of you, after all."

I held out my hand. "Hey, wait a minute. I didn't kill anyone."

"What? No, of course not. Just meant that because it happened in your greenhouse, you should receive some of the credit for me getting the award. Perhaps you could give me some more details? You know, about what happened."

This was getting way out of hand. "As happy as I am for your, uh, award, I'm afraid I can't give you details. It's still under investigation."

"How disappointing. Well, there is something else I heard."

Really wanting to get the group finished with their tour so I could get back to work, I tried not to sound as irritated as I was. "And what was that?"

"A rumor is floating around your little town that over in that park, there's a buried treasure."

I shook my head. "No, that's not true. That rumor has been spread for as long as I can remember. Just somebody wanting to stir something up, I'm sure."

He frowned. "Well, that's a shame. I was thinking of maybe leading a tour next month to investigate that theory. Oh, well, there's still the news of the murder that happened here in your greenhouse."

Though I didn't plan it, my gaze wandered to the spot.

Blinking rapidly, Richard eyed that area on the cement, then focused again on me. "Miss James, is that the site?" He got out his camera and snapped a couple of pictures.

I groaned. How could this day have gotten so out of control so early?

Thankfully, some of the group had sudden nap attacks, a lot like Winifred did, and were ready to leave. By the time the last person was seated on the bus, I felt like I'd worked an entire day. But there was still so much to get accomplished. And I didn't have the luxury of taking a nap right now.

# Chapter Thirteen

After making sure Annie was still working with the caterpillars, I headed out to check on the doused milkweed. It was dry. And I was alone. No sign of my turncoat neighbor or the creepy surveyor. Good. Before I left, I made sure Winifred was still shut in the house. She hadn't been pleased, but there's no way she would have enjoyed being so close to a huge, smelly, smoky burn pile any more than she would have liked being fawned over by touchy-feely senior citizens.

I hooked the trailer to my truck and drove over the beaten-down grassy path to the far edge of my property. Venturing to this corner was something I only did every so often. There wasn't any milkweed here, so monarchs weren't in abundance.

Plus, a small portion of my land met the edge of the park, although all that was back here was a tangle of scrub trees and wildflowers. All the better for me, though. Park visitors weren't as interested in that area, so they pretty much stayed away.

The previous park ranger had once given me a lecture on fire safety since my land was so close to Pines Park. Even though I'd assured him it was safe, that the pit was far away from the park's trees, that I kept the pile contained in a cement basin with high sides, and I never, ever left the fire unattended, he'd regarded me with a scowl the entire time.

Showing him my fire pit and how safe it was, finally convinced him to leave me alone about it. I didn't blame the man for checking up on a close neighbor who burned brush. That was his job. I just wished I hadn't had to jump through so many hoops to assure him it was okay.

The crazy thing about when I burned brush was the butterflies. For some reason, they seemed to like the smoke. They flitted through it over and over, hung close by, like they wanted to see what would happen next. I'd never found a reason for it. But every single time, as soon as I got a good fire going, monarchs and other butterflies showed up when they hadn't previously been around.

That was okay. It was nice having their company since Winifred would have spent all her time either hiding in the truck or hissing at the fire.

It took me a little while to get all the stalks unloaded and into the pit. I retrieved my matches from the truck. No way I was going to leave them here all the time. Someone might come along and decide it would be fun to set fire to the trees in the park. Then Ranger Nelson would really have had something to worry about. Now, though, that would be Jesse's job.

Ready to get this over with, I struck a couple of matches and tossed them in the fray, stepping way back, respectful of impending fire. Not to mention the fact that if I came home smelling too smoky, Winifred would have nothing to do with me for days. Her nose might be tiny, but strong smells sent her scurrying away to the nearest hiding spot.

After walking to my truck, I opened the door and sat on the driver's seat to monitor the pile. With nothing else to occupy myself, my mind gleefully took over. Sudden images of Mr. Morton made me cringe. The blood. The mess. The pain he must have endured before breathing his last. Poor guy. Who killed him? And why?

Before I knew it, the flames had died down to embers. With the stalks so thin, the pile had shrunk in no time. I grabbed a large container of water from the truck bed, doused the remaining sparks, and waited a few more minutes to be sure it was out.

I was glad to have that done. But the reason for it, Hal's senseless destruction, still burned in my gut. What a waste of time, effort, and money. Not to mention the most important thing of all—the monarchs he chased away or destroyed.

With a sigh, I climbed into the truck to head back. I hadn't gone too far when I gasped, slamming on the brakes. A flash of gray and brown.

Something—a coyote maybe—had raced past, barely missing my front fender, his fluffy tail sailing straight behind him as he ran. Where was he going in such a hurry? Nothing was chasing him. He'd come from an area where several blue spruce pines huddled together on the edge of my land, next to the park. The animal trotted off. If he ended up in view of my house, Winifred would have a puffy fit that lasted a week.

A long, dark splotch lay on the ground in the direction from which the coyote had come. What was it? I squinted as I visually followed the path of the mark back to the pine trees. A line.

A red line.

Blood?

Maybe another animal had died there, and the coyote saw an opportunity for a quick meal. Or maybe… My mind went into overdrive. Flashbacks to the puddle of blood and Mr. Morton in the greenhouse.

Not again.

Panicked, I put the truck in park and jumped out. Pine branches snagged on my shirt as I pushed my way through to the center of the trees.

A woman, thirty or so, lay sprawled on her side, her back toward me. She seemed familiar, but from this angle, I couldn't tell for sure who it was. As I crept forward, I had to stifle a scream. It was Millie King! Mouth gaped open, hands clutched together near a hole in her midsection. That's where the blood had come from. It was everywhere. Had she been stabbed? For a moment, as I stared down at her, I saw not her pale skin, open eyes of light blue, but Mr. Morton's coarse features. His weathered skin and prominent nose.

*Stop it, Seneca.*

I forced myself to see what was there. Stepping forward slowly, as if something or someone might leap out at me, I avoided the blood as best I could. Leaning down, I felt for a pulse on the side of her neck, not surprised when there was nothing but cold, lifeless skin.

Poor Millie! Who would have done this? Everyone liked her, always had. Her sunny disposition when working at the park's department office made it a pleasure for visitors to stop by. If it wasn't for the stab wound, I'd wonder if she'd had an accident. But no. There was no way. And I didn't think she could or would have stabbed herself like that.

No, someone killed her. My heart ached for her family and close friends. How would they take the awful news when they heard?

What was she doing here at the very back of the park? From where she was, she was just over the property line on Pines Park land. Odd that she'd end up way back here since there wasn't much to see.

Most people headed for the trails and campgrounds. To get back here, though, a person would have to brave waist-deep grass and overgrown foliage, along with no clearly marked trails. Because that happened so infrequently, I didn't worry much about anyone coming onto my land.

Standing, then backing away, I gave her one last look before reaching for my phone. Cody would never believe this.

This time, I remembered to call the sheriff's office instead of his personal line, although my fingers fumbled for the number. Since there was another dead body, it seemed like keeping it official was more appropriate. I was in shock. Finding Mr. Morton had been bad enough. But Millie? She was someone I spoke to nearly every day. Such a nice woman. So many people would miss her.

"Sheriff's office."

I jumped when Dana answered the phone. "Hi, Dana. It's Seneca James."

"Hi, Seneca. How can I help you?"

"Well, there's a body. Dead. Body. Back of my land. Near the park." I pointed, obviously more for me than for her.

Two seconds of silence. Though it was her official duty to take and process all calls, ones about murder weren't normally received. Maybe I'd shocked her with my call. "I'll send Cody right out. He knows where you'll be, exactly?"

"Tell him it's close to my burn pile. He'll know."

"I'll make sure he gets there as soon as he can."

"Thank you." I ended the conversation and stuck my phone back in my pocket. Then, I went back to my truck to wait. I'd briefly considered staying there with Millie, but the more I looked at her wound, her expression, it

94

hurt my heart so much. If I were to keep my wits about me long enough to show Cody where I'd found her, I needed to take a few moments to calm down and collect myself.

Several minutes later, his truck came bouncing along the path I'd taken earlier. He pulled up next to me, then got out.

I expected him to ask where the dead body was first thing, but he surprised me. Without a word, he walked to me, opened his arms, and enfolded me close to his chest. I blinked. Not that I minded, or necessarily wanted it to end, but what was he doing?

A few seconds ticked by. Cody gave me a final squeeze and made eye contact as he pulled away. "Are you all right, Seneca?"

"Um…" Still taken off guard by the long hug when I'd expected something totally different, I nodded. "Yeah. I'm okay."

Cody shook his head. "Another one."

"Yes, another one. And… It's Millie King."

"What? Holy cow. What's happening to Maple Junction?"

I gave a shrug, wishing I had the answer. Something nefarious was going on in our little town, and I had the feeling it was only going to get worse.

I headed toward Millie in the trees. If I let myself think about it too much, I might end up in a fetal position on the ground. Why was this happening? Two people dead. Me finding them. One in my greenhouse and the other close to my property line. It couldn't be coincidence, could it? "I can't believe this has happened to Millie. And I'm still reeling from Mr. Morton. And, by the way…"

"What?" He gave me his full attention as he walked with me.

Swallowing hard, just wanting to get it out in the open, I said, "Payne said I might need him. In an official capacity."

"Why?"

"That maybe, I might be a suspect in Mr. Morton's death."

He grabbed my shoulder, but gently. "Don't be absurd. Since I'm the one who's investigating the man's murder, I'm the one hunting for suspects. And sister, you ain't it."

Relieved, I relaxed my shoulders.

"Were you seriously concerned that I suspected you?" he asked.

"Honestly? No. Not until Payne put the suggestion into my head. And then, it only bothered me if I let myself dwell on it."

"Here's some advice. Don't dwell. And ignore advice from your ex."

It wouldn't do any good to remind Cody that Payne was representing me in the case against Hal for the land. He'd never liked Payne. Would never like him. I let it go. Giving a shrug, as if to say, what're you gonna do?

We reached the spot where Millie lay motionless. Though I knew her expression couldn't have changed from a few minutes before when I'd found her, somehow, she appeared to be more frightened, more in shock.

Cody edged closer, taking in the body, the scene, the awful truth of what was before him. After a deep breath in and out, he knelt beside her. He felt for a pulse, standard procedure, I was sure, since she was obviously dead. If I had to guess, I'd say she'd been gone a little while. There was a slight odor. Her arms and legs appeared stiff. Must have been what had attracted the coyote. Either that or he smelled the blood and came running.

Cody repeated the same steps he'd taken with Mr. Morton. He took pictures from every angle, collected evidence with gloved hands and, dropped it in small clear plastic bags, then called the funeral director.

Wasn't it sad that I knew what to expect when Cody showed up? Most people never would know. I wished I didn't.

When that was done, we both walked out between the trees and back toward the vehicles. Cody stripped off his gloves and stashed them away. "Need to check out the area. See if anything pops up."

"Mind some help?" I asked.

Cody grinned. "Not at all. I'd never turn down your offer of help. And you're much cuter than Bud."

I smiled, embarrassed, as heat traveled up my neck. I wasn't used to Cody talking about my appearance. To cover, I said, "Well, I would hope so. Bud's pleasant enough, but not much to look at."

He winked to show me he was teasing, then said, "Guess we better get to the real reason we're here. I'm not hopeful to find any useful clues, but you never know."

Someone had deliberately done this to Millie. But who? And why?

Unsure what I was searching for, I walked around the inside perimeter of the trees. Having been back here before many times since it was right next to my property, I didn't see anything out of place. Just the usual dirt, pine needles, grass, a couple of birds' nests. I wouldn't be much good at spotting anything minuscule, like he would. But surely, I'd notice if it was outlandish or obvious. And then I saw something. "Hey Cody?"

"Hmmm?" He was visible through the thick trees on the park's property, bent over, examining a tree branch.

"Could you come here for a second?"

Pine branches swished as he angled between two of them. "Find something?"

"I think so."

"Do you think it has to do with the murder?"

I shrugged. "Maybe."

A car horn sounded, making us jump. The barrier of the trees must have covered the vehicle's arrival. We hurried out. Arnold Wellings was out of his vehicle and heading our way. He stopped when he reached us but said nothing, just watched Cody and waited.

Probably knowing he'd have to take the verbal initiative, Cody said, "The body's back here. In the trees."

Arnold's signature head bob was his reply. I chose to wait beside my truck, because seeing Arnold brought back memories of Mr. Morton in my greenhouse. Would I ever stop thinking about it? About finding him?

Then there was the part of me that worried about Mr. Morton's cause of death. If it was an accidental slip, hit of the head, and a fall, then I could move on. But if the autopsy proved murder…

With a mental shake, I opened my truck door and sat down sideways beside the steering wheel, my feet hanging over the seat toward the outside. No good would come of dwelling on the what-ifs. We'd know soon enough. At least there wouldn't be anything to tie me to Millie's murder. She'd died in the park, really close to the line, but still, not on my property.

Cody and Arnold came out with a bulky body bag. Seeing two of those in such a short time was way more than I needed. After Cody helped load it into the back of the hearse, he came to stand by me. We watched as Arnold's car bounced down, then up when he hit a deep rut.

I cringed, thinking about Millie in the back getting jostled.

*Seneca, what does it matter now? The poor lady won't feel it.*

"Let's go take a look at what you found, okay?" Cody's eyes were filled with concern as he studied me.

"Yeah." I followed him back into the trees.

Once back in the spot, I pointed to what I'd found. It was a half sheet of paper, like maybe part of a letter. The paper was caught on a low branch, flapping in the breeze. The letter's handwriting was nearly illegible in places, but one corner was stained with blood. Had Millie been clutching this when she was killed? I knew it might not be connected to the murder at all. But what if it was? Clues were hard to come by. If this was one, we didn't want to overlook it.

I reached out to touch it but pulled my hand back. Cody wouldn't want my fingerprints on it. It was then I noticed he'd already slipped on another pair of gloves.

He shook his head. "If she was killed for this, why didn't the killer take it with him or her?"

I pointed toward a crevice between two branches where I'd first noticed it. "And why in a tree?"

"Maybe there was a struggle. Could have gotten flipped in there somehow."

I bit my lower lip, trying to picture that scenario. A thought occurred, harsh enough to make me shiver. "You don't suppose the killer left it there for safekeeping to come back and get later?"

Cody's gaze snapped down to mine. "Maybe I'll have Bud do a stakeout, see if whoever it was comes back for it."

# Chapter Fourteen

A quick trip to the café gave me the information from Murray, although I'd hoped for more. According to Murray, Lorna's interest in Mr. Morton had been romantic in nature. Knowing her crotchety, complaining self as I did, I couldn't imagine any man seeing her in that light. Apparently, though, that had been the problem. Lorna had wanted something to happen with Mr. Morton, but he hadn't wanted any part in being with her. I didn't know if that tidbit of information would come in handy, but I'd hold onto it just in case.

When my phone rang later that day, I snatched it up. Anymore, it wasn't good news. Maybe it would be best to just get it over with and find out what it was this time. "Hello?"

"It's Payne."

I hadn't taken time to check who was calling, or else I might have ignored this call. "What's up?"

"Nice to talk to you too."

Glancing out my living room window, I muttered, "Sorry. Just busy."

"I spoke to Hal again. He's not budging."

Why was I not surprised? "Okay, and...."

"And...he's contemplating suing you," said Payne.

"What for?"

"According to him, you've been a nuisance to him, keeping him from getting his work done, accusing him of things he hasn't done."

Sarcasm dripped from my words as I said, "Gee, that sounds an awful lot like what he's been doing to me. As a matter of fact, there was even a surveyor over there, saying there was a buyer for Hal's property, to build a shopping mall. His name was Lonny Gibbs."

"Interesting. Still wanting to take him to court over the contract?"

Not wanting to involve going to court, I said, "Do you think it's come to that?"

Something tapped against his phone. A pen? "Let's wait a little longer. See what happens."

I was shocked. Payne had never been a see-what-happens kind of guy. He was more calculating, trying to figure out how something might best benefit him. But I needed his professional advice. "If you think it's best."

"Just for now. If he's serious about suing you, and we're in the middle of suing him, it might get messy."

"Might?" I hated messy. In anything. Especially blood on the floor of.... Gritting my teeth, I forced my thoughts back to our conversation.

"Let me think about how best to proceed so you'll get the most benefit of whatever happens," said Payne.

My mind went straight to the fact that Payne would also get maximum exposure and payment out of the deal.

"All right." I was ready to end the call. "So, I need to go now, and—"

"Wait."

"Wait for..."

"There's something else," he said. "Something we talked about the other day. During our date."

"That wasn't a date."

"It was to me," said Payne.

"Good for you. But it wasn't."

He huffed out a breath, having always hated when I disagreed with him. "Anyway," said Payne, "we need to strategize about your defense for the murder of Herman Morton."

"Um...wait a second. Where did that come from? I haven't been charged or—"

"But you're a suspect."

"No, I'm not," I insisted.

"How could you not be? It happened in your greenhouse. You were the only one with a key to let someone in. You knew the deceased and were in the middle of doing business with him for your contract dispute with Hal."

"I'm telling you. I am not a suspect."

Silence. Then, "Oh, I get it."

"You get what?"

Payne let out a grunt. "It's because your boyfriend is investigating."

"Hey! That's not how it is. Not at all. He and I aren't—"

"Skip the theatrics, Seneca. I will never believe you and he aren't a thing."

Anger caused heat to race straight from my chest up to my face. If Annie showed up now, she'd diagnose me with high blood pressure. Or the bubonic plague. "You're totally wrong. Even though it doesn't do any good to tell you that because you're too stubborn to listen to anything I have to say."

"Is that so?"

Why were we doing this? All too much like the fights we had right before we divorced. "Payne, for the last time. I'm not a suspect for Mr. Morton's death, and I'm not any more than friends with Cody. Not that it's any of your business."

He kept quiet. Probably a good thing. Any more snide comments from him, and I might just fire him from being my lawyer. Then I'd have to go find someone I didn't know anything about from another town. Not worth it. Not when so much was going on, and I needed representation now.

Hating to, but knowing I should, I said, "There's something else."

"Aww. Ready to tell me you still love me?" he asked.

"Hardly."

He laughed. "Someday. It'll happen. You'll see."

Ignoring his comment, I went on. "What I needed to tell you is that there was another murder."

"What? Who?"

"It was Millie King. I found her body just over the line from the back of my place. She was on Pines Park land though."

"What is going on with you?"

Clutching the phone tighter, I said, "It's not like I planned to have two people killed nearby. Not like I invited a murderer to do his dirty work where I'd have to deal with it."

"You are in a boatload of trouble," he said.

Like I didn't know that? "Thanks for the uplifting words."

"No, I'm serious. Not only are you in a contract dispute, being possibly sued by that same person, you've now discovered two dead bodies on or very near your land. Don't you see how other people might see this as more than a little suspicious?"

Imagining it from another person's point of view pointed out the likelihood of what he'd said. It really annoyed me that the man was right. "All right. I see your point."

"Is your boyfriend investigating this one, too?"

"He's not my..." I gave up. "Cody is investigating."

"Okay. I'll need to check in with him then."

"I only told you about the second murder as a precaution. Nothing is going to come of it, but I knew you'd hear about it from someone else. It seemed better to just tell you about myself."

"No, you did the right thing. I'll start working on my strategy for that one, too."

That one, too.

Great. I'd keep my ex busy with all my legal woes for three lifetimes. Not at all what I wanted to do with my spare time. Or money. "Payne, you're getting ahead of yourself."

"And you're not taking it seriously, Seneca."

Was he right? Though I'd been horrified at finding the poor woman, I hadn't thought I'd be considered a suspect. With Cody having checked it out, the fact that she died on the park's land, not mine, what would be the reason someone would think I'd killed her?

Doubt crept in. But Payne did have a point. I had so many things going on with contracts, disputes, and murders. Those weren't everyday occurrences for anyone. And the fact they were all happening to me at the same time cast more suspicion that I might somehow be involved at least in some way.

What should I do? The main reason I'd clued Payne into finding Millie was so he wouldn't hear it from someone else and get false information through gossip. Also, in the remote—and in my mind, it had to be very remote—chance that someone down the road might point the finger at me, I might need Payne's services.

Now, however, hearing it from an attorney's view, even though that attorney was Payne, it pointed out how others might see the situation. How they might think of me. Would people I'd known all my life suddenly begin to doubt my honesty? Integrity?

Surely not.

"Seneca? Still there?"

"I'm here."

"Just think about what I've said, all right?"

"I will," I said.

"Don't fret about it. But if things do go south, I'll have a defense prepared just in case."

Don't fret? Was he kidding? I'd been doing okay until he started painting the worst-case scenario about everything illegal being dumped on my doorstep.

"Hey," he said. "I gotta go. Keep me in the loop."

Even after the call ended, I still held the phone to my ear, unable to move. If Payne was right, I might be in more trouble than I'd ever imagined.

Before I could change my mind, I punched in Cody's cell number. I didn't want the call to go through Dana, as I probably had already freaked her out enough with the call about finding Millie. Our sheriff's department wasn't used to dealing with anything more serious than pickpockets, broken streetlights, and cavorting, half-naked senior citizens.

He picked up right away. "Hey, Seneca."

"Hi. Got a question for you."

"Sure. Shoot," he said.

"Maybe don't use a murder term like shoot. Kinda affects me wrong lately."

I could imagine him grimacing. "Good point. Sorry. What's up?"

"Just got off the phone with Payne."

A few seconds of silence, then, "There's your first mistake."

"Listen, I know you don't like him. I don't either, but he's my lawyer, and I need him right now."

His sigh traveled through the phone. "You're right. Okay, what did he have to say?"

"I told him about Millie."

"You did?"

"Shouldn't I have? It's not a secret."

"No, it's not," he said. "Sorry. Go on."

I began pacing from my couch to the TV and back. "Anyway, he was concerned that I might be a suspect in that murder."

"First, Mr. Morton, and now this. Is he determined to get you charged with something you shouldn't be? Or just trying to mess with your head because he can?"

"I think, as an attorney, he's trying to stay ahead of any future trouble. Wants to keep me, as his client, in the best position possible." Wow, I couldn't believe I was defending Payne, but I was especially shocked I'd said those words about him to Cody.

"Listen, you are not a suspect in Morton's death. Nor, as far as I can see, will you be a suspect in Millie's. I know he's your attorney, and you need his legal advice, but consider the source. This is Payne we're talking about. You know better than anyone what he's like."

"True. Yeah. I'm just..."

"Don't worry about it. Anybody who found themselves in your current situation would have doubts and questions. Right?"

"Yeah, I guess."

"They would," said Cody.

I stopped pacing. "Everything is so crazy right now. Sometimes, I don't know what to think or do. Afraid of what might happen next."

"No, don't think like that. I know that's easy for me to say, but things always seem worse when you're under stress, you know?"

"I know."

"Maybe the best thing would be to keep busy with work, let me handle the investigations, let Payne handle the dispute with Hal. Is that doable?"

Letting out a long, slow breath, I said. "Yeah. Doable. Why do things always make more sense when I talk them over with you?"

"You are one lucky girl to have a friend like me." He laughed. "You good, now?"

"All good. Thanks."

"Anytime."

I ended the call, hoping his *anytime* wouldn't be necessary, at least as far as discussing murders went. Hadn't enough happened as it was? Then I realized what I'd done. As much as I insisted on doing things on my own, not depending on a man for everything, I'd done it again. Instead of trying to sort out my feelings and problems for myself, I hadn't wasted any time running to Cody for his advice.

Would that ever change?

Did I really want it to?

# Chapter Fifteen

After I'd checked the monarchs in the greenhouse the next morning, I left the farm to venture into town for some groceries for me and Winifred. The most important item on my list was cat food. Canned. Tuna. Slathered in gravy. And smelly. If I ran out of Winifred's favorite meal, she'd complain for a week.

The store was small, and I knew where to find everything I needed without hunting it down. It didn't take me long. Once I'd picked up the needed items, I headed toward the checkout. Right before I turned into the checkout lane, someone who'd been looking at a magazine rack turned and nearly crashed into me. It was Lorna.

She glared at me. "Watch where you're going!" She pushed past me and practically ran from the store. Shaking my head at her weird behavior, I made my way to the checkout site and placed my purchases on the conveyor belt.

Tonda, the checkout girl, scanned my groceries, then bagged them. Knowing the girl had big ears for taking in gossip and an even bigger mouth for spreading it, I tilted my head toward the exit.

"So," I said, "what's up with Lorna Watkins? She nearly plowed into me just now."

"Was she looking at magazines?"

"Yeah. That's right," I said.

Tonda rolled her eyes. "Old bag comes in here at least once a week to look at the bridal magazines."

"Really?"

"Yep. Always mutters something about being left at the altar. I mean, who says that anymore?"

"Do you think that's what happened to her?" I asked.

"Definitely." She leaned closer. "I heard she was dumped by that lawyer guy. Morton." Her eyes widened. "Wait. The one who was murdered in your greenhouse, as a matter of fact."

Oh great. Tonda knew about Mr. Morton's demise and where it happened. I rolled my eyes. It occurred to me who'd told Tonda. It must have been Gretchen, Tonda's best friend. Gretchen was also Arnold's assistant and had the biggest mouth, even worse than Tonda. But now that she'd mentioned it, I couldn't very well deny it or ignore what she'd said, "Yeah, sad thing about Mr. Morton."

Tonda waved her hand while holding a box of my mac and cheese. The dry noodles rattled together like maracas. "Old news."

"Huh?"

"I meant Millie King. The one who was stabbed or something."

Frowning, I stared at her. So, that news was already out? Arnold's assistant Gretchen must have called her the second Arnold got back to the funeral home with the dead body in tow. It always struck me as odd that the mortician never said anything to anyone. At least not that I'd ever noticed. Surely, he spoke to people at some point. Wouldn't he have to say something to his assistant to give her directions about a case? Either way, did the girl have no scruples? Not care that when she spread gossip, it might get back to family members and upset them?

Tonda had stopped scanning my purchases, was now openly staring at me, chomping on her ever-present, green-apple scented gum. "Wonder why bodies are piling up out your way all of a sudden."

Piling up? I didn't like the sound of that. Was she using that term to every shopper who came in the store when she discussed the dead people? Would the listeners, then, attach that term to me, to my being involved in the deaths? Checking behind me, I was relieved that no one else was in line. But that wouldn't deter Miss Looselips.

Giving a shrug, hoping Tonda wouldn't tell everyone who came through her line today, I handed her money for my purchases. "Guess we'll never know." Hurrying out before she asked any further questions, or I was waylaid by another person wanting to know the juicy details, I tossed the bags in the passenger seat of my car and left the parking area.

I was going to throttle Gretchen.

As soon as I got home, Winifred attacked the grocery sack. Literally ripped it from my grasp and dove on the bag. How did she know there was canned food inside? Surely, she couldn't smell it through the metal containers. Before I could do anything else, I popped the top and placed the food on the floor. My cat pounced on it, stuffing her face inside the can, her whiskers smashed up against the sides of her head.

I sat down on a nearby kitchen chair. "You know, the way you carry on, one of these days someone's actually going to believe I never feed you."

She froze, mid-gulp, chunks of food stuck to her chin, and stared at me. Good grief. "Uh, sorry. Carry on."

With a loud huff, she resumed gorging on her meal. As I watched her, I fumed about my current circumstances. I loved the small town I lived in, but did everyone have to know details about my life and tell every person they knew?

I jumped when someone knocked on my door. Probably Cody since he stopped by most days. When I opened the door, I got a surprise. And not a nice one. A group of men stood on my front porch. Cody. Jesse. And Lonny Gibbs.

That couldn't be good. Sweat trickled down the back of my neck and under my sleeveless top. I must have been staring, because Cody, his hand halfway toward the screen door, said, "Seneca? Can we come in?"

Jolted from my reverie, I opened the screen door so fast, it cracked against the side of the house. Jesse's eyebrows rose, but he didn't look at me directly. Winifred's eyes lit up when she saw Cody, but one look at the other two had her hissing, running in place, then racing from the room.

Cody angled his head toward the table, then waited.

"Please, sit down," I said. They sat, but I was too nervous. Instead, I paced back and forth across the narrow vinyl floor. What did they want? And why were they here all at once? Especially Lonny. I glared at him.

Remembering my manners, I twisted my hands in front of me and said, "Can I get anyone anything to drink? Or—"

"Seneca." Cody held up his hand. "This isn't a social visit."

I knew that, of course. Part of me wanted to put off knowing the real reason a little longer, to save myself from whatever they'd come here to say. Still jumpy, I leaned against my kitchen counter, hoping it would hold me up if these three men told me something that would try to knock me flat.

Cody took the initiative. "Some things have come up since I investigated finding Millie in the...park."

Why had he hesitated? Or had I only imagined that he had? "What's that?"

"It seems...." He eyed first Jesse, then Lonny. "It seems that there's some question as to whether she died on park property. Or yours."

Holding up my hand, I said, "Wait a second. You know very well she wasn't on my land, Cody. How many times have you been back there? You know where the—"

Jesse shifted in his seat. "Um, Mr. Gibbs says the property line might not be where you think it is."

"And just how would he know that?" I focused on Lonny. "Have you been on that part of my property too?"

Eyes wide, Cody leaned forward. "Too?"

With a huff, I lifted my chin in the surveyor's direction. "As a matter of fact, I caught him on my property with surveying equipment."

Lonny's face reddened. "Now, hold on. I told you I'd been mistaken when I was on your land. I'd thought it was Hal Atkins'."

Crossing my arms, I smirked. "Wow. You must be some special kind of surveyor not to even know where you were. Like I'd really trust what you'd have to say about where the park ends and my farm begins."

Jesse frowned. "Listen, this is all getting out of hand."

With a sigh, I said, "I agree. It's pointless, since I know my property lines better than anyone."

Jesse flicked a glance toward Lonny and back to my shoulder. "I was all set to turn the investigation over to the state police since it's a state park.

However, since the question of the property line has been raised, I'm afraid the murder may have happened on your land. Until we know for sure where the body was found, we'll have to assume there's at least a possibility the woman died on your farm. I'm so sorry." His face reddened, making the rest of his skin match the color of his burn.

I shook my head. How could this be happening? Not only one person but possibly two died on my property. Now I had Lonny breathing down my neck. Again. Was this retribution for me telling him to vacate my farm when I'd caught him? By the expression of victory on his face, I'd say yes. It seemed I was outplayed. Even though I knew it would turn out that the surveyor was just blowing smoke, he'd still have accomplished his goal of deflecting the place of death from the park to me.

I didn't know why he'd bother. What was in it for him? Was he somehow in with Hal, wanting me not to get Hal's land, instead preparing it for sale as a shopping mall? None of this made sense. Nevertheless, I'd have no choice but to watch as Cody, the state police, Jesse, the surveyor, and who knew who else, tramped all over my property to get to the truth.

"Fine." I crossed my arms, trying to appear in control, but I'm sure I wasn't fooling anyone. "When do you want to do the survey of the property line?"

Lonny said, "Now. If that works for you. Although, you don't really have to even be there. We could always—"

"No way. I'm coming."

I rode with Cody. Neither of us said anything about it, I just climbed into his car. He went first, the other two following back to the edge of my property. My hands shook, so I clenched them together in my lap, hoping Cody wouldn't notice.

He reached over and patted my arm. "Don't worry, Seneca. We'll get to the bottom of whatever happened and where it took place." His dark eyes searched mine for an instant before he focused on driving again.

"Why is this happening?"

"Wish I knew. Strange that we've now had two murders."

I waited for him to say more. Did the fact that he didn't add near your property mean anything? Was he concerned what might happen if the state police somehow thought I was connected?

We reached the area where we'd found Millie and stopped. Vehicle doors slammed as the other two men got out of theirs. But I didn't budge.

"Seneca?" Cody squeezed my hand. "If you'd rather, you can stay in the car. I'll be glad to—"

"No. I need to find out what's going on." I turned toward him. "Since they think it might somehow involve me."

"Honestly, I don't think anyone suspects you. And if it helps, I didn't call you beforehand to warn you because they showed up at my office right before they insisted we come over. I didn't get the chance to even text you."

I nodded to let him know I understood why he hadn't given me the heads up, something I would have otherwise expected. "No, I mean... just that I'm connected, unfortunately, because of where it happened."

By the time we got out, Lonny already had his tripod in hand, lugging it to the dreaded area. Jesse was still beside his truck. I couldn't read his expression. Was he angry about the situation, or concerned?

Cody and I walked in his direction. Since Jessie had glanced toward me, then down, it seemed like he was trying to get my attention. I stopped. Cody, without a word, trudged past us.

"You wanted to say something?" I asked.

Jesse's arms hung limply at his sides, like he was tired and out of options. "Listen, I'm really sorry about this inconvenience."

"You're thinking this is just some minor glitch?"

"I hope it is," he said.

"What if it isn't? What then?"

He spread his hands and shrugged. "We worry about that later."

"It's not your land that might have had a stabbed woman found on it."

"Listen, I just wanted to make sure you're okay," he said. "Now, with a second murder connected to you..."

My shoulders and arms stiffened. "Hey, wait a second."

His face turned beet red. "Sorry, that came out wrong. Not at all what I meant. Just concerned about you. I think if you can—"

"Hey, Ranger Vance?" Lonny had his head stuck out from between the trees, waving Jesse over.

Jesse shook his head. "Really wish we didn't have to do this. I'm on your side. You know that, right?"

I nodded, hoping it was true. When I reached the crime scene, I gasped. I'd been the one to find the woman, yet was startled at seeing the yellow tape again, and the space where she'd lain now broken up by taller blades of grass. As if some foreign object had landed here, leaving a terrible reminder of what had happened to a woman I'd known and liked.

Cody turned and studied me but didn't say a word. His attention went back to Lonny. Ordinarily, I might have been fascinated, watching someone do a job that was new to me. But after catching the surveyor on my land before and now having him here for a bogus reason, I just wanted him to get it done quickly.

Lonny had already set up the tripod and was checking out the property line. He held some sort of paper. A map?

I stepped a little closer. "The property line was surveyed a very long time ago. Way before I inherited the farm. Since the farm has been in my family for generations, it may even predate the park. I don't understand why you need to do this. It's a waste of everyone's time."

Never making eye contact, he answered, "It's like you said. It was done a long time ago. Technology has made advances so that now, we can pinpoint the accuracy of a property line much better."

"But why?" I asked. "I mean, who told you to do it?"

He glanced at Jesse and back.

I whipped around so fast, I nearly fell. "You?"

Jesse held up his hands in a defensive pose. "It's not what you think."

"Believe me, you don't wanna know what I'm thinking right now."

"With all that's at stake, making sure we know where she was killed so the correct agency can do the investigation, is important," said Jesse. "When I contacted the state police and told them where in the park it had happened, they were concerned about it being so close to private property. It was my responsibility as the park ranger to make sure the land was surveyed to get the right information. I had no choice. I'm really sorry about this."

Lonny huffed out an annoyed breath. "Are we doing this, or what?"

As Jesse nodded, I clenched my jaws together, tight. There was no way Millie had been killed on my land. No way. But it seemed there wasn't any alternative to doing the survey since it involved government land.

Cody came over to stand beside me. I gave him a small smile, grateful for his support. Keeping his voice low, he said, "It will take a few days to know the results. Not as long as it might have, if they were surveying a large piece of ground, but still."

"Okay." I could do this. I had to. But everything in me knew she hadn't been found on my property.

# Chapter Sixteen

I was still fuming over the events from the day before, when someone parked out on my driveway. A glance out the door showed Jesse's truck. Though he'd said he was on my side, and I wanted to believe him, part of me was severely annoyed that he'd called the state police about Millie.

Waiting at the door, since he may have already seen me looking out anyway, I removed my dusty apron and wiped my hands off with a nearby towel. I opened the screen door when Jesse approached.

He stepped in. "Hope this is an okay time."

"It's fine." I let the screen close, then crossed my arms, facing him.

"You're still upset." He looked somewhere past my right ear.

I lifted one shoulder up, then down. "I know you did what you had to. Did your job, it's just…"

Jesse stuffed his hands in his front jeans pockets. "I get it. Really. If I were in your shoes, I would have been irritated too."

My chin lifted until I could watch his face, see if he was serious. "You would?"

"You probably felt backed into a corner, like everyone showing up at your house unannounced was out to get you. That it wasn't fair that we thought one thing and you something else. And had given you no choice in the matter of having the land resurveyed."

Blinking, I said, "That's it exactly." Maybe he really did understand how I'd felt. And he would have to do his job, after all. Was I being too critical, since it was so personal for me?

He glanced around the interior of the greenhouse. "Was hoping that if you had a few minutes, we could talk about that possible collaboration between your farm and the park? Ever since it came up, I've been thinking of little else."

"I'd like that." Talking about something positive sounded pretty good right now. Tilting my head toward the corner table, I said, "We could sit down, if you'd like."

With a look around, he said, "I'm okay here. That is, unless you need to sit."

"I'm good."

"Great." His shoulders relaxed, like he was relieved. Maybe he'd been anxious coming over here, afraid of what I might say. "You probably have lots of ideas," he said. "I'm sure better than any of mine—"

I waved away his words with my hand.

"—but what about, for starters, you could come to the park, say once a month? And give a talk and guided tour of the monarchs and the milkweed? I've learned quite a bit about monarchs just from the little we've talked. I have no doubt others would feel the same. We could also combine that with a field trip from the park to here, where people could see the caterpillars in the pens, really see the whole life cycle of the monarchs."

"Those are great suggestions, Jesse."

"You think?"

"Absolutely." I thought for a few seconds. "You know, aside from seeing you yesterday, it's been a while since I've spent much time at the park. I can't remember, does it have a gift shop?"

"Yes. A small one. Open at least a few hours every day, and all day on Saturdays. Why?"

"If it doesn't stock butterfly-related items, maybe you could consider that? Offer several books, both nonfiction and fiction, especially something for kids. There are lots of homeschooled kids who come through with their parents, who are always hunting for new ideas to teach their children about science and nature. Along with that, how about toys—stuffed butterflies and coloring books. Those are big right now."

He nodded. "More good ideas. Another thing I wanted to ask was about a butterfly release. For Millie King. I didn't get to work with her for very long, but I liked her. What happened to her was a terrible tragedy, and she needs to be recognized. I was thinking of having a memorial service for her since she'd worked at the park."

"I love that idea. Why don't I—"

Something scratched across the cement floor. It sounded like claws. Right then, Winifred made an appearance. I'd forgotten she'd been asleep in the back room in a sunbeam on the floor. She strolled in, tail waving high like a flag in a slow breeze.

Jesse glanced down, blinked twice, then gave a small smile. "Hello."

Then, I realized why he'd smiled. I was so used to seeing Winifred in butterfly costumes, but there was a good chance he'd never seen a cat wearing anything but her own fur. It must have seemed odd, to say the least, since most felines wouldn't dare be caught in something like that.

Winifred noticed Jesse and froze, staring up at him. Fur puffed to twice its normal volume, eyes wide, whiskers sticking straight out to the sides like toothpicks. Not an uncommon reaction from her to strangers. The fact that she wasn't screeching or running away was a good sign. She adored Cody, but she'd known him since she was a kitten. Sometimes, it took her a while to warm up to people she hadn't officially met.

Jesse crouched down, hand outstretched. Maybe he was more comfortable with animals than people. Animals wouldn't judge his appearance or limp the way humans might. He stayed still, barely moving. Winifred crept closer, neck craned, nostrils flaring. Right before making physical contact, she took a step back and sat down, staring at him.

After watching them for a minute, I said, "Don't worry if she doesn't come right to you. She can be skittish. The way she's acting, I think she likes you."

"She's beautiful." He stood, then pointed to the wings of her costume. "Does she always wear—"

"Yep."

"She doesn't mind? Doesn't put up a fuss when you put it on her?"

"Nope. As a matter of fact, she has a fit if she doesn't get to wear one every day," I said.

"Seriously?" He stood, crossing his arms over his chest.

I laughed. "Yes. She's a great advertisement when people come to the farm."

A smile tugged at one side of his mouth. "I can see that."

Winifred sauntered toward the back room again, as if proud that she'd done her duty as official watch cat. I knew she'd go take another nap. I wouldn't see her again for hours. We both watched her until she'd disappeared around the corner.

"Very pretty cat." Jesse turned back toward me and clasped his hands in front of him. "So, getting back to our collaboration. Any other ideas for me to try at the park?"

"Not so far, but I'm sure I can come up with more. Always glad for new opportunities. Anything to do with monarchs and their well-being is where I put my efforts."

His eyebrows lowered, and he looked toward the side wall. "Um, I wasn't going to bring this up now."

"What?"

"There's something—"

"Obviously, it's bothering you. If it will help, you can tell me."

Eyeing the table in the corner, he said, "Maybe we should sit down."

That sounded serious. "Okay." We made our way to the table and took seats across from each other.

"It's about Cody," said Jesse.

I gasped. "What about him?" Had something happened? I would have heard if he'd been injured on the job. Or something worse. *No, don't think about worse. Just don't.*

Jesse didn't make eye contact as he said, "I overheard something. Earlier today. Thought you should know."

I was getting seriously antsy. And a little annoyed. But I forced myself to wait. I did grit my teeth, though.

"I was in the grocery. I don't usually eavesdrop, especially since I don't know that many people in town. What would be the point?"

Nodding, I hoped he'd get on with it soon.

"Anyway, two women—no idea who they were—mentioned Cody's name."

"Okay...and?" Why wouldn't Jesse just come out and say it? Was this the real reason he'd stopped by today?

"Well, the gist of it was, he'd done something a long time ago that wasn't aboveboard," said Jesse.

"Cody? I can't imagine that." He was the most trustworthy, honest, straightforward person I'd ever known. "Go on. What did they say he did?"

He got a pained expression as he said, "It involved you."

"Me?" I jerked back, my arms sliding over my chest. I needed to wrap them around my middle, to brace myself for whatever it was he'd heard. Maybe it had to do with the murder investigation. I shook my head. No, Jesse had said something had happened a long time ago.

"If you'd rather me not tell you... maybe I shouldn't have even brought it up. Have left it alone. It might not be true anyway."

"No." The word popped out forcefully, louder than I'd intended. "I need to know."

"All right." He ran his hand through his hair, leaving his bangs slightly mussed. "These women, I didn't see them, but from the sound of their voices, I'd guess them to be about my age. Does that make sense?"

I nodded. Fairly easy to guess an approximate age of someone elderly or very young. The rest fell somewhere in between.

"They said that a long time ago, Cody did something to try to prevent you getting married."

That stopped me cold. It was beyond belief that Cody would have done that. Or if, for some strange reason, he had, he would have told me by now. "That doesn't make any sense. Why would he have?"

Jesse shook his head. Of course, he wouldn't know. He was new in town. Didn't know everyone's history like those of us who were born here. "One of the women said that Cody never liked your husband." Glancing at my bare ring finger, he said, "Now, ex, I assume?"

"Right. Ex."

"She also told the other lady that Cody had tried to scare—Payne, was it—?"

"Yes."

"—to scare Payne off right before the wedding."

Shaking my head, I frowned. "It doesn't make any sense. If Cody had done something like that, he would have told me." We told each other everything. At least, I thought we did. A tiny doubt crept in.

"Maybe he was ashamed after the fact. Didn't want to hurt you."

"Stopping a wedding of your best friend would be hurting someone, don't you think?" Try as I might, it was still hard to imagine Cody doing that.

He sighed. "I'd think so."

Anger welled up in my chest. Could it be true? It was so hard to believe of Cody. But why would Jesse make up something like that about a person he hardly knew?

And it was true that Cody had never liked Payne. Though he hadn't come out and said the words, I knew he hadn't wanted me to marry him.

"Listen…" Jesse's voice pulled me back from my thoughts. "Hey, I shouldn't have told you," he said. "But I figured you would want to know if people were saying something like that behind your back. I'm sorry if—"

"No. You did the right thing. Thanks for letting me know. I appreciate it."

He nodded, then glanced down at his watch. "Hate to say it, but I've been gone from the park too long already. I have a meeting in a little while. We can talk more about your ideas later?"

"Yeah, I'd like that." I stood at the door, watching him leave. As soon as the last of the gravel dust settled back down to the ground from the departing truck, I clenched my fists tight. What was going on with Cody? I didn't think it was true. Didn't want to believe it. I'd give Cody the benefit of the doubt, but I still had to know. The not knowing might kill me.

# Chapter Seventeen

There was a knock on the greenhouse door, then it creaked open. Not many people walked in without permission. Under the circumstances lately, I was a little wired. It wouldn't be Cody, because he didn't knock, and Annie was already here working with some caterpillars in the other part of the building. Until the killer was caught, were we in danger here? Cody had harangued me, telling me even more frequently to be cautious and careful. Maybe I should take him more seriously instead of blowing his warnings off, chalking it up to his overprotectiveness when it came to me.

Grabbing the first thing nearby—though what damage I thought I'd do with a butterfly net I didn't know—I waited. From the angle where I stood, I couldn't make out who was on the other side of the glass in the door. Hal wouldn't come here to try to do more damage, would he? Could it be whoever had killed Mr. Morton? Or maybe it was—

My breath came out in a whoosh when Dana, Annie's mom, entered. Quickly, I set the net down on the counter and forced a smile. Maybe she hadn't seen me holding it. *Don't be an idiot. Why would holding a butterfly net in a butterfly greenhouse seem strange?* With effort, I smiled. "Hi, Dana."

"Seneca." She stepped all the way inside and stopped. Her face was pale, her hair messy, like she'd run her hands through it several times. And her clothes were wrinkled over her trim frame. "I hope you don't mind me just dropping in."

"Of course not. You're welcome any time, you know that." I took a deep breath, hoping my heart would stop slamming against my ribs. From now on, I had to do better at keeping calm, or lock the door even when I was inside working.

Briefly checking over my shoulder, I saw Annie in the back, her red hair a flash of color in the shadowed room. Her lips were moving, though I couldn't hear her. She was probably talking to the caterpillars, as was her habit. "Did you need to see Annie? She's—"

"No." Dana's throat moved as she swallowed. "I…" She came closer, her hands twisted in front of her middle. The same thing Annie did when she was distressed.

"Are you all right?" I'd never seen Dana upset before. She was one of those people who was perpetually cheerful, almost disgustingly so. Always complimented whoever she spoke to, asked the other person if he or she was doing all right. And seemed genuinely interested in whatever their answer would be, tried to pump them up with positive comments if need be. If Dana hadn't been a cheerleader in school, I'd have been shocked.

She reached up and brushed her strawberry blond bangs from her forehead. "I'm concerned about Annie."

Ah. Should have seen that coming. What parent wouldn't have concerns about their child spending time where something so awful had occurred? "Of course." I touched Dana's shoulder and gave it a squeeze. "Because of what happened here."

"Yes."

How could I blame her? Her only child was working in a murder scene. For any mother, it would be frightening, disturbing, and creepy all at once. If I didn't own the place, I might not want to work where I'd seen a dead body and lots of blood either.

Dana's eyes were wide as she said, "Do you think Annie is doing okay? I mean emotionally."

My eyebrows lowered. Annie hadn't said a whole lot about it, which was odd. But then, so was Annie. "She hasn't seemed too upset. I mean, I'm sure she's horrified that someone was killed right here, but only as much as anyone else would be. I haven't noticed her crying or asking a lot of questions about the crime scene." Although, I wouldn't have been surprised if she had. Anyone else might have, right?

Dana let out a breath. "Good. Annie is…" She bit her lip as she seemed to search for the right term. "Spirited."

Leave it to a mother to find an adjective that smoothed over the rough edges of her child's personality. But then, that was a mom's job. Or, in my case, it was more my Gram who'd always taken my side no matter what.

I pressed my lips together, trying not to smile at Dana's answer. Spirited was putting it mildly, but at least Dana recognized her daughter as being unique among kids her age.

Stepping closer, Dana whispered, "Does she seem to have a problem with the spot… um… with where it actually happened?"

I turned, eyeing the place in question. "She hasn't seemed to. Her work has gone on without a hitch. Haven't seen her try to avoid walking over the place or stand close to it." When I turned back, Dana was peering around me. Maybe she, like everything else in town, was curious about the murder. Hopefully, she didn't suspect me, like some in town appeared to. And if she did, maybe she'd keep her opinion to herself at work. Cody might not take kindly to someone badmouthing me. That fact both warmed and annoyed me. I loved that he cared, but sometimes his big-brother behavior was a little smothering.

Dana was still staring past me. Did she want to see where Annie was right now, or see the spot where the crime occurred? Though she might be curious about the actual place where Mr. Morton was attacked, I couldn't come right out and ask if she'd like a tour of the morbid location. Instead, I said, "If you'd like to see Annie, she's…"

She blinked and focused on me again. "Yeah, if that's okay. Just want to make sure she's all right. And safe."

It hit me like a punch in the middle. I should have spoken to Dana before now. Assured her Annie was protected here during the day. But also give her, both of them, the option of Annie taking off work for a while until the matter was settled and the murderer was behind bars. How thoughtless of me. No wonder Dana appeared so pale, so freaked.

I put my hand on her shoulder, briefly. "Dana, you must have been so worried about Annie, still being here after… Listen, if you'd rather she not stay here, find another part-time job, I—"

"No," came from behind me.

I whipped around to see Annie standing a few feet away, hands on narrow hips.

"No," she said again. "I like working here, Mom. Don't make me leave."

Her mother let out a long breath. "Are you sure? I was afraid that—"

"It's all fine," Annie said as she came closer. I moved back, nearer the counter, so mother and daughter could converse more easily. The aisle we stood in was narrow, but with three people crowded together, it was claustrophobic.

"Maybe you two need a minute to talk?" With a tilt of my head toward the back, I stepped that way. "I'll finish up with the caterpillars, Annie. You take as long as you guys need, okay?"

Dana sighed. "Thanks, Seneca. I won't take up much of her time."

As quickly as I could, I left the two women alone and made my way to the caterpillars. Even though I now stood in the back part of the greenhouse, the overall space of the building wasn't that big. I could hear every word. Why hadn't I just gone outside to give them privacy? Their conversation wasn't something I wanted or needed to hear. A glance over my shoulder showed them standing right in front of the door. To go back that way to get out now would be a rude interruption.

With effort, I tried to ignore them as I cleaned out the bottom of the caterpillar pen. My hands worked seemingly on their own, doing a job that came as natural as breathing. The little guys looked great, none appearing diseased or in distress. Soon, they'd be producing silk to build their cocoons. Though they were healthy, the fact that there should be more, many more, poked at my thoughts. To run my farm effectively, the numbers had to increase. Without Hal's property, I was landlocked. I couldn't expand in another direction because of my proximity to the park.

Seeing what Jesse had shown me with his butterflies came back. I'd nearly cried that day at the beauty of his swarm. The numbers. The fluttering activity. The sheer volume of active life cycles of egg, larvae, cocoon, and then flight. Also, I'd had a heavy heart. If I didn't get Hal's land with the milkweed, and soon, what would become of my monarchs?

Running the farm was a joy, but it didn't come cheap. It was imperative that I expand my operation, or I might not be able to continue financially. But even more important than that, since the monarchs were in danger of becoming extinct, without enough milkweed to feed them, they wouldn't have a chance to survive.

Why had Hal tried to destroy them with the hose? Tried to break milkweed as well as attack the butterflies. And what about the fact that he'd previously agreed to sell to me, even to the point of a signed contract? Something had changed, but I didn't know what. Would I ever?

I shrugged. As long as I acquired his property, did it matter why? Though if I never knew, it would bother me. People, kind ones like Hal had always been, didn't change suddenly for no reason. Gram had always trusted him, liked him, and I had too. Having him turn on me felt a deep betrayal. Like I didn't know who to trust anymore.

Like how I now questioned Cody's honesty.

Annie and Dana, their voices now raised, grabbed my attention. Because I cared about both of them, everything in me wanted to go over there, see if I could help in some way, but no... Whatever it was needed to be discussed between them as a family. And since I didn't want to interrupt by barging through, I'd have to stay here and pretend I couldn't hear them. Not an easy task. They had to know their voices carried through the small area.

I busied myself as best as I could, finding the broom that Annie had abandoned, and sweeping dirt from the floor in front of the pens into a dustpan.

"Mom," said Annie. "Why haven't you checked out the website link I showed you for med school yet? We have to get things rolling for me to go as soon as I graduate. Get finances in order for tuition. Do you realize how many students there are I'm going to be competing against to get a spot? How hard it will be just to be admitted. If we don't hurry, I'll have to wait until the following year even to apply." Her voice had taken on a panicked pitch.

"Honey, I've told you. We can't... can't afford med school." I could imagine Dana reaching out, trying to soothe her daughter with her touch.

Something like a shriek came from Annie. "No. I have to go. Have to. Can't you see? It's all I've ever wanted. You'd promised. Promised! And a mom should never go back on her word to her daughter. You've told me that all my life. Since it was only just you and me and no one else."

"I know I did." Dana let out a loud sigh. "Maybe... maybe someday later down the road. I don't know when. But not now. The timing is all wrong. Things aren't coming together as I'd hoped, honey. I'm sorry."

"Please." Annie's voice came out sounding like a young girl, begging for her heart's desire. "If I don't go to medical school, I'll just die."

*Don't say that. Not that word. Not here, after...*

The silence in the greenhouse engulfed me. It was then I realized I'd stopped sweeping and had been standing there, actively listening. What an idiot. *It's none of your business, Seneca.* Hoping they hadn't noticed I'd halted my work, or think I was trying to eavesdrop, I angled the broom underneath the raised pen, pulling dirt and dust out toward me so I could get it easier.

Something thwacked hard against the cement, like a loud clap. I'd witnessed Annie's tantrums before, stomping her foot like an angry bull. Once she did that, things usually spiraled downward. Was Annie going to have a full-out meltdown? Though she was normally good-natured and said silly, nonsensical things, she did occasionally have a bad temper when something didn't go her way. Maybe it was her hair. I'd heard redheads could sometimes be moody.

Annie's hair made me think of Winifred. How she was afraid of the girl. I smiled. Silly cat. I never knew what would set her off, and she'd have a meltdown of her own. Then, I nearly laughed out loud. With Winifred's orange fur, she was a redhead too. Maybe she and Annie didn't get along because they were too much alike? Both likely to throw a fit in a sudden pique of anger.

Voices ceased, and the door creaked open, then shut. Had they both left? Or was one of them still around?

Dana approached me. "I'm so sorry you had to hear that."

125

Guilt swam over me. Why hadn't I just gone outside, or to the house when this whole thing began? "I...um, is everything okay?"

Pointing her thumb behind her, Dana said, "Annie's upset. About maybe not going to med school."

"Oh." I didn't know what else to say. 'I'm sorry' didn't seem right, neither did asking any kind of further question for clarification.

"As you know, all she's ever wanted to be was a doctor."

I nodded. That was true. And everyone in town knew it. Because Annie told them.

"But, as a single parent, it's hard to make ends meet sometimes," she said.

"Sure." I set the broom aside and focused on Dana. Though I didn't have a child to support, I did know something about financial difficulties. It had taken every dime I could scrape together to get enough money for the down payment for Hal's land. And it hadn't been easy. I tried to sound upbeat when I said, "You never know. Maybe things will turn around. Something turn up to change your circumstances."

Dana gave a half-hearted smile. "Maybe. Thanks for letting me steal her away for a little while." Then, she headed for the door.

After Dana had walked outside, I noticed Annie sitting on my stone wall, petting Winifred. How had that happened? The cat usually didn't get within twenty feet of her. Maybe, because Annie was visibly upset, Winifred decided to be kind, allowing someone the privilege of petting her fur. How weird.

Dana, with slow steps, using a cautious approach a person would use with a scared animal, reached her daughter.

For a minute, the two women spoke. Voices rose and fell, and Annie's arms flailed about. Her mom put her hand on Annie's shoulder, rubbing it gently. Relieved, I watched as Annie stood and hugged her mom.

Crisis averted. At least for now. Though I did feel sorry for them both. Annie, for maybe losing her life-long dream. And Dana, for not being able to give her child what she most desired. I wanted to help them but had no idea how. Just being a friend was all I could offer. All anyone could offer.

126

# Chapter Eighteen

As I often did before the café closed for the day, I made my way down to check-in. Evie was wiping down tables as she nodded and made occasional eye contact with Mable Kane. Had the older woman spent the entire day here? But then, maybe she had nothing else with which to occupy her time and sought out the company of others.

When Evie finally glanced over and noticed me, she gave me a wink. My cousin was perfect for working around the public all day. So personable and friendly—I looked at Mable, who was still talking—and patient.

The kitchen lights were dimmed, so Murray must have already left for the evening. Poor Evie. She'd never get out of here. I headed to the counter, stepped around to the back, and snagged a cleaning cloth and spray bottle. Evie gave me a shake of her head, but I nodded back, then grinned.

From the day we'd agreed she would run my café, she'd taken ownership, not wanting help from anyone if she didn't have to. I admired that, and normally would have respected it. But with Mable now literally hanging on Evie's arm, she wouldn't get away from here before midnight without assistance.

I scrubbed down tabletops, then the chair seats. Tidying the condiments on the main counter came next. Then, I wiped down the plastic-coated menus stacked on the counter. Finally, I hunted down the broom from the back closet and started to do the floors.

Footsteps came from behind me. "Thanks so much, Seneca. Mable just left. Bless her heart. I think she just gets lonely sometimes." She rubbed the back of her neck. My cousin worked hard. I'm sure she was sore by the end of each day.

I stopped sweeping and faced her. "You're so good with her. I'm not sure I'd be so patient."

"But you have so many other good qualities."

I narrowed my eyes. "Are you saying I'm not patient?"

Evie bit her lower lip as she studied me. "No. You are. But only with butterflies. And cats."

I tried to hold my fake scowl but couldn't. We both laughed. Evie was so right about me. Give me animals or butterflies to spend my time with. I understood them, and they seemed to connect with me, too. Not sure why. I'd just always had a kinship with beings covered in fur or wings.

"Hey," said Evie, "I was talking to Murray, and he filled me in on your conversation about Lorna Watkins."

I nodded. "Isn't that wild? Can you imagine Lorna and romance in the same sentence?"

"No. Never. But here's something interesting."

I propped the broom against a nearby chair and waited. "About Lorna?"

"Yep. Earlier today, I'd stepped outside to take a quick break. I walked around the area to stretch my legs, and I saw her."

"What was she doing?"

"I'm not sure exactly, but she was kind of crouching down near the back of your greenhouse."

I jerked. "She was? I never saw her." When people came to the café, it was rare they ventured near the greenhouse unless they had business with me or had requested to visit the butterflies.

"I think you were out," Evie answered. "Pretty sure I remember you driving past a few minutes before then."

I thought for a minute. "Oh, right, I had to run a package to the post office. So you couldn't tell what she was doing when she was crouched down?"

"No, I wish I could. I wanted to go closer and see what she was up to, but several cars pulled up, and I needed to rush back to the café. After having talked to Murray, I thought I should tell you, even though it isn't much."

I reached out and squeezed her hand. "Yes, I'm glad you did. Thanks. You never know what might turn out to mean something later on."

My mind wandered to possible explanations, but I couldn't come up with anything. Lorna had never struck me as the outdoor type, so I couldn't imagine her down near the ground to pick up a pretty rock or watch a bug crawling around. She didn't even like the butterflies that floated into the café, which made me wonder why she even bothered to come in there. Maybe she just liked to spew her unpleasantness to as many unfortunate people as she could. Still, whatever Evie saw might be valuable later, if I could figure out what Lorna had been up to.

"Here," Evie said, holding out her hand for the broom. "I'll finish sweeping."

"No, that's okay. We need to get you out of here so you can go home."

"All that's left is this and a final check under tables and chairs to make sure no one left anything behind."

Shrugging, I said. "All right. I can do that, then." I handed her the broom. "Thanks."

The broom swished against the wooden planks as my cousin finished sweeping. I started at one corner and bent down to peer under each set of tables and chairs. So far, nothing out of the ordinary except for the occasional ketchup packet or napkin that had gotten wedged beneath a chair leg. I threw those in the trash and went back to my checking. I'd made it completely through the room before I found something under the very last table by the door.

It was a piece of paper that had slid over next to the wall. A streak of dirt and a couple dots of mustard marred what turned out to be a clipping from a newspaper article. Hopefully, it wasn't something important the person would need back, because it wasn't in the best condition anymore.

I stood up, then took a closer look at the page. The print was faded and appeared to be several years old. Why was this in the café? Sure, older customers sometimes brought in newspapers and magazines to read while they ate, but this one.... No, it wasn't current.

With some of the lights now dimmed from the back—Evie must be nearly done sweeping over there—it was difficult to read the tiny print. But one name did stand out from beneath a black-and-white picture of several men standing together in front of an office building.

Herman Morton.

Why was there a picture hiding under a table of my recently deceased lawyer? Quickly, I amended my thought. The poor man was recently murdered. How soon before the whole town was buzzing about that? If Tonda's customers at the grocery spread the word after listening to her, it wouldn't take any time at all. Even that odd little man from the bus tour had heard about it.

I went on to read the article. It was mostly about Mr. Morton, his long legal career, and subsequent success, financial and otherwise. Beneath the paragraph was a second photo. This one was smaller and was of several people. Below the picture in tiny letters, it listed the names of those in the picture. One looked an awful lot like a much younger Dana Hastings.

I stepped closer to the exit, where the lighting was better. Now I could read the small text better. One of the names listed was Dana Morton.

What? They were related? Why hadn't I ever known that? With Dana working for Cody, he would have mentioned it at some point. That is, if he'd known. Why would Dana live and work in the same town as her brother and not tell anyone about their relationship?

I scanned the rest of the article below her picture. According to that, she was his younger sister.

I shook my head. In a town as small as ours, it was amazing that I'd never heard anyone link Dana and Mr. Morton together as family. It was rare for any secrets to be kept around here. At least to be kept for several years. No, something was wrong with this picture. Literally. Because as I looked closer at the photo, what I'd thought was a smudge was now obviously deliberate.

Mr. Morton's face had been crossed out. Had Dana been the one to do that? Or could it possibly have been Lorna, if she'd been scorned by the man she'd loved.

For whatever reason, whoever had this picture seemed to have had a grudge against the lawyer. If it was Dana, Cody should know. Because with her brother dead and her keeping their relationship a secret, not to mention that her brother had been murdered, did that make Dana a suspect?

Probably not a good thing for an employee of the sheriff's office.

I waved at Evie as she turned out the rest of the lights, then I headed back to my house. I'd fill my cousin in later on what I'd found, but at the moment, she looked like all she wanted was to head to her own home and put up her feet.

No, the person I needed to talk to was Cody. And it couldn't wait.

As I walked back to the house, I tried Cody's number. I got his voicemail. I'd rather have spoken to him in person, but wanted to let him know about this as soon as possible. After leaving a message, I stepped inside my house.

Winifred was sitting right inside the door. She was frowning. As I glanced at the wall clock, I could see why. I was a little later than usual after spending more time in the café.

"Okay, little one. Supper's on the way."

With a haughty sniff, my cat followed me to the cabinet where I kept her food. I had a fairly good idea she'd open the cabinet door and get it out herself whenever I was late. That was, if she had thumbs.

She chowed down on her dry food, making grunty-slurpy noises. I couldn't really blame her. I was hungry, too. I'd just made myself a peanut butter and jelly sandwich when my phone rang.

It was Cody.

"Hey, Seneca. I listened to your message, but it didn't make a lot of sense."

"What's to make sense? Dana's brother is, well, was, Mr. Morton."

"How did you find that out?"

I explained about finding the newspaper article in the café.

"And you say that his face was crossed out in the picture?" he asked.

"Yep. Looked intentional to me. Not like someone accidentally spilled something on it. More like marked up with a pen."

Silence. Then, "Hmmm."

"What's that mean?"

"It's odd she never mentioned he was her brother," said Cody.

"That's what I thought too. See? Maybe I should work in law enforcement, getting all the clues."

Cody sighed. "Or maybe you should stick to what you're so good at."

131

"Being a great friend to you?"

He chuckled. "Yeah, that. But I was thinking more along the lines of your monarchs."

"You mean, the ones Hal didn't manage to destroy."

"Don't worry," he said. "We'll get to the bottom of that. And of the murders. All of it."

As we said our goodnights, I desperately hoped he was right.

# Chapter Nineteen

Once again, Winifred was sitting in the greenhouse when I entered the next morning. I'd let her outside from the house but hadn't watched where she'd gone. I needed to keep a closer watch on her. The little magician had a way into the greenhouse that wasn't duly authorized by the owner. Me.

"How are you doing this, kitty? I know you don't have a key to the door. Besides, you're not tall enough to open it. And don't have thumbs to turn the knob."

She squinted her eyes half-closed, an expression of satisfaction on her face. Even if she could tell me the secret, I don't think she would.

There had to be some opening in a wall. Or maybe something had made a tunnel underneath and came up through the floor. Though the floor was concrete, the greenhouse was so old that the foundation did have some crumbly spots. Maybe Gram had never had the time to get them repaired. If that were the case, and some animal had tunneled below, the hole could be hidden underneath some shelves against one of the walls.

Time to find out.

With my cat on my heels, seeming a little too interested in what I was doing, I searched under and behind shelves, most of the time down on my knees, with my head stuck in cobwebby places.

Blech. Really needed to clean down here, in my spare time, when I wasn't in the middle of a bizarre murder or two.

Lying on the floor, I reached under a shelf as far as I could. Some old paint cans had been shoved under there that I had to move. Might as well haul them out and away. Who knew how old the paint was, since I hadn't even known it had been there. As I tugged on one can, the metal scraped across the concrete, the noise so loud, I felt it in my fillings. There were four cans in all, and I'd pulled out three so far. Winifred climbed up and sat on one, flicking her tail at the spider webs now attached to her tail.

I watched her. "Serves you right for being nosy."

With a loud sniff, the cat glared at me with narrowed eyes, as if I'd been the one to place her on the can and cover her backside with sticky webs.

"Whatever." I rolled my eyes, realizing I'd used Payne's favorite term. At least he hadn't been here to hear that. I wasn't enjoying the icky cobwebs either, but to find Winifred's secret entrance, I had to check everywhere. I didn't mind her coming into the greenhouse when I was working, but there were some chemicals around that would be dangerous were she to investigate too closely. Every time I found her already in the greenhouse, anxiety shot through me that she might be doing just that.

With a cough against the dust I'd stirred up, I scooted closer to the shelf, reaching in as far as I could. I finally snagged the paint can handle and gave it a tug.

Something screeched. It wasn't me or Winifred. So who—

A mouse, large and brown, darted right past my nose, so close its tail whipped across my cheek.

"Ack!" I sat up too fast, banging my head on the edge of the shelf. Stars swirled in my vision.

Blinking hard, I could finally see more than celestial bodies engulfed in darkness. As my vision cleared, I gasped. A mouse. And where was...

Claws on concrete came from the other side of the room. Cautiously standing in case the darkness would return, I held onto one of the shelves and glanced around. I hurried around some monarch pens and found my cat.

She was peering into a bucket that had turned on its side in the scuffle. Her tail lashed back and forth. So did her backside. I knew that posture. Winifred was ready to pounce.

The last time she'd caught a mouse, she'd left the headless carcass on my pillow. I'd woken up the next morning with it tangled in my hair. We were not doing that again. After gently toeing Winifred away, I grabbed the bucket, mouse inside, and ran to the door. Once outside, I carried the bucket a few yards away, then set it down. The mouse jumped out and landed on the grass, its tiny paws running in place a couple of seconds before shooting off into nearby bushes.

A growl came from just behind me. There stood my cat. She wasn't looking in the direction of the shrubs, but right at me. With a loud hiss, she turned around and purposely gave me a view of her back.

"Sorry, kid. But it had to be done." I sighed. She'd be in a snit for the rest of the day. The only thing that would get her out of it was a can of people tuna from the store. But that would have to wait. First, I needed to find her greenhouse entrance.

More cobwebs and dust, but thankfully no more mice, brought nothing out of the ordinary. There was some crumbling cement, but nothing that seemed big enough for a cat to climb through. How was she getting in?

Maybe it couldn't be viewed from inside. It had been a while since I'd walked to the back of the greenhouse since there wasn't much reason for me to do so. All that was back there was a row of overgrown bushes that desperately needed trimming. Another job I didn't have time for.

I brushed off the front of my apron, now grimier than usual, and headed back outside. Winifred was sunning herself on a nearby stone wall, but she still wouldn't make eye contact with me. I was the traitor. The woman who ruined the cat's fun for the day. Possibly for her entire existence.

"Just wait. Tuna will get your attention."

She didn't bother to look at me, but her ears had perked up. With a smile, I headed around one side of the greenhouse, certain that she and I would be back on speaking terms as soon as I made good on giving her a treat.

The temperature dropped a few degrees from a nearby towering maple tree that put off plenty of shade. After my eyes adjusted to the absence of the bright sunshine, I began my search.

When I'd been down on my knees inside the building, it had been bad enough. Now, though, I crawled through the narrow path between the bushes and greenhouse. Winifred wouldn't have had any trouble, though. Too bad I wasn't her size right about now.

The dirt, damp from dew that the sun hadn't reached to dry, clung to me. Soon, the knees of my jeans were wet through to my skin. Everything down here smelled like mud. And worms. Although I adored butterflies, I'd never been fond of other insects. None of the worms, flies, or other winged or creepy crawlies were as graceful or beautiful as my monarchs. No, I'd stick with the butterflies.

A couple of branches got caught in my hair, while a longer one scratched my cheek. Great. Swiping away the dirt and wetness from the bush leaves, I forced myself to keep searching for Winifred's secret opening.

In truth, I didn't have time for this right now, but my maternal instinct toward my cat forced me onward. If she ever got into something that harmed her, I'd feel responsible for the rest of my life. Even though she was snooty sometimes, I loved her so very much and would do anything to keep her safe.

After crawling a few more feet, I had one wall checked out. Nothing there. Rounding the corner, I squinted as a ray of sunlight angled through a break in the bushes. I'd have a headache later, for sure. Being so close to the ground, I also scanned the area for anything Lorna might have left there or have been interested in. But it was the same old bushes, dirt, and rocks as usual. What the heck had she been doing back here?

A few feet into the path, my knee sunk down, and I pitched forward, my chin smacking a large rock on the ground. What had happened?

Rubbing my sore chin, I checked behind me. A deep hole was nearly hidden right beside the wall. Had I finally found the opening?

I studied the area. While there was a hole in the ground and a crack in the cement, there didn't seem to be an opening large enough for Winifred to wiggle through.

But as I leaned closer, I spotted it. There wasn't one crack, but two, three feet apart. After digging my fingers into the bottom of the cement, I gave a yank. Small pieces of cement rained down on my knees as the large area gave way. This had to be it. Then I frowned. Winifred might be able to claw out a damaged section of cement to crawl inside, but she wouldn't be able to push it back in place afterward after leaving the greenhouse.

My cat wasn't the only one getting inside. The other one did indeed possess opposable thumbs. Was that how Mr. Morton's murderer had gained access to the inside of the greenhouse without having a key or breaking in the door?

It made sense. I felt around the bottom edge of the broken piece. Another opening was below, which explained the hole dug in the dirt. Maybe the killer had used the opening in the cement, but Winifred had shimmied underneath the loosened area, crawling up that way.

I sat back on my heels before I remembered the bushes behind me. Several branches poked the back of my head and shoulders before I crouched down again. Upon further inspection, I noticed something else. Stuck to the top edge of the broken-out cement were mud-encrusted pine needles. But Winifred never had those on her fur. She must not have been close to the top of the concrete when she dove under the foundation. The person who'd killed my lawyer must have left them there.

But there weren't any pine trees close to my greenhouse. Only farther away, next to the park.

The park.

Had whoever murdered Mr. Morton also killed Millie?

And why couldn't I have seen the cracks in the wall from the inside of the building, where I'd spent time I couldn't spare, hunting for the opening? I tugged the concrete piece all the way out.

Ah-ha…. It sat behind the cart where I kept reference books on monarchs and their habitats.

The cart was on wheels.

Whoever had made the opening must have pulled the cart to the wall to cover their entrance once they were backing out.

*Raise your hand if you're the idiot who wasted time crawling around, checking under dusty shelves when you could have simply rolled a cart out to visibly see the hole. And could have avoided crouching behind bushes like some frog outside as well.* I wiggled my fingers in the air.

*Idiot, thy name is Seneca.*

With a frustrated sigh, I crawled past the opening until I could scramble out through a break in the hedge. As I finally stood, my knees and back popped. After stretching out my sore muscles for a few seconds, I headed around to the front of the greenhouse. Time to clean up, call Cody about the latest development and head to the store for concrete to repair the opening.

# Chapter Twenty

When I reached the hardware store, Mr. O'Hurley, the owner, was in a chatty mood. Though I didn't want to hang around longer than necessary, out of politeness, I did and ended up hearing more about his wife's hysterectomy operation than anyone should know. After giving details about her puffy incision twice, he finally ran out of gory adjectives.

I found the aisle with the concrete. The price was more than I thought it would be, and I'd end up paying too much for too big an amount of concrete, but it was the smallest bag Mr. O'Hurley sold. The sack weighed so much, I had to have his stock boy place it in the truck for me. That grated on me since I prided myself on doing everything I could without help. And since it was so heavy, there was no way I'd be able to get it out of my truck without dropping the bag and fracturing at least one foot. Maybe Cody could help me unload it once I was home and ready to do the repair.

Maybe he'd help me with the repair itself.

*No. You can't depend on a man for every little thing. You know that.*

Memories of living with Payne and his giant male ego came, unbidden and unwelcome, into my mind. What a nightmare that period of my life had been.

Interesting how my mind had jumped straight to Cody when I needed something. After what Jesse had told me, maybe I shouldn't be so quick to do that. But this was Cody. I had to find out for myself if what Jesse had said was true. Maybe he got it wrong or misunderstood. That was my hope, anyway. The thought of Cody doing something even a little underhanded and then not being truthful about it to me was unthinkable.

Shaking off the bad thoughts, I headed down the tool aisle to get something to apply the concrete with. Not knowing much about the task, I browsed through several items, still not finding what I needed.

I leaned down to the bottom row. Maybe there was something different farther below. My back protested, bending over so far again. Why was I spending my day crouched over shelves? Didn't I have better things to do?

Finally, my luck held. At the very back of the shelf, wedged against the wall, were two trowels that would be about right for the job. I snagged both. It wasn't a bad idea to be prepared with an extra in case one of them broke or bent. One thing I hated was shopping. If I could save myself a trip by purchasing an extra of something in case of emergency, I was all over it.

As I stood up straight to toss the items in my cart, I heard my name. Had someone seen me enter and needed to talk to me? Occasionally, people, not locals, wanting directions to the farm for tours stopped in the store for directions. But right when I opened my mouth to call out where I was, I stopped, my jaw hanging open like some trout's.

Because what the person was saying wasn't some innocuous inquiry as to where I might be now. Or giving some tourist directions to the Majestic Monarchs. Did the speaker even know I was there? I edged closer to the end of the aisle and waited for my name again.

"Sid, I'm telling you something funny is going on."

Sid...must be talking to Sid Fairchild. The other voice had to be Norman Gates.

"What have you heard?" asked Sid.

"That she has something to do with those killings."

I rolled my eyes. I guess they'd gotten past their theory about either the butterflies or Winifred killing Mr. Morton. I'd have to tell Winifred that. She'd be so relieved.

"Seneca James? Come on. She's good people. You know that."

*Yes, I'm good people.*

"I'd always thought so," said Norman. "The first body, that nasty lawyer, I could have chalked up to a freak accident. But the second one?"

"What about it?"

"Didn't you hear?"

"Guess not," said Sid. "And I guess you're gonna tell me."

"There was a second murder. In the park."

"Didn't know 'bout that one. But what's that got to do with Seneca?"

Norman went on. "Hear tell it was actually on her property, not the park's."

"Is that right?" asked Sid.

I frowned. How was that out to these guys already? It wasn't as if they were the social butterflies of Maple Junction, always in on the latest news. Did people not have better things to do but gossip? First, Jesse heard something about me, now this.

"It's what I heard."

Sid went on. "I gotta say, your information usually pans out, don't it?"

"Darn tootin'" said Norman.

*Tootin? What did that even mean?*

"Okay, but still...that don't mean she had anything to do with them."

"Don't it?" asked Norman. "I think maybe she snapped. Went on some kind of killing spree."

*Snapped? Spree?*

"Ya think?"

"Stranger things, ya know?"

Their voices grew fainter as one asked the other, "S'pose we should start locking our doors at night, in case she's not done racking up her body count?"

Lock their doors? Like I'm gonna stalk around town wielding a pickaxe just for the pleasure of watching someone's blood spurt out? Go after my neighbors whom I'd known my whole life? Did more people than Sid and Norman feel that way?

Fuming, I glanced down to see both of my hands had curled into fists. And my face was heating up. How dare they? How dare anyone who knew me, who'd known me since I was born, ever think I could do such a thing? Was the tiny town so starved for drama it manufactured its own? And why did I have to be the unfortunate star of their show? I would've loved nothing better than to confront the old codgers, but all I wanted to do was get home and repair my greenhouse. Besides, I highly doubted anything I said would change their minds about me.

After the stock boy had loaded the concrete into the bed of my truck, I shut the tailgate, ready to head home. When I turned, Jesse stood a few feet away, looking in the window. He spotted me in the reflection and angled around.

Even though he and I had cleared the air about the survey of the property line, there still might be some lingering ill will. And I didn't want that, if he and I were to collaborate on things to benefit the monarchs.

I leaned with my back against the truck tailgate, really needing to get home and also still miffed about what the two older men had just said about me. But my small-town polite gene kicked in. "Hi. What're you in town for?"

"Needed some supplies." He pointed to the store, then edged closer. "I'm still learning my way around, though. Who carries what items. Has the best prices."

I shrugged. "As small as Maple Junction is, that shouldn't take you long."

A fly buzzed near my face, then landed somewhere on my head. No matter how much I tried to wave it away, I could still feel the little winged fool buzzing around. My hair was already a wavy rat's nest. Would the stupid insect get trapped in my untamed curls? How embarrassing.

"Wait." Jesse reached out and waved his hand over my hair. "It's gone now."

Relieved, I brushed the bangs from my face and said, "Thanks, I—"

Loud, fast footsteps approached. "What's going on here?"

Whipping around, I was not pleased to see Payne. What in the world did he want? If it was to talk about the case, surely he wouldn't do it in front of Jesse. "Payne?"

My ex stood with his arms crossed over his chest, his glance moving slowly from me to Jesse and back.

After a few moments of awkward silence, Jesse stuck out his hand. "I'm—"

Waving away the other man's gesture, Payne said, "I know who you are."

Getting tired of the sudden negative testosterone level coming in waves from Payne, I tapped my foot as I said, "I don't know why you seem so upset, but—"

He grabbed my hand, tugging me toward him, nearly causing me to stumble. "I'd thought after we'd had that date the other night...."

"Date?" I tried to pull away from him, but he held tight. As he blew out a frustrated breath, I caught a whiff of alcohol. He was drinking this early in the day? Perfect.

Something shuffled behind me. Jesse had moved closer. "Do you need help here?"

Payne's voice came out as a growl as he said, "Back. Off."

Why were men so crazy sometimes? Taking a deep breath, trying to remain calm, I looked straight at Payne. "Please let go of me. Right now. You've obviously been drinking."

And just my luck, Norman and Sid had stopped a few feet from us on the sidewalk, openly gawking at us. I couldn't really blame them. Our voices were getting loud, and I could feel a public altercation brewing. Norman elbowed Sid. Then, heads close together, they whispered like a couple of twelve-year-old girls.

With lowered eyebrows, Payne opened his grasp on my hand and took a step back. "What does it matter if I tossed one back? I'm allowed. And yes, what we had was a date. Thought we were rekindling something between us. So why is this guy—" he glared at Jesse "—pawing at you?"

I moved farther away. Payne was clearly delusional. Besides, my ex was good-looking and knew it. Why would he act jealous of a shy older man with a burn across one side of his face? "It wasn't like that," I said. "I had a fly in my hair and—"

"Please. Spare me the inane explanation. If you wanna be with some other guy, then..."

I pounded my fist against the side of my thigh. When would this guy get it? "There's nothing going on. Besides, you and I aren't a thing. Not anymore. Not for a long time. Kind of thought the divorce papers took care of all that."

The two bystanders watching us elbowed each other again, seeming to thoroughly enjoy the encounter. Did they want popcorn with the show?

Again, Payne eyed the close proximity of the park ranger to me. His eyes narrowed. The way he acted, maybe he'd tossed back more than one drink.

Several more people had gathered on the sidewalk, wide-eyed and open-mouthed as they took in the spectacle before them. Didn't they have anything better to do? Letting out a groan, I shook my head. Anything other than the old, boring ordinary stuff was an opportunity for a little excitement in Maple Junction. That would never change.

# Chapter Twenty-One

"All right. Break it up, people."

I knew that voice all too well. I watched my friend over the heads of several older women who stood in a clump a few feet away. Of course, the confrontation wouldn't be complete without my well-meaning but overprotective friend, Cody.

He made his way through the growing crowd, then reached the three of us. Eyeing me, he said, "Seneca? Is there a problem?"

It wouldn't do any good to act like nothing was going on because of all the bystanders who were still gawking. Any minute now, one of the shopkeepers might start selling tickets to see the show. "Cody, it's okay. Just a misunderstanding."

"That's all?"

I nodded. "Yep. Fine. Everything is fine."

Cody glanced at Jesse, then focused on Payne. "Is that your story, too? No problem?"

Payne shrugged, like we were all having a friendly chat, but as red as his face was, a sure sign he was still angry, the gesture came off as not believable.

Then, Cody turned to Jesse. "I'll ask you. Is there a problem here? Something I should be concerned about?"

"The only problem is with him," Jesse said as he quickly glanced toward Payne. "He stormed up here, tossing out accusations that weren't true."

"What about?" asked Cody.

"Me. And Seneca."

"Is that so?" Eyeing Payne again, Cody said, "Is that true?"

Obviously having trouble holding in his anger, Payne narrowed his eyes and glared at first Jesse, then Cody. "My wife seems to have way too much male companionship to suit me."

I stomped my foot, not caring if it appeared childish to the onlookers. "Ex. Wife."

"Whatever." Payne clenched his jaws together, something I remembered all too well as a sign he was about to blow a gasket. His expression when he stared at Cody was so venomous, I was afraid he might take a swing at him. Wouldn't the onlookers get a real show if that happened, and Payne ended up in jail?

Why couldn't he just let it go? Let me go? He'd signed the papers ending our marriage, or had he conveniently forgotten that in his inebriated fog?

With a glance at Payne, Cody said, "Why don't we break this little party up now? Go our own ways." He stood there, one hand by his side, the other resting lightly on his firearm. I'd never seen him do that before. Never even seen him draw his weapon. He wouldn't actually use it on Payne, would he? Maybe he knew him well enough to see how ticked off he was, too.

Time to end the spectacle we had created. I could only imagine the gossip that would run rampant the moment people left the scene and spread the titillating rendition of what they'd witnessed. How embarrassing. And mortifying. I was a business owner in this town. It wouldn't help matters any to become an object of ridicule. Wasn't it bad enough there'd been murders on my land?

As I took a step back, I distanced myself from all three. "Listen, I need to get back to the farm. There's lots of work to do. I've wasted too much time already on something that never should have happened."

I turned and walked around to the driver's side of my truck. Tired of dealing with men in general, I started the truck and drove away.

With my foot pressed on the gas pedal so hard, it didn't take long to reach the farm. Slamming the door after I climbed out, I took a few deep breaths. Maybe that would help me calm down.

Nope. It didn't help.

I'd stashed the sack with the trowels on the passenger seat, so I grabbed those. After I'd set them on the counter in the greenhouse, I came back out. Eyeing the bed of my truck, I groaned. Why was it now, at this moment when I needed a guy to take the cement out, I was miffed at men in general?

Truth be told, I couldn't be mad at Cody for what had happened in town. He'd been doing his job. Except for his putting his hand on his gun as some sort of subliminal threat, he hadn't done anything out of the ordinary. Jesse had been innocent in the whole thing. And Payne. Good old obnoxious Payne. Saying I was still his.

Anger resurfaced, the accompanying heat burning a path down my back. Why did men assume I was helpless? Think I needed to be taken care of, that I couldn't run my own life?

The huge package of concrete mocked me. Sat there, waving. *Hello, Seneca. Too bad you can't do everything for yourself. Remember me? The thing that was too heavy for you to load into the truck by yourself.*

I let out a sigh.

Not this time.

I climbed into the bed, studying the situation. It would have been nice if the stock boy hadn't shoved the thing all the way toward the cab, but I'd just have to work with what I had.

Glancing around to make sure no one was headed up the drive, I bent down and grabbed the edge of the package with both hands.

And pulled.

And landed on my butt.

Which, on a metal surface, doesn't feel all that great.

Standing and brushing off the back of my pants, I tried again. Bending down, grabbing the edge, yanking.

Back on my butt.

There had to be a better way. What if I tackled it from the other end? I smiled. Sure. Use force from behind it instead of in front. Stepping over the concrete, I managed to wedge one boot between it and the cab. I had strong legs, so I should be able to—

A pain shot up my leg. The concrete hadn't moved. Not an inch. And it still mocked me.

"Fine." I walked to the opened gate and hopped to the ground. "We'll see who's boss around here."

After I went into the greenhouse, I rummaged around until I found what I needed. My old shovel. I used it for everything around the farm. It had been around for decades. Gram had used it, too.

Hauling the heavy tool outside, I carried it to the truck, gave it a toss into the bed— cringing when metal clanged on metal—then climbed up after it. This time, I'd get that cement out of my truck. I just needed to be smarter than the concrete.

Placing the edge of the shovel where I'd previously had my boot, I applied leverage. Using every muscle, gritting my teeth against the pull in my leg muscle from before, I pushed, pulled, and otherwise persuaded the concrete into submission.

It moved an inch.

*Seneca, you can do this. Keep working. Applying pressure. Pretty soon, you'll have it off the truck. Who needs men? Not this girl.*

Encouraged, I kept at it, using all the force I could manage, moving the container an inch at a time. I was out of breath but refused to give up. Doing it this way would take forever. Time I didn't have to waste. But I was determined to do this myself.

Deciding I needed to increase my efforts, I put my whole body into it. Leaned all my weight on the handle until I was standing on my toes.

When something cracked, I stared down.

And when the shovel broke off from the handle, I groaned.

Defeated, I sat glumly on the tailgate. Maybe I needed to accept that I couldn't do everything for myself. That I didn't have to. And shouldn't feel bad about the fact that sometimes it was okay to depend on someone else. On a man. So, the concrete would stay in my truck until the next time Cody came over to see me.

With a sigh, I jumped down and got back into the cab to drive to town.

I needed a new shovel.

# Chapter Twenty-Two

On his day off, Cody volunteered to help me fix the opening where Winifred had been getting into the greenhouse. Though my first inclination had been to tell him I could do it myself, I didn't. Having come to the realization that every person has limitations, I gladly accepted.

Somehow, I needed to bring up what Jesse had overheard about him. But I didn't want to do it in a way that would put him on the defensive. Especially since I doubted it was true. Still, for my peace of mind, if nothing else, I needed to clear the air.

"I feel guilty," I said, "having you here, doing this when you could be off doing something fun."

"Fun...like what?"

"Don't know," I said. "What do you usually do on your time away from work?"

"Visit you."

The two words hung in the air. *Visit you.* It was true. Hardly a day went by that Cody didn't stop by to see me, or at least call. Had I taken him, our friendship for granted all this time? I shook my head. No, I didn't think so, but hoped I'd been as good a friend to him. I knelt beside him, ready to help push the old concrete piece in place so Cody could seal it in along with some of the new concrete.

"Well," I said, "I really, really do appreciate you doing this. I would have tried on my own—"

"I know. Just like you always do."

Though I knew I had limitations, it was still hard to admit them to someone else. Taking the tack of inexperience over inability took some of the bite out of it. "But I've never done it, so—"

"So, who knows how terrible it would turn out?"

If I'd had a free hand, I would have smacked his arm. Instead, I hissed.

He smirked. "Not bad. Winifred's still got you beat, though."

"She's a cat."

"Good point."

Part of me didn't want to bring up the gossip, because I never wanted to lose the closeness that Cody and I shared. However, if I left it like it was, the uncertainty would fester, and it wouldn't be long before it hung between us, changing the way we were with each other.

We sat there, shoulders touching, until Cody finished. "Now," he said, "if you can hold this in place for, say, a couple of hours."

"What?"

He laughed. "Only for a second, until I can drag that big rock over here to press against it."

Letting out a breath, I glared at him. "You're not a nice man."

"Sure I am."

"Not right this second. I thought you were serious, that I'd have to try to hold this heavy thing in place for that long."

Cody sat back and crossed his arms.

"What are you doing?" I asked.

He raised one eyebrow. "Sitting."

"Why aren't you getting the rock? I'm starting to lose my grip." Panic shot through me. "Hey...stop kidding around."

"I'm gonna sit here until you admit I'm a good guy."

"Joking again?"

"Afraid not," he said.

I narrowed my eyes, trying to ignore my cramped arm muscles from holding them in an awkward position. "Okay, fine. You are a good guy."

"You mean it?"

My arms were quivering from staying in the same position. "Yes!"

He stood up. The sound of footsteps, then the rock rolling across the ground. "All right." He edged the rock closer until it nudged my arm. "Very slowly, pull your hands away."

I did, relieved when he had the rock in place, and I could relax. That also left me with my hands-free, so I whacked him in the shoulder.

Cody gave me a sheepish grin. "Guess I deserved that."

"Yes." I sighed. "No, you didn't. Like I said, I really do appreciate you doing this for me."

"I don't mind. Honest."

Wanting to say something but not quite ready to ask about what Jesse heard, I filled Cody in on Lorna being Lonny's sister and having a past romantic interest in Mr. Morton. When I mentioned Lorna having been close to where we were sitting now, Cody's eyebrows shot up.

"What do you think was going on?" he asked.

"I have no clue. It's so odd. But then, so is Lorna."

Cody wiped some moisture from his forehead. "Good point. I'll keep an eye on her, though, just in case."

Silence surrounded us when I didn't say anything more.

"Seneca? You okay?"

Though I didn't want to tell Cody what Jesse had said, the information threatened to burn a hole in my innards if I kept it inside. "Something..."

He touched my shoulder. "What? What's happened?"

"I heard something."

"Like—"

"Jesse stopped by," I said.

His hand slid from my shoulder. "All right. So, something happened?"

"He... he'd overheard some talk. About you."

"Me?"

How could I get the words out without just blurting them? I didn't want to say it. But I had to. Our future friendship depended on us being open and honest with each other.

"Seneca, you're killing me. What's going on?"

Giving him my full attention, I said, "He was in the grocery. Overheard two women talking but didn't see what they looked like. Said he only paid attention because they mentioned your name." Letting out a sigh, I forced myself to go on. "According to them—whoever they were—you tried to... right before I got married, you tried to scare Payne off. That you didn't want me to marry him. I told Jesse I didn't think it was true, that—"

Cody's face turned white. He swallowed hard, his Adam's apple moving in his throat. Then he turned his head and wouldn't even make eye contact.

No. It wasn't possible. I grabbed his arm. "Cody? What's going on?"

He faced me again, placing a hand on each of my shoulders. "I should have told you a long time ago."

"You mean it's true? You did that?" My heart plummeted in my chest. My world threatened to shatter. If I couldn't trust Cody...

"Listen to me, okay?" He squeezed my shoulders. "I did talk to Payne. Told him I didn't think he was right for you. Not good enough."

"You knew I loved him. Why would you do that?"

"Seneca, he...even back in high school, he'd talk about how stupid it was for you to be all into the butterflies. He made fun of you. All the time. It made me so mad. I knew how much they meant to you. Shouldn't the guy you were dating have thought the same thing?"

"You never said a word. Sure, I knew he felt that way after we were married, but I figured he was jealous because of the time I spent with them. But in high school, when I was dating him? He never said anything to me."

"Of course, he didn't back then. He wanted to make sure you married him. I didn't tell you for the reason you said, because I knew you did love him. I didn't want you to get your heart broken. We were all kids. I figured, at some point, you'd figure it out for yourself and dump the loser."

"Then why did you try before the wedding?"

"Because dating someone and pledging your life to them is totally different."

His words, so full of wisdom and maturity, were the opposite of our usual teasing conversations. Sure, we talked about everything. At least I thought we had, until I learned about this. But our friendship was easy and comfortable. Like my grandma's warm shawl, I used to drape around me on cold evenings at her house when I'd visit. Now, he came out with this.

"Why aren't you saying anything? You always have some kind of comeback." He playfully nudged my shoulder with his fist. "Okay, I'm getting nervous now. Please, say something."

When Jesse had told me what he'd heard, at first, I hadn't believed it. I'd only partially accepted it might be true later, but still had serious doubts. Cody, confessing it was true, had knocked me for a loop. Until he'd told me why. He was right. Dating someone and contemplating spending the rest of your life with them were like comparing a fluttering butterfly—fragile, with a short lifespan—to a soaring eagle—a symbol of power and freedom. Since I'd been married, although briefly, I knew it was true.

The fact that Cody understood that was amazing, the guy never having been married or even in a long-term relationship. I guess that said something about the man himself. Though he liked to come across as funny and playful, a deep, rushing river flowed beneath the lighthearted veneer. "Oh, Cody. And all this time, you've thought about this? Carried this around?"

"Don't make me sound like some kind of saint. I'm not. I only wanted what was best for you. And he wasn't it. Didn't matter, though. He wouldn't listen to me."

"But you should have told me then."

He watched me intently for a few seconds. "Your Gram told me to keep quiet."

"What? She knew?"

"Yeah. But she said it had to be your decision. That we weren't going to try to influence you in any way if Payne was who you loved."

I shook my head. The more I thought about it, that did sound like her. Gram always had my back. Always believed that a woman should be strong, decisive, make her way in the world, and live with her decisions. She never failed to let me make my own choices, even when those led to mistakes.

Knowing what she did about Payne, hadn't she been worried that it would turn out badly? Or was she counting on my strong desire to be with him, my overpowering love for my new husband, to turn things around? I'd never know.

I shrugged. "Sometimes I forget how much time you'd spent with my grandmother, hanging out lots of time when I was visiting her. It shouldn't surprise me that you and she confided in each other about me. That she'd leave the decision up to me, without trying to interfere by injecting her own opinions or wants. Now, though, I feel like such a fool. Think of all the time I wasted being married to him because I didn't want to see the truth. Didn't want to see what was right in front of me. That he didn't care about what was so important to me."

Cody fastened his gaze onto mine. "Can you forgive me? At least try?"

The man in front of me looked like he might shatter if I refused. It was Cody. The person I treasured the most. The one person aside from Gram who'd stood up for me my whole life. Though he'd kept a secret from me all these years, hadn't he done it to try to protect my feelings? To not interfere with what I'd had my heart set on? Knowing now that he'd wanted to change things for me but hadn't, it gave me a new appreciation for the depth of his love as a true friend.

I threw my arms around his neck. "Of course."

With a sigh, he gave me a big squeeze, then released me. "Thank you. It's way more than I deserve."

Smiling, ready to lighten the moment, get back to our comfortable comradery, I said, "Yeah, it is."

Cody laughed.

"But..." I pointed at him. "From now on, no more secrets. You got that?"

"Yes, ma'am." He gave me a mock salute. I was glad to see him smile, see that he'd gotten color back in his face.

We were going to be okay. We had to be. Because a life without Cody wasn't something I could imagine.

He swatted something away from his face, a large insect. Cody looked annoyed that nature took that moment to interfere with a special moment.

Watching him finally shoo the tiny beast away, I said, "Well, now that we've done manual labor and sorted out anything that might come between us, are you ready to take a break? How about—" Something buzzed near my ear, and I waved my hand at it. It did a dive right over my head, then circled back to my face. I smacked at the air but missed hitting it. "What the heck?"

Frowning, Cody glanced up. "It's wasps. Maybe there's a nest close by."

"Then I'm not sticking around to find out. Not in the mood to meet more of their wicked little friends."

"Agreed." He stood, then reached down and helped me up. "So, you said something about food? I think..." Something landed on his cheek.

"Hold still." I flicked it away with my hand. "I don't remember seeing wasps much. Good thing since they're predators for monarchs."

"After we eat, let's see if we can find the nest. Do you have insecticide?"

"Yep. Locked in a cabinet in the greenhouse. You know, so a certain nosy cat won't get into it."

"Great. Then let's—"

All at once, four wasps buzzed around my head. Good grief! I took off running around the greenhouse, trying to get away from them. Cody's heavy footsteps followed mine.

When we rounded the corner, I got a shock. Wasps. Everywhere. Like a giant dark cloud that moved from side to side, up, then down. The noise was like a hundred tiny buzz saws started up all at once. "Where did they come from?" I shouted.

"Don't know. Let's get inside the greenhouse." He opened the door partway so we could squeeze in, hopefully not letting any of them in with us.

The problem was, there were already a ton inside.

My mouth dropped open, but I quickly snapped it shut when a wasp tried to fly in. I swung my arms violently around my head and smacked my bare arms and face when one landed on me. "What are we gonna do?"

Cody grabbed my hand and tugged. "We have to get to the house. And call an exterminator!"

I let him pull me toward the door. "Wait! Where's Winifred?" I slipped free of his grasp, waving aside wasps that came from every direction. "Winifred! Are you in here? Winifred?"

Doing my best, I fought against the insects as I tried to locate my cat. Finally, near the back of the building, there was a high-pitched screech. I found her cowering next to a caterpillar pen. Her eyes were huge and round.

She howled even louder when she saw me. After lifting her up, I covered her face with my hand and ran for the door. Cody was there, waiting for us.

"Why do you have it open?" I frowned at his hand on the doorframe. "Won't you let more in?"

"I think there's more in here than out there." We left and rushed to the house, slamming the door shut once inside. Standing perfectly still, we listened. Silence. There didn't seem to be wasps here.

Winifred struggled to get down, so I let her. But when she tried to walk away, she wouldn't place her left front paw on the floor.

Panic shot through me. A wasp sting on a cat could be dangerous. "Cody, she's hurt. I bet she got stung."

He leaned forward and watched her. "You're right. Is Doc Cummings open today?"

The only veterinarian in town was eighty if he was a day, but he still loved to treat the animals. "I think so."

"Why don't you take her, then? I'll stay here and contact an exterminator and animal control. Whoever can get here the fastest to get rid of these wasps."

I stopped mid-stride as a horrible realization took hold. "The monarchs. The wasps will kill them."

Cody sighed, then swallowed hard. "I know. I'll get the pens and take them around the other side of the house."

Grabbing his arm, I said, "You'll get stung. I can't let you do that. There's so many of them out there."

"I'm doing it anyway. Besides, I've already been stung. Haven't you?"

As if his words conjured it up, a couple of stings on my arms began to ache. "Yes, but..."

"Let's take care of Winifred and get someone out here, then we can assess the..." His voice drifted off as he grimaced.

But I knew what he'd been about to say. "Assess the damage," I finished for him. The poor monarchs. I didn't even want to contemplate what this might do to them.

Tears blurred my vision as I grabbed Winifred and headed to my car. In shock about the wasps and worried about Winifred, I hadn't even stopped to get her carrier. That left me steering with one hand and clutching her to my chest with the other. Thank goodness I didn't have to drive far.

# Chapter Twenty-Three

The only vehicle in the tiny lot was the vet's. His old Chevy truck appeared nearly as ancient and wrinkled as he did. I stuffed my keys and wallet in my pocket, then held Winifred tight as we headed into the small brick building.

A tinny sound of a bell dinged overhead as I opened then closed the door. Dr. Cummings himself came from the back. His daughter, Penny, who had to be near sixty herself, must be off today. She had been his receptionist for as long as I could remember. Wondered if either one would ever retire.

"Miss James. Nice to see you." He glanced down. "You too, Winifred."

My cat hissed, then growled.

I held her close and set my chin on top of her head. "Sorry."

"Not to worry. I'm scolded by something with fur every day. Nothing new. What seems to be the problem?"

"I think she got stung by a wasp." Please let him know how to help her. Know what to do. The thought of something happening to her, especially something like this, was nearly unbearable. She followed me everywhere, and this time, it seemed, since I'd let her out of the house, it might do her terrible harm.

His mouth turned down at the corners. "Poor kitty. Let's bring her to the operatory. Lighting's better there, so I can check her out."

A growl, low and feral, came from my cat, growing louder with every step I took toward the back. For Winifred, only painful, scary, or mortifying things happened here. Guess I couldn't blame her for not wanting to visit.

Dr. Cummings turned on a bright overhead light, making Winifred and I both squint. "Here," he said, reaching out. "Let me see her."

I made the hand-off of angry fur to the doctor, then crossed my arms and waited.

He pushed his thick glasses higher on his nose and leaned closer to the cat. "Ah, yes. Right there. See?"

When I studied it more closely, I did see it. A tiny red mark surrounded by a welt forming, causing her fur to look like she had a grape beneath the skin.

"We'll get her fixed right up."

Comforted at the vet's confident, easy manner, I said, "Thanks so much." I watched while he gave her a shot—producing another growl—and put some salve on the wound. Winifred hissed so loud and so long, I think both the doctor and I were covered in cat saliva. "Being a cat, won't she just lick that salve off?"

"Of course." He grinned. "But if you can keep her from getting to it until you get her home, I think enough of it will soak in that she'll get the benefit."

"I'll do my best."

He smiled. "That's all any of us can do."

I returned his smile. "Yep." Winifred was already lifting her paw to her mouth, ready to wash off the offending goo. "Oh no, you don't." I picked her up, pressing her to my chest, making sure I kept my other hand beneath her chin so she couldn't get to it. I was, of course, rewarded with a growl. "I really appreciate this, Dr. Cummings."

"Glad to help."

"How much do I owe you?"

"Penny takes care of the billing. She'll send you one. Won't be much, though."

"Okay. Thanks." I started to leave.

"By the way," he said. "You'd mentioned what she got stung by was a wasp?"

"That's right."

"Strange," he said.

"What is?"

"About an hour ago, some man, a stranger, brought in a German Shepherd.

Same thing had happened to the dog."

"Wasp sting?" That was odd.

"Right. Haven't seen one of those in a pet all year, now two in one day."

Until now, I hadn't had time to think it through. But all those wasps appearing out of nowhere, it couldn't be a coincidence, could it? Had someone let them loose on my property to kill the monarchs? Maybe Hal had done it. But no, Dr. Cummings would have recognized him. What about the surveyor? I tilted my head. "You say the person wasn't someone you knew?"

"No. In my profession, I'm mainly acquainted with people who bring their pets to me. 'Course, you know I'll still treat any animal, even though they're not a regular client."

"Yes." I nodded slowly. "Could I ask, what did this man look like?"

He lowered his eyebrows. Did he think the question was odd? That I was being nosy where I had no business asking about another person who'd brought a pet into the office for treatment?

After clearing my throat, I said, "See, I think maybe I've met him before. Walking his dog through town, um, a couple of weeks ago. Seemed like a nice guy. And the dog was beautiful. I… thought I'd catch up with him to see if his dog was okay."

Dr. Cummings tilted his head, considering, then gave a slow nod. Had he decided I was only being thoughtful, inquiring about another person's pet? Finally, he smiled and said, "Oh, that's nice of you. Yes, it was a beautiful dog."

I hated lying, but needed to know. It couldn't be a coincidence with the wasps, could it? No one would do that, release a hoard of stinging insects unless he wanted to do some harm. To me or to the monarchs. Or both? I tensed my shoulders, hoping he'd answer my question about the guy's appearance.

The doctor lifted his chin, raising his eyes toward the ceiling. "Let's see. He was maybe fifty-ish, heavyset, balding."

I blew out a breath. That awful man, Lonny. Had to be. "Yep, that sure sounds like him." I cuddled Winifred closer when she tried to reach her paw again. "Well, thanks so much. I'd better get her home."

"You're welcome. Good to see you. Take care, Winifred."

Instead of growling or hissing for once, she winked.

Dr. Cummings laughed and waved. I turned and headed back to my truck.

Driving home was even more challenging than before. I once again steered with one hand and held onto her with the other, but also kept hold of her chin so she wouldn't lick her paw. "Just wait 'til we're home, Winifred, then you can lick it for hours." And she would.

When we reached my lane, I drove up slowly, afraid of what I'd find. There were two unfamiliar trucks with writing I couldn't quite make out on the doors—exterminators I assumed— parked near the greenhouse. Cody stood watching them. As I got closer to the house, he turned and waved. Then, hurried toward us.

"Is Winifred okay?" How like him to care so much about someone else's cat.

"Yeah. She did get stung, but Dr. Cummings took care of her. I'm going to take her in the house and close her in my bedroom, so she won't get out again."

"Good idea. With the help of the exterminators, I was able to get all the pens out before they used any chemicals."

His quick thinking and actions might have saved at least some of my army and immature swarm. "I can't thank you enough. What would I have done if you hadn't been here already?"

"Called me."

I smiled. "True. I don't deserve you."

"True." He laughed.

I took Winifred inside, trying to ignore her yowling as I closed her in my bedroom. Though I'd given her treats out of the drawer in my nightstand—a must for when she wanted a middle-of-the-night snack, and I didn't feel like trudging to the kitchen—she was decidedly unhappy. A few minutes later, I stood beside Cody again. "What happens now?"

"The guys are inside the greenhouse with the windows closed, killing the wasps."

Suddenly tired from all of it, the stress, the rushing around, the worry about Cody, Winifred, and the monarchs, I leaned against him, comforted when he wrapped his long arms around me.

"I hate to say this," he said, "but maybe we should check the monarchs by the milkweed too. Who knows if whoever did this didn't get to them as well."

Closing my eyes, I took a few seconds to try to calm down. When I opened them, he was watching me. "You're right," I said. "Better check it out."

We took my truck. I drove faster than normal, but if there were wasps in the milkweed, I'd want the exterminators to take care of them out there, too, while they were still working on my property.

When we arrived, everything seemed okay. No buzzing or anything flying around except my orange and black beauties. I jumped out of the truck, and Cody followed. He pointed to the patch. "I don't see or hear any wasps. Do you?"

"No." I shook my head. "Thank goodness. These guys are okay. I just hope the caterpillars and—"

"I know." He stepped close and rubbed my shoulder. "But it's good news the adults are all right."

"Definitely."

When we got back in the truck, I didn't start it right away. Just sat, finally having a minute to sort out what had just occurred.

"Seneca?"

I angled around to see him better. "When I took Winifred to the vet's, the doc told me something interesting."

"Interesting can be good." He folded his arms over his chest.

"In this case, I hope so. He said a man, a stranger, brought in a German Shepherd an hour before I was in. Said the dog had a wasp sting."

He lowered his eyebrows but didn't respond.

"According to Dr. Cummings, he hadn't seen a pet with that all year, then bam, two in one day."

"Anything else?"

"I asked for a description of the guy. It might be that surveyor."

Cody shook his head back and forth slowly. "Very interesting indeed."

# Chapter Twenty-Four

When my phone rang, I knew it was bad news. Or I should say, more bad news. Glancing at the screen, I saw it was Cody. "Hello?"

"Hey," he said. Then, silence.

"What's up?" Though I truly didn't want to know, I had to ask.

"The results of the land survey are in."

"And...."

"Millie King. It turns out she was on park property—"

I let out a breath, relieved that at least something was going right for me.

"—and on yours," he said.

"What? But how?" All those years of thinking the property line was in one spot, but it had been wrong. Somehow, I felt betrayed by that, though I couldn't come up with a good reason why. Maybe with everything in an upheaval, it was just one more thing I couldn't trust.

"Not to sound morbid, but her body was on the line, half on, half off your side."

"This can't be happening."

"I'm sorry to be the one to give you more bad news."

"Not your fault." I ran my hand through my hair, already a mess from hauling caterpillar pens around in the greenhouse. It was a few seconds before I realized Cody hadn't said anything else. "So...what happens now?"

He made a noise like he was swallowing or maybe giving a slight cough. "Since she was partly on your side, the state police want to talk to you."

A weight pushed down on my shoulders, like hands of an oppressor, never letting me break free from all that had gone on. "If it's not one thing..."

"Yeah, I know."

I pictured large men in dark suits, donning sunglasses and stern expressions. "Are these state people going to just show up at my house one day, pounce at me when I walk out my door, or what?"

"Not quite that scenario." I heard a chuckle in his voice. I hadn't been joking, but maybe he was trying to find a little humor in a bad situation.

"Then, what?" It had come out harsher than I'd intended. "Sorry, not mad at you."

"It's okay. Blame the messenger and all that."

"No. I didn't mean that. You're just doing your job," I said.

"Kidding about the messenger thing. Sorry. Um, since I'm the sheriff in this jurisdiction, they've asked me to set it up with you. At the sheriff's office."

"Will you be there?" I clutched the phone tight, hoping.

"Watch them try and stop me."

I smiled. It was true. Cody was a papa bear when it came to me. Had been that way since we'd been little. If anyone had ever bothered me on the playground or in school, Cody was ready to put up his fists and duke it out, no matter how big or mean the other person was. "When do they want to..."

"Today, Seneca."

My shoulders hunched, as if a plug was pulled, forcing me to deflate. "Wow. Today."

"I know. Quick. Can you..."

"Do I have a choice?" I asked.

"Probably not. Sorry to say."

I clutched the edges of my phone tighter. "Should I be worried about this?"

The three-second silence nearly knocked me flat. My heart clenched in my chest. If he was concerned, it really was serious. "No. I don't think so," he finally said. Was he hoping to keep me calm in the face of a scary situation?

Whatever his intentions, it sounded like I had no choice but to go. Glancing down at my dirty apron, I said, "Can you tell them an hour? I'll need to clean up and change and..."

"Don't go to any trouble for them. They're not worth it." His voice sounded angry, but I knew it wasn't aimed at me.

"It's not that. Just... If I feel better about my appearance, maybe it will give me a little confidence, you know? Going into something scary. Kind of like donning armor."

"Yeah, I get it."

Then I had a thought. If this turned out to be something serious, would I need my own representation? "Wait. Do I need to call Payne?"

"What for?" His voice sounded grumpy.

"As an attorney."

"They said no. That you wouldn't need one. It's just an informal question and answer time."

Should I take them at their word? I forced my bunched shoulders to relax. Cody would be there. That was at least comforting. I could always call Payne if need be.

"Want me to pick you up?" Cody's question jolted me back to our conversation.

The thought was appealing, but I needed to do this myself. Besides, Cody would be at the station with me once I got there. "No, I'll meet you."

"Sure?"

"Yep," I said.

"And Seneca?"

"Hmmm?"

"It's gonna be okay."

I bit my lip, then said, "Thanks." And pressed the end button.

When I entered the house, Winifred was sitting by her empty dish, an accusatory expression on her furry face. I glanced at the clock. Later than I thought. Sometimes, I really thought my cat could tell time. Either that, or she had an internal feed-me mechanism in her tummy. I hurried and dumped food in her bowl. A small piece bounced out and hit her on the nose. She gave me another glare that would have curled my hair had my locks not already been wavy and attacked her food.

After a quick shower, change, and half-fluffing my hair into some semblance of order, I grabbed my purse and keys and hopped into my truck. When I started it, I checked the gas gauge. Almost E. Why now? A fast emergency stop at Maple Junction's only gas station, then I hightailed it to the sheriff's station.

I parked right behind a state police car in front of the building, where it was a no-parking zone. Figured if someone tried to give me a parking ticket, I could always claim innocence that I thought it was okay since the state car was there too. I'd like to see someone argue with that logic. And the way I was feeling lately, anyone getting in my way might regret it.

Practically running, out of breath, and overheated, I went inside, skidding to a stop in the main lobby. Dana sat at her desk, her brow lowered. "Seneca, are you okay?"

I took a gulp of air and edged closer to her. "I'm supposed to meet—"

She held up her hand to quiet me, which gave me another second or two to catch my breath. With a low voice, she said, "They're all back there in the conference room. Cody, too."

"Okay, thanks."

"Hey," she said, "I'll be thinking of you. Fingers crossed. It will be fine."

She was, had always been, such a positive influence when it had come to me. I tried not to think about the newspaper picture I'd found in my café. Cody was going to talk to her, but I didn't know how far he'd gotten. Wasn't up to me to bring it up. I gave her a nod, stood up straight, and marched down the hall toward the only conference room in the small department building.

The door was closed. I knocked, which seemed silly because I was the one they wanted to speak to, yet small-town politeness demanded I use my big-girl manners.

The wooden door opened. I let out a relieved breath when Cody stood just inside. He'd said he'd be here, but I was relieved just the same. "Hey," he whispered. "Got a little worried." He angled around toward the clock on the opposite wall. Ten minutes past when I said I'd arrive.

"Sorry," I said back.

"No, it's okay." He motioned me in.

Once he stepped aside to close the door behind me, I got a look at who all was in the long, narrow room.

Two men in suits who I'd never seen before were there, plus Lonny, and Jesse. I should have guessed he'd be here since he oversaw the park, and Millie had partly been found on that property, but still, seeing him here with the others who were, at least to my way of thinking, the enemy weighed my heart down.

"Seneca James," said Cody, "this is Frank Biggens and Alec Ridge. They're here on behalf of the state." The suits both stood. Frank, a tall, burly man with a burr haircut and meaty hands, nodded. Alec, so thin, his white shirt collar appeared loose around his neck, gave a partial smile, which disappeared nearly as soon as he'd given it.

"And," added Cody, "of course, you've met the county surveyor, Lonny Gibbs, and Park Ranger, Jesse Vance."

I nodded back. Saying 'hello' felt a little friendly, for what I gathered might not be a friendly meeting. We were talking about a murdered woman, after all.

Jesse wouldn't make eye contact. Instead, he kept his head lowered, eyes on the tabletop. Lonny, however, seemed gleefully pleased I was here.

Frank gestured with his huge paw toward an empty seat nearest me. It was by itself on the end of the long table. With only one other seat available, Cody watched me for a second, then turned and went to that chair. It was halfway down the table. Oh, how I wished I could have sat beside him. Just knowing he was in the room would have to do.

Slowly, as if my joints and muscles protested, I tugged out the chair, set my purse on the table, then sat down.

Alec leaned forward, elbows on the table, and focused on me. "Miss James," he said. "I'm sure you know why you're here?"

Suddenly self-conscious, I brushed some hair away from my cheek. "I assume because the woman was found to be partly on my land."

He nodded. "That's right. The woman…" He held out his hand toward Frank, who handed him a piece of paper. "Millie King was indeed found dead on the property line. Which puts this investigation in two courts. State and County."

Was I supposed to say something? Nothing was forthcoming, so I clutched my hands together in my lap, under the table, and waited.

With a scowl, Frank said, "In the interest of time, I suggest we get straight to the questioning."

Questioning. In my mind, the word equaled Guillotine, or Noose.

Alec glanced at Frank, giving him a disapproving frown. "We can at least be civil, don't you think?"

Good cop, bad cop. Rehearsed, or were they really at odds? Did it matter? I didn't much care how they spoke to me if, by the end of this little discussion, they let me walk out of the room free and clear.

Frank tapped a pen on the scarred wooden table. "Now, why don't we start with what happened when you claim you found her already dead?"

Claim? My throat went dry. This guy didn't mess around.

"Miss James?" Frank's bushy eyebrows were lowered over narrowed blue eyes.

Shoot, I hadn't answered his question yet. Something caught in my throat. "I..." Coughing, I tried again. "I was burning some brush."

"That close to state property?"

"Not that close. I'm always careful. Had cleared the practice with former Ranger Nelson."

Frank shook his head, like it was something he'd need to check out.

*Good luck with that. Ranger Nelson left, and no one knew where he went.*

"Proceed."

"Anyway, I finished burning brush and had gotten back into my truck to leave. Something ran in front of my truck."

"Wait. Something or someone. Is it possible you hit Miss King with your truck?"

I gasped. "No." The word came out like a squeak.

Cody leaned forward, "That's not what she's saying, she—"

"Sheriff Bales, this is the state's investigation; kindly keep your personal remarks to yourself."

His face darkened as he glowered at the other man.

"Now," said Frank, "you were saying?"

After a quick glance at Cody, I eyed Frank. "The thing that ran in front of me was an animal. Probably a coyote. It went by really fast, so it was a blur."

"And then what?"

My mind went blank. What had happened next? I hated when my thoughts fled, just like when I'd had to give speeches in high school. Fear often did that to me, wiped out any coherent thought. *Think!* Finally, the fog cleared. "After the coyote ran past, I noticed something dark on the grass."

"Which was?"

"I wasn't sure at first. Looked like...blood."

"Blood?" Frank's eyebrows shot up like he'd never heard the term before. Like when he did more research, he might just discover that saying the term was a jailable offense.

"Um, yes. So, I got out to see."

He narrowed his eyes. "Why did you get out? Why not call the sheriff instead?"

"I did call him."

"But not right away?"

"I wasn't sure what it was." My voice came out shrill. Did I sound as panicked as I felt?

"So, you took it upon yourself to do some detective work?" His intense stare, aimed right at my eyes, seemed to go straight through me. My head began to pound.

"No, I... It just seemed like the thing to do. I didn't really think about it. Just..." Why was he twisting my words around? Was he trying to make me look guilty? Suddenly, this didn't seem like informal questioning. Maybe I should have called Payne, after all. Was it too late? Opening my purse, I eyed my phone. One edge of its purple plastic case was visible next to my sunglasses.

Alec glared at Frank. "Maybe we should let Miss James tell us what happened in her own words. Then we can perhaps ask more questions."

Muttering something, Frank stared back at Alec.

Perfect. Were we going to witness a state police catfight right here on the table?

"Fine," Frank said through clenched teeth. He waved his hand in my direction. The royal summons to continue.

Maybe Alec would keep a tight enough rein on Frank so that I could get through this without having to involve my ex. I closed my purse and rested my hands on it. "Anyway, I followed the trail of blood until it was in the pine trees. On the park side." Though they'd said the property line was different than I'd told them, I didn't quite believe they were right. Without a way to prove them wrong, though, I was stuck.

If Lonny was in on all that was going on, had he falsified the findings of the survey? But why would he? Unless they wanted the state police involved, hoping someone other than my good friend, the sheriff, might seriously consider me a suspect.

No one said a word. Or moved. Every eye was on me. Were they even breathing?

I wanted to get this whole thing over with, so plunged ahead. "When I got inside the grouping of pine trees, Millie was lying there. Lots of blood. And...it looked like stab wounds across her midsection."

"Are you a physician? How could you possibly know that?" Frank had practically shouted the words.

"Really, Frank." Alec shook his head. Then to me, "Please go on." He folded his hands on the tabletop, his expression calm.

I nodded, the movement shaky. Alec's serene demeanor did nothing for my quaking heart. Would they believe what I told them? Understand that I had nothing to do with the woman's death? If they didn't, it might be my and Cody's word against theirs. "I checked for a pulse. There was none. I called Co-uh, Sheriff Bales. He showed up. He checked for a pulse too. We walked around, searching for any clues—"

Holding up his hand to stop me, Frank said, "Please just stick to what you did. We'll have a separate discussion with the sheriff about his findings later."

"Okay." I sat there, silent, feeling chastised and small. How could one man be such a bully? Make me question what I knew to be true. *No Seneca, you told it just like it happened. Relax.*

"That's it?" Frank was leaning onto the edge of the table so hard, I half expected it to break beneath his large frame.

"That's it."

"I find it difficult to believe there was nothing more. That it happened as you've said."

Cody tightened his hand into a fist on the table. "Seneca is telling the truth."

"Sheriff, were you there when she found the woman?" asked Frank.

Cody's eyebrows lowered, causing a crease between them on his forehead. "No, but—"

"Then please keep quiet."

Would Cody explode? His face turned tomato red. A vein bulged in the side of his neck above his shirt collar.

Jesse finally spoke. "Listen, I don't think Miss James is making anything up. Maybe this is getting all blown out of proportion."

"Blown out of..." Frank's already florid face grew darker. A sheen of perspiration appeared above his eyebrows. "A woman has been killed. Every avenue must be addressed. Don't you think we should take this seriously? Find the person responsible?"

"Yes, I-I—" stuttered Jesse.

"Please. This is a state police discussion. You, Sheriff Bales, and Mr. Gibbs, as the one who did the official survey, are here as a courtesy from us." He'd said the word courtesy like it tasted bad, and he wanted nothing more than to spit it out on the table.

As Frank and Alec sat, writing something down on their legal pads, the rest of us didn't move. We waited, though I didn't know what for.

A couple more minutes went by, then Alec addressed Frank. "Do you need anything else? Have any more questions for Miss James?"

"Not at this time." Frank flipped his pad over, face down, like he didn't want anyone checking his answers to cheat on a test. He sighed deeply, as if the whole world's problems rested on his thick, wide shoulders. "That will be all, Miss James."

All as in, that's it for now, but don't leave town? Or we never need to bother you with this again? Was I supposed to stand? Leave? Curtsy?

Thankfully, Cody got up from his chair and tilted his head toward the door, then walked that way. He opened it for me, and I stood, glad for direction, and followed him out.

When he shut the door on the other men, I nearly collapsed against the wall.

"You did fine," he said.

"Did I?"

"Yes."

I wrapped my arms around my middle, suddenly chilled. "So, what now?"

"Gotta go back in there. They'll now want to ask me about my findings. And you...." He squeezed my hand, his warm fingers curling around mine. "...go back to the greenhouse. Work with your caterpillars. Try to relax."

I nodded. Yes, I'd go back home, but couldn't imagine a way I'd be able to concentrate on anything besides what had just happened.

# Chapter Twenty-Five

The results of Herman Morton's autopsy came the next day. Apparently, Arnold would give us the results on behalf of his cousin, the pathologist, Dr. Reynolds. After Cody had received a call from the mortician's assistant, Gretchen, he called me to meet him at the funeral home office. Probably a good thing she hadn't called me directly. With all the gossip she seemed to be spreading around about me, I might have given her a good scolding.

Believe me, I knew how to scold. I'd learned from the master, Winifred.

When I got there, Cody was standing inside the funeral home vestibule, talking to Gretchen. For such a tiny, spindly creature, she had a huge mouth. Determined to be polite, I smiled and said, "Hi, Gretchen."

She left Cody's side, raced to me, and grabbed both of my hands in her icy ones. It was like being accosted by the Goddess of Snow. "Seneca, how are you holding up?"

"Um…" I slid a glance to Cody, who watched, eyebrows raised. But he kept quiet. The traitor.

The girl dragged me to stand beside one wall. She released my hands but pressed her back flat into the wood paneling. Was she expecting a stampede to come through the door?

"Arnold told me what's been going on. How bodies keep appearing on your property." Gretchen whispered the word 'appearing' like some type of apparitions had floated overhead, were enamored of what they saw on my farm, and decided to stay for a bit.

I took a step back, wanting a little breathing room. "I'm doing fine. Really."

"But how can that be?"

What was she getting at? "Not sure what you've heard—" *or repeated* "—but things are fine with me and my farm." I held up my fingers in the Girl Scout honor sign, though I'd never joined them as a kid. Maybe she'd believe I had been, though. She seemed to suck in all information like a sea sponge.

"Well, when Arnold mentioned there'd been two murders, I was so concerned about you. Aren't *you* concerned about *you?*"

First, it was difficult trying to imagine Arnold saying or mentioning anything to anyone. As far as I could remember, I'd never personally heard the man utter anything. At all. Of course, common sense told me that unless he was mute, he spoke to some people at some point. He had to in order to do his job, didn't he? "Gretchen, don't worry. Everything will be fine."

"If you say so. But maybe in the meantime, you should avoid trying to do anyone else bodily harm."

"Now wait a second, I never—"

"It's all over town about the two killings," she said. "And about the connection to you."

I fumed as I bit my tongue, longing to blurt, *yeah because you've told them that.*

"With all the dead people, we might not be able to keep up with the work," she wiped her brow, as if exhausted.

Two people was an overload? I frowned, though, because as slow as Arnold moved, maybe it was. "I don't think you have anything to worry about, Gretchen."

She placed her hands on her hips. "How do I know even more deceased persons might not show up on your property?"

My hands clenched into fists at my sides. Cody must have noticed, because he caught my eye, shook his head rapidly back and forth, then lowered his gaze to one of my hands.

Oh, for goodness sake. Did he really think I would do something to her? Though I had to admit the idea had a small appeal, he had to know I'd never actually harm someone. With effort, I unfolded my fingers, instead tapping them against my thighs.

As Cody let out a breath, he turned to check behind him. Was he looking for Arnold? Where was he anyway? Hadn't Gretchen intimated to Cody with her phone call that Arnold needed to see us right away? We did have lives, after all.

Lives. Maybe a poor choice of wording, considering where I stood now.

Cody cleared his throat to get my attention. When I took my focus off the skinny assistant who was still peering at me with huge owl-like green eyes, I saw Arnold had joined our fun little group.

Without a word—big surprise—the mortician gave a head tilt toward the open doorway behind him. Gretchen scurried after him, nearly tripping in her haste to get inside. Cody gave a shrug, motioned for me to precede him, and we entered the small office. Then I realized that since the moment Arnold showed up, no one had said a word. Was it rubbing off?

Cody and I took the two chairs facing the large mahogany desk while Gretchen perched her skinny backside on the edge of a table against one wall. Surprisingly, the wallpaper was cheery. Yellow sunflowers on an off-white background. Did Arnold need it to brighten his otherwise dreary existence?

His job would be depressing at times, I would think, but it was more than that. The man's demeanor gave off waves of despair. The long, narrow face, sad eyes, and drooping mouth. Had he chosen this line of work because it suited his personality, or had he changed from someone more positive into what he was now because of his vocation?

When he raised one eyebrow at Gretchen, she jumped up like she'd been shot, rushed to a pile of papers on a nearby shelf, and delivered it to him with a flourish worthy of a serf to a king.

I eyed Cody. Did he think this was as odd as I did? He rolled his eyes.

Oh, right. He'd been here before, many times, due to being sheriff. He'd most likely witnessed Arnold's strange way of communication in the past.

The rustle of papers being flipped over pulled my attention back to the man behind the desk. His head was lowered over them, eyes squinted. Did he need reading glasses but wouldn't wear them? Or was he so interested in the subject matter he felt the need to nearly press his face onto the page?

Beside him, Gretchen stood, bony hands clutched together, the rapid rise and fall of her narrow chest an indication of something exciting—frightening—to come.

Unable to stand, not knowing yet what was in the autopsy report, I reached over and clutched Cody's hand, gave it a quick squeeze, and released it. He smiled, but soon went back to watching the others.

Finally, Arnold pointed to something on the top page, then stared right at Gretchen. She bent over the page, pushing her long, lank hair away from her face as she did. Why did he want her to read it, but wouldn't tell us what it said? I was seriously starting to doubt the man's ability to speak. I'd always assumed it was just an oddity. Cody had never said otherwise, but why wouldn't he have mentioned it?

It wasn't like I'd ever had much opportunity to deal with Arnold before now, thankfully, except at Gram's funeral. Since my parents had handled the arrangements, I hadn't even seen Arnold until the day of the service. He'd stood off to one side, his expression mournful, watching everyone who passed by.

Gretchen finished reading what he'd pointed to, nodded at him, and turned to us. "He wants you to know that from what the pathologist could ascertain, Herman Morton was indeed murdered."

A shock rolled through me, even though I'd known deep down it couldn't have been an accident. I guess a small, hidden part of me had been still hopeful it wasn't murder. But what did that mean for me? Though Cody didn't think I'd be a suspect, would someone else step up and make a stink about the fact that the man had been killed in my greenhouse?

"Wait." Gretchen leaned down to where Arnold pointed again at the page.

Wait? She dropped a bombshell like that, then expected me to sit tight, hoping it wouldn't get worse? My heart rate increased, thrumming through my veins, speeding across my chest, getting ready to catapult me into a full-blown panic.

Cody scooted forward on his chair. "What's going on? Is it murder or accidental?"

Arnold scowled at Cody. Was it for interrupting Gretchen's perusal of the paper or the fact that the missive contained nothing but bad news?

Stabbing again at the page, Arnold huffed out air through his nose. He stared at Gretchen until she read something further. With a nod, she focused on us again. "He wants you to know that though the pathologist feels this is murder, his findings weren't totally conclusive."

What did that mean?

Cody's frown said he felt the same way I did. He eyed them. "Why don't you just say what the findings are so we can move this whole thing along?"

While I was surprised at his tone, bordering on rudeness, it also helped me calm down, knowing Cody was on my side no matter what occurred.

One more point with Arnold's long, skinny finger had Gretchen reading once more. She nodded at him, which earned her a nod in return.

She straightened, smoothed down the front of her knee-length dress, and looked straight at me. "He's almost certain it was murder."

Almost?

"How certain?" asked Cody.

"Eighty-two percent."

What kind of weird setup was this place? The man didn't talk, communicated to his assistant by pointing, which somehow translated to her full sentences, that she in turn conveyed to us.

With a twitch of his hand on the side of the chair, Cody said, "Is that the final conclusion?"

Arnold nodded.

With an expression that said, *it's about time*, Cody stood and motioned for me to do the same.

Gretchen rushed in front of us, stepping ahead. Was she going to usher us to the door like we wouldn't know how to find the exit we'd just come in a little while ago?

She and Cody had already gone out. I was halfway out the doorway when, from behind me, Arnold said in a raspy voice, "Have a nice day."

I bolted for the exit.

# Chapter Twenty-Six

I sat at my table in the greenhouse, doing one of my more unpleasant jobs—paying bills. Necessary, but I'd rather be catching up on work with the monarchs.

The door opened and closed, but I didn't glance up. Annie had been in and out, doing work, but she'd also seemed more restless than usual. I didn't ask what was going on because I knew if she really wanted to talk about it, she'd bring it up. Before long, her steps came closer to where I sat.

"It was me." Annie's voice came out timid and small, like a little kid's.

I glanced up from my laptop, where I was paying some of the bills online. "What was you?"

Annie twisted a strand of red hair around her finger so tight the end of her finger turned purple.

Since she'd come to me, and it was obvious she was upset, I stood up. "Are you okay?" That was a loaded question, considering I never knew what she'd say next.

She wouldn't meet my eye, instead, seemed too interested in something behind me, though I knew the only thing back there was a filing cabinet. "See, here's the thing. That lawyer? The deceased guy?"

"Yeah...." Though she'd heard about the murder, of course, a couple of questions posed to me and some from other people she'd overheard, we hadn't talked about it at length. I hadn't wanted to upset her any more than was necessary, considering it had happened a few feet away from where we stood. Had Dana talked to her about her brother?

"I'm the one who... killed him."

My mouth dropped open, but I snapped it shut. She'd said some outlandish things before, but this was beyond the pale. "Why would you say that?" Maybe she was on some new kick. Instead of giving people her uninformed diagnosis, she was now confessing to crimes.

She stepped closer, her eyes huge in her pale face. At least she'd released her finger from its hair trap. "I'm saying I did it because I did it."

This girl was a piece of work. I liked her, really did, but sometimes I wasn't sure what to do with her. Was she doing this to get attention? Cause more drama? Or maybe she was concerned about me. Afraid that since it had happened here, I might get the blame. "Honey, listen, you don't have to say you did something if you didn't. Are you just trying to help me out? Afraid they'll charge me for it? That's really sweet, but—"

"No!"

I jerked back. What was going on? Should I call her mom and have her come over? "Annie, should—"

"You have to believe me." Now her hands were twisted together, fingers interlocked, in front of her midsection.

Maybe she was stranger than I thought, wanting to say she was a murderer. That wasn't normal. Could she possibly benefit from seeing a psychiatrist? It wasn't my place to tell her that, but I might have to speak to Dana about her. Surely, this behavior would only escalate, causing more problems for her in the future.

With quick steps, she hurried to me and knelt in front of my chair. Her hands were ice cold when they grasped mine, her grip so tight I winced. "Seneca, I'm not crazy. I know what I'm saying, and I mean it. Will you call Cody? Please?"

My eyes widened. She was serious. Really thought she was guilty. I still didn't believe her, but apparently, there wouldn't be any calming her down until I did as she asked. "Okay. I'll call Cody. But I'm going to be with you when you talk to him." It was the least I could do since Dana wasn't here.

She nodded, a big fat tear streaking down her freckled cheek. "Thank you."

"Listen, maybe we should call your mom. Have her come by and—"

"No, please. Just the sheriff."

With a sigh, I nodded. I called Cody, asking him to come out. However, I didn't say why. With Annie still sitting right beside me, I didn't want to get into a complicated explanation over the phone. Explaining to him that she wanted to confess to a murder would be hard to pull off convincingly. She'd know I didn't believe her. Who knew what she might do?

Ending the call, I studied Annie. "He's on his way."

She swallowed hard. "Good." Her hands shook, and her shoulders trembled. Was she regretting having me call him now? Did she want to take back what she'd told me? There was no way I'd believe her capable of murder. But something was going on. I still wanted to speak to Dana about it. Maybe after Cody had spoken to Annie and talked some sense into her, I could convince Annie to let me call her mom, too.

Neither one of us would be able to concentrate on work, so we passed the time by petting Winifred. The cat, of course, took the attention as her due, being royalty and all. Only a few minutes passed before tires crunched on the gravel outside.

After slipping past Annie and Winifred, I hurried to have a quiet word with Cody. As he was getting out of his car, I was already standing by his door. He got out, shading his eyes from the sun. "You know I love seeing you and all, but I'm hoping you didn't call for yet another murder?"

"Nope. Same one."

"What?"

I took Cody's arm and gently tugged him farther away from the green-house. "Annie just told me...I can't believe I'm even saying this."

"Is she all right? Do I need to—"

"She isn't all right. Listen, just now, right before I called you, that girl confessed to killing Mr. Morton."

Cody blinked, long and slow, as if his reactions had notched down to half-speed. "I don't understand."

"Neither do I, but it's what she said."

"Do you believe her?"

"Of course not. But she wouldn't calm down until I promised to call you.

181

And when I suggested having her mom come too, she got upset. Did you say anything to Dana about it at work?"

He shook his head. "Wow, this is…."

"I know."

"I can't imagine why Annie would say that. With Dana not having a relationship with her brother, did Annie even know him?" he asked.

I sighed, hating to drag Cody into this when there was already so much going on, he had to investigate. "Would you mind talking to her? She's in the greenhouse. I want to be with her. Is that okay?"

"Sure. Let's… let's go."

I went in first, wanting to offer support to Annie. She was waiting just inside the door, so I put my arm around her shoulders.

Cody tilted his head as he watched the girl. "Seneca said you have something you wanted to tell me?"

Annie nodded, her hair bouncing in ringlets around her face. "It's… You see…"

He stepped closer. "Annie, if you need to tell me something, it's okay. Just go ahead."

She glanced quickly at me and away. My earlier thought returned, that maybe she was trying to protect me, like she thought I wouldn't be charged if she confessed. I rubbed her shoulder. "You don't have to say anything if—"

"No. I have to. I want to." As she took a long, slow breath, her narrow chest rose, then fell. "Sheriff, I'm confessing to the murder of…Herman Morton."

Even though I'd told Cody what Annie would say, it must have taken him off guard. He sucked in a breath. "Annie, you do realize what you're saying, don't you? This is very serious."

She bit her lower lip and nodded.

Cody glanced to his right, toward my small table and chairs in the corner. "Why don't we sit down?"

We took our seats, me and Annie on one side, Cody opposite. "Now," he said, "why don't we back up, and you give me a little more detail?"

I nodded my approval. Maybe once she was forced to say more, she'd admit her confession wasn't true. Would admit she hadn't meant it.

"Okay." Annie placed her forearms on the table and grasped her fingers together. "The man, the murdered one. You refer to him as Mr. Morton."

"Um, sure." Cody scrunched his brows lower.

"Well, I call him something else." She squared her shoulders and addressed Cody. "I call him Uncle Herman."

Though I'd recently discovered she was related to Mr. Morton, I hadn't been sure she knew about him. Since her mother didn't seem to socialize with her brother and hadn't even acknowledged him publicly, I wondered if her daughter was even aware. "Why didn't you ever say anything?" Oh, this put a new, terrible spin on her confession. Could she really have done it for some reason having to do with family?

"Seneca," she said, "Uncle Herman and I have never been close. I barely knew him. He and my mom—his younger sister—haven't spoken much since my grandparents died. And I never met them."

Was Cody starting to believe her now? He leaned forward. "Annie, you say you murdered him. Tell me why."

This was all so surreal. The concerned expression on Cody's face had me worried now. He must believe her. At least somewhat. Enough to continue the conversation instead of waving it off as a strange girl's weird ramblings. My heart raced. What I'd thought would be a short-lived conversation, with Cody talking a dramatic girl down from the proverbial ledge, was morphing into something frightening and unbelievable.

"Because," said Annie, "when our grandparents died, they left their estate to him and mom equally. But Mom never got a dime. We've never had much. Mom always had to work so hard to support us."

Cody and I both nodded. It was true. I'd never met Annie's dad, had never known him to be in the picture. I wasn't even sure of his name. But Dana did work hard. Always had. Cody adored having her in the office. He depended on her and gave her his complete trust. If Annie was telling the truth, this would crush Dana.

"So," continued Annie, "I knew we deserved half of that money. Mom has tried for years to talk to her brother, to make him see reason. But he wouldn't budge. Selfish man wanted it all for himself." Her face reddened. "When my uncle found out the truth… that my mom was actually the product of an affair my mom had a long time ago, he was able to finagle things and put the brakes on mom getting her share."

"So, you, what…took matters into your own hands?" Cody tapped the tabletop with each word. His face had gone pale, eyes opened wide as he studied her.

Her expression turned defiant. "That's right. I did. The only way I could see to get the money was for him to be gone. To die."

I took Annie's hand. "But honey, you do realize that you'll never see any. If what you say is true and you're convicted, you'll go to jail. For a very long time."

Tears pooled in the girl's eyes. "I know. But my mom will get the money. She'll be okay, right? That's what matters."

When I glanced at Cody, he was already staring at me. Annie had just confessed to a murder. If it turned out to be true, and she was convicted, her life would never be the same. What were we going to do?

# Chapter Twenty-Seven

Dana, in tears, showed up at my door. As soon as I opened it, she fell into my arms, wailing. Poor woman. I couldn't even imagine how torn up and worried she must be about Annie and her confession.

She finally pulled away, wiping her eyes with her fingers. I reached toward a nearby end table and grabbed some tissues.

"Thank you." She dabbed her eyes and nose, then stuck the wad of tissues into her pants pocket. "I…I can't tell you what a shock it was…when Annie… "

"I know."

But did I? Yes, I'd been stunned when Annie had told me and Cody the news, but to have your child say it, then possibly later on be charged with murder? Go to prison? A chill ran over my shoulders. The girl's life would never be the same.

"Here," I said. "Why don't we sit down?"

Nodding, she followed me into the living room. We sat on the couch. At first, she said nothing, just stared around the room, as if searching for answers, hope, someone to take away her current circumstances. "I know this whole thing, this terrible ordeal, is going to take a while to sort out."

"Yes, I imagine so." Even with what I was going through, my life and daily routine changed in ways I'd never imagined. Mental images seared in my mind of blood, faces frozen in horror, townspeople talking behind my back, accusing me without having all the facts. But what Dana and Annie must be going through…

"I, we, will need a lawyer. Since my brother…since he died, was killed…"

Dana wiped away a few more tears. "Not that he would have been the lawyer for us. I guess that doesn't even make sense, does it? The only reason we need one is because he's dead."

I reminded myself that not only was her daughter charged with murder, it was of Dana's own brother. Though they hadn't been close, he was still her sibling. "Yes. There's either Payne, or someone from another town." I would be keeping Payne busy for a while with my predicament. Would he have time to take on another large case as well?

Knowing him, he'd jump at the chance. More work meant more money for him. No matter if he had to give up sleep to get it.

Dana angled toward me a little on the couch. "I thought since you know Payne, um... I realize you're divorced and all. Still, I hoped that maybe..." She glanced away.

Reaching out, I touched her hand, hoping to offer at least a little comfort. "Did you want me to call him for you?"

"Would you? I'd be so grateful. Then, if there was anything you needed, I'd be glad to help. With whatever. Any time. You'd just have to ask."

"Oh, Dana, that's not necessary." Another small-town thing. You always wanted to pay back favors. Try to help out where you could. Be available to your friends and neighbors in times of crisis.

She gave my hand a squeeze. "Thank you. So much."

My gaze wandered wistfully toward my front door, knowing I had work to do. But this woman, someone I liked and respected, who worked for my best friend, needed help. So, help, I would give. I studied Dana as I said, "Let me call him right now."

Her shoulders slumped in obvious relief.

After locating my phone on the entryway table beside my purse, I put in the call. I didn't go into detail, wanting Dana to tell Payne in her own words. Coming back to the living room, I set the cell phone on the coffee table. "He's on his way."

Dana bolted upright, like she'd had a shock. "Right now? That was fast."

"I told him it was important."

She let out a long, audible breath and leaned against the back of the couch.

"I just can't believe this. Any of this. That Annie would actually…" She stared in my direction, but not really at me, as if she were somewhere else. Maybe she wished she was.

I sat back down next to her. "I'm sure it was a shock, to say the least."

"You have no idea."

I nodded. Although, I had a small idea of shock. But to have one family member kill another over money? No. That I couldn't quite wrap my mind around. It was the stuff of movies. Not something that happened in a quiet, friendly, small town.

When I offered to fix her some coffee while we waited, she gratefully accepted. After it brewed, I went back to the living room. To my surprise, Winifred sat next to Dana, rubbing against her hand. And purring. What was it with my cat lately? First, cozying up to Annie, now her mom.

Not that I was complaining, I liked this new side to Winifred. I just wondered why she'd changed. And how long it might last. Moody felines were unpredictable at best. Dana petted her, but, understandably, the woman appeared distracted, mouth turned down at the corners, eyes unfocused, staring into space.

When I heard tires on my drive, I hurried to the door and opened it. Payne, briefcase in hand, closed his vehicle door and headed my way. He stepped inside. "Dana's here?"

"In the living room."

"And Annie?"

I shook my head. Payne frowned. I said, "She wanted to see you first. Before Annie. Does that work?"

"That's not how it usually goes, but…." He made a face. Was he mentally adding up possible client payments? "Yeah, all right. We'll make it work."

He followed me there, stopping just inside. He set his briefcase on the coffee table and joined her on the couch. Reaching out, he shook her hand. "Hi, Dana. I'm sorry to hear what's going on. Would you like to tell me more?"

Surprised, I nearly collapsed into a chair. Who was this gentle, kind man, and where had he stashed my jerk of an ex? I knew what the man was really like, having lived with him and put up with his crabbiness and mean streak. I couldn't believe he'd changed overnight. Must be his professional persona to gain trust from his fee-paying clients.

Winifred, in close proximity to Payne, leaped from the couch and tore out of the room.

As I watched the two people get better acquainted, I sat up straight. Suddenly uncomfortable and not wanting to intrude, I said, "Listen," I pointed to the doorway. "I should go. Give you some privacy so you can—"

"Please," said Dana. "Could you stay? I know that's asking a lot. I just... Since you know Annie and me, and my...brother was found on your property."

"Sure. Of course," popped out of my mouth. I wanted to be anywhere else. Not to hear more conversation about my former attorney who I'd discovered in my greenhouse. Wouldn't all of this be conflicting interest on my part, on Payne's to represent both of us? But I didn't know the law. And whether it might not be appropriate for Payne to take it on, that wasn't for me to say. Though I couldn't stand my ex, he was doing me a service, and I needed to be grateful he could take my case.

Payne watched me for a few seconds. Was he deciding whether to veto Dana's request? With a slight shrug that I knew to mean, *what's the worst that could happen*, he focused again on Dana. "Let's talk about Annie. Okay?"

With a nod, she agreed.

He opened his briefcase and removed a legal pad of paper and a pen, which I recognized as the one I'd given him our first Christmas together after we'd gotten married. Why was he still using it? Did it hold some sentimental value?

Wait. This was Payne. He has no sentiment. For anyone.

"All right, Dana," he said. "Let's start with what Annie had to say about what happened."

A visible shudder rippled across Dana's shoulders. "She... said she killed him. My brother. In the—" She pointed toward my greenhouse. "—in there."

He nodded and wrote something down. "And her reason for committing the crime?"

Crime. I was really starting to despise that word.

"She said...it was because of the money."

Payne's eyes lit up at the last word. Was it because he loved the stuff in general, or he caught onto something interesting to defend Annie? "Tell me more about that."

"Well..." Dana clenched a tissue in her hand. She must have retrieved it from her pocket earlier. "When my parents passed, they'd left us, me and my brother, some inheritance."

After jotting down more on the legal pad, Payne glanced up. "Go on."

"I was supposed to get half of it. For me and Annie. To help us out. You see, we've never had much, always scrambled to keep up with bills. Sometimes, as a single mom, I had trouble making ends meet. Never knew where the funds would come from to take care of us."

Though he was good at covering it up, I could tell by the slight tic in Payne's jaw that he was getting impatient. It never took long for him to want to get past something he considered trivial. Something he had no desire to deal with or work around. "Yes, of course. Had you tried to get your share of the funds from your brother in the past?"

"Yes. Several times."

"What happened?" asked Payne.

"Um, the circumstances surrounding my birth were... complicated."

"How so?"

Dana wouldn't make eye contact with Payne as she said, "My mom had an affair, making me only a half-sibling. Herman was adamant that I wasn't a legal heir because I was illegitimate. Since he was a lawyer, he had ways to get around it. To find loopholes to keep from me what should have been legally mine." She gave a small gasp as if realizing what she'd implied. "Uh, no offense, about the lawyer comment, since you're—"

"None taken."

And there wouldn't be. It was more likely Payne would find it admirable that someone had gotten something over on a person for his own gain. Even on a family member.

"Anyway," said Dana. "I tried and tried. But every time, Herman kept me from getting it. At first, it was excuses. That the executor of the will hadn't had time to meet with us. Or that there was some holdup getting us the money because of a glitch in the final will. Things like that. And since I don't know anything about the law, I accepted that as truth. My brother and I hadn't been close, but it had never crossed my mind that he'd do that. Not then."

"But since then?"

"Oh yes. The longer this has gone on, the more I saw how devious he is. Um, I mean, how he was." She darted a quick look in the direction of my greenhouse again.

Poor woman. No wonder she'd been so upset when she'd gone there to talk to Annie. The body that was discovered had been her brother, someone she should have been able to trust. What puzzled me was how no one in town had known that they were related until now. Had Dana not wanted anyone to know because she and her brother hadn't been close?

Of course, with what he'd put her through with their inheritance, I couldn't blame her. Maybe something happened a long time ago to create distance, and she wanted nothing to do with him until they came into their inheritance, and she had no choice but to see him.

I wondered if Annie had ever had any kind of link to her uncle past the simple acknowledgment that a family connection existed. How different her life and Dana's could have been had Mr. Morton been a decent man. Had given them the money that was rightfully theirs and had been a supportive family member. Now, everything was one colossal mess.

Payne wrote a few more things down, then flipped the paper to start a second page. His handwriting had always been large and showy, so filling a page didn't take much. It had always struck me that his style of writing was like his personality. Wanting everyone to notice him. Give him the attention he thought he deserved.

He stopped writing and addressed Dana. "Did Annie give specifics on how she did it?"

"Did... it?" Dana's expression showed confusion, lowered eyebrows, tilted head.

"Committed the murder."

Oh boy. Here we go. I didn't want to know all this. Squirming in my seat, I longed to jump up and head to the greenhouse where I felt safe, where I was comfortable in my own little world, working with my tiny charges. But right then, Dana peered over at me, begging me with her eyes to stay, support her as I'd promised. So, I forced myself to relax, allowed my hands to stop clenching the sides of my chair. I gave her what I hoped was an encouraging nod.

Seeming satisfied I wouldn't bolt from the room, she turned back to Payne and swallowed hard. "I...she didn't actually say how...." Dana blinked back tears. "I'm not sure what...."

He patted her hand. "It's okay. I'll speak to her right after we're finished here. Normally, I'd have wanted to see her first, talk to her, but when Seneca had called, she'd said you wanted to see me immediately."

"Yes, that's true." Dana cleared her throat. "Maybe I should have had her here. I...it was just that I wanted to make sure you'd take her case. Because I...she and I so desperately need your help. I wasn't sure how she'd take it if you'd said no. Didn't think she'd bear any further bad news." More tears ran down her cheek.

Payne gave a tiny sigh that I hoped Dana hadn't noticed, then wrote down a few more things on the pad.

"So," said Dana, "you'll take Annie's case?"

"Yes. I will."

Dana flung her arms around Payne's neck.

Payne patted Dana's back a couple of times, then reached up to grab her arms and gently push them away. Again, I couldn't believe how well he'd taken it. That someone he didn't know well had just made such a spectacle of herself, of him. The guy must have some sort of switch to turn on his career persona, so different from the real person I knew.

Dana's face reddened. "Oh, forgive me. I'm just so grateful. So—"

"It's not a problem." Payne smoothed a few creases from his button-down shirt. "Why don't we go talk to Annie? Do you know where she is right now?"

"She's at our house. Scared to death to leave. Afraid the sheriff will pounce on her and take her right to jail." Then, her eyes widened as she focused on me. Everyone around knew Cody and I were close friends.

I smiled and shrugged, hoping she'd know I wasn't offended on his behalf.

"Seneca," said Dana, "I just realized, with all that's going on, and if Annie is arrested, what will you do? I mean, since she worked here and helped you."

Waving it off, I said, "Don't worry about that. I'll be fine. Really." That wasn't true. I did rely on Annie to take some of the workload from me, but that couldn't be helped now. If she was arrested—and a confession was a compelling reason—I'd be forced to find someone to replace her.

# Chapter Twenty-Eight

When my phone rang and woke me, it was early. Seven a.m. I jumped up to grab it. With all that had happened lately, I feared the worst. I pressed the answer button but didn't have time to even say hello.

"Just wanted to tell you," said Cody, "that I'm formally arresting Annie today."

My heart sank. I'd expected it to happen, probably soon, but still… "Oh."

"I figured you'd want to know."

"Yeah." I rubbed some sleep from my eyes. "When?"

"About an hour."

I rubbed my eyes again, trying to wake up. "I want to be there."

"Figured that too."

"At their house?" I asked.

"Yes."

Then it hit me how hard this must be for him. Though Annie was odd, she was likable, and Cody had always had a soft spot for her. Like a big brother would.

Like he did for me.

"Cody, you okay?"

A long sigh, then, "I guess. It's just…never thought I'd be doing something like this."

I nodded. What could I say? It was all so surreal. The murders. Finding out Mr. Morton had been Annie's uncle and that she'd killed him.

"So," said Cody, "I'll be over there in about an hour. You're welcome to be there for her and Dana's support, as a friend. But when I speak to them, make the arrest—"

"I know. Keep quiet."

In my mind, I could almost see one side of his mouth quirk into a smile. "Right." Then he said, "See ya there?"

"Yep." I ended the call and set down my phone. When I turned, Winifred sat staring up at me, her eyes doleful, her meow pitiful. "Come on, dear, time for breakfast."

She and I clattered down the stairs, her beating me to the bottom, as usual. When it was her time to eat, my cat didn't mess around. Almost on autopilot, I grabbed her dry food from the cabinet, filled her dish, got her some fresh water for her drinking bowl, and pressed the button on the coffee maker.

As I leaned against the counter, watching Winifred gorge herself like she wouldn't see another morsel of cat food for months, I shook my head. How had it come to this for Annie? If convicted, her life was pretty much over. Spending who knew how many years in jail would end any plans she ever had for becoming a doctor, at the very least.

Not to mention, even being in jail for a short time would change the girl. Would change anyone. How could it not? But Annie was especially overanxious and flighty. Being cooped up in a cell was essentially a cage was unthinkable.

Finally, the coffee was ready and poured. I carried it upstairs. A quick shower and change later, I was ready. Not that I usually cared that much about my appearance since I spent most of my time with the monarchs who didn't care what I looked like, but the urgency of Annie's plight had me back downstairs and in my truck in minutes.

The short drive to their bungalow in a quiet neighborhood made up mostly of retirees seemed to go in slow motion. Anxious to get there before Cody actually said the words, *you're under arrest*, I jammed down on the accelerator. Obviously, Cody wouldn't arrest me for speeding, and if for some reason Bud happened to, I'd just tattle on him to his boss, and it would all go away.

When I got to the Hasting's residence, Cody's car was parked out front. Panicked that he was already inside, had told Annie and Dana why he was there. I slammed to a stop behind his car and got out.

I'd made it halfway up the drive when someone called, "Hey!"

Cody opened his car door and got out, waving me back toward him. Letting out a breath of relief, I joined him.

"Seneca, I know how much you want to be there for Annie. For them. When I have to arrest her. I thought you might like to go in with me."

"Thanks." I reached out, giving his arm a pat. "I just wasn't sure how it would work. You know, that it might not be legal or whatever for me to be there when—"

"Since I'm the one in charge, I guess I can make the rules." He smiled, but it was sad. How hard this must be for him. With a head tilt toward the house, he said, "Come on, let's get this over with."

We walked side by side up the short drive. He waited until I went up the narrow porch steps first, then followed. Right before he knocked on the screen door, decorated with a cheery wreath of daisies and green ivy, his eyes found mine and held them for several seconds. Cody's chest rose slowly, then fell, almost as if he deflated right next to me.

I gave an encouraging smile and bumped his side with my shoulder. He raised his fist to knock but didn't have a chance.

The door opened before he could. Annie stood there, eyes bright, like she could barely hold in the tears, but mouth set in a determined, stubborn line. "Guess you might as well come on in."

With a glance at me, Cody nodded, and we stepped inside the small but tidy living room. Dana stood near the entrance to their tiled floor kitchen, her hands wringing together, face white, eyes red from a recent cry.

All four of us stood there, silent. No one wanted this to happen, and none of us, obviously, wanted to start the inevitable process that would change the lives of the two women who shared this house.

As if we'd just come over for a friendly visit, Dana waved her hand toward the couch. "Please. Have a seat."

I stepped forward and sat, Cody joining me. We waited while Dana and her daughter took the chairs opposite us.

Annie smoothed down her hair with her hand, though the red curls sprang immediately back up. I eyed her unruly locks. How would she care for her wild hair in prison? I happened to know she bought a special conditioner to help tame it, though it didn't always give Annie the results she hoped for.

Why was I thinking about something so inconsequential as a person's hairstyle? Maybe it was easier to dwell on something like that than what the horrors of prison might be.

And how would she fill her days when she couldn't study biology, spend time with her mom, or help me with the butterflies? Thoughts of being cooped up in a cell, scared to death, made a ripple of fear run across my shoulders.

Cody sat forward, forearms on his knees, hands clasped. His knuckles were white, like he was barely holding himself together. "You know why I'm here."

Dana and Annie nodded, identical in their movements and expressions. "Yes, we know why," said Dana. She turned to study her daughter, her eyes blinking rapidly, lips trembling. She reached over and grabbed Annie's hand and didn't release it. Was she thinking how this might be one of her last chances to do so? Before Annie was carted off for who knew how many years?

"Since Annie has given compelling evidence of how and why she let her uncle into the greenhouse and that it all seems to fit with what I discovered at the scene, I'm afraid I've got to take her in. She said she'd found a crack in the foundation of the greenhouse and worked the opening wider until she could squeeze through, then she unlocked the door from the inside to let him in."

Dana gasped and shook her head. Was she having trouble taking it all in?

Cody went on. "Annie showed me where she'd gotten in around the back of the greenhouse. That part checks out since Seneca, and I found the opening and recently repaired it."

Cody went on, "And she'd already told me her reason for killing her uncle when she confessed, which, from conversation with you, Dana, checks out as well. I'm sorry to say, I'm afraid it's time for Annie to come with me."

A wail came from Dana as she grabbed her daughter, pulling her into a clenched hug. Annie sat very still, too still, to the point I wondered if she really understood what was happening.

I didn't budge, taking my cues from Cody. He sat motionless beside me. Was he giving them a minute to absorb the reality of the moment? Letting the two women have the brief comfort of physical closeness before he officially arrested Annie?

My heart raced, though the rest of me didn't move. Fear shot through me for Annie, possibly living decades of her life in jail. For her mom, watching her only child suffer through something so frightening, so unthinkable, that it would, for all intents and purposes, stop her own life in its tracks as well.

Finally, Dana released Annie, and they shared a look that must have conveyed all their thoughts, feelings, dashed hopes, and broken dreams. Then, they both stood and faced us, hands gripped together between them as if their physical connection could save them from what lay ahead.

With a long sigh, Cody pressed his hands to his thighs and pushed on them to stand. The corners of his mouth were tugged downward, and his eyes were sad, as if he'd aged several years in those few seconds. I rose from my chair as well and waited for what would happen next.

Moving slowly, Cody stepped closer to the women. "Annie Hastings, you're under arrest for the murder of Herman Morton."

Annie's face whitened, surprising since I hadn't thought she could have gotten paler than she already was. Her nod was short, more like an uncontrollable jerk.

As Cody informed Annie of her rights, I let out a small breath, grateful he hadn't reached to the back of his belt to retrieve his handcuffs. At least Annie would be spared that mortification as he took her to his sheriff's vehicle.

Once Cody had finished speaking, I tentatively edged closer. When he gave me an encouraging nod, I hugged Annie briefly, making eye contact. There were no words. At least, I couldn't seem to find any that would make this situation any easier. After I stepped away, Cody and Annie moved toward the door, his hand gently on the girl's shoulder.

Dana stood, her stare fixed on them, then, slowly, so slow I wondered if she was even aware of it, she turned her eyes to mine. She sucked in a huge gulp of air, and her entire body seemed to fold in on itself. When she fell into my arms, I wrapped her in the tightest, warmest hug I could manage, hoping to convey my sympathy, friendship, support, and encouragement. Even though anything I could say or do would never be enough.

Without speaking, we followed them outside, watching as Cody gently assisted Annie into his car. Dana glanced at me, then her car. I nodded and got into her vehicle with her. I didn't know how I'd be of help, but I wanted to go along. Hoped, in some way, my presence would be an encouragement to Annie, facing jail. To Dana, who would be without her daughter. And to Cody, who, though he'd rather do anything else at the moment than arrest a young woman for murder, was doing his duty in the eyes of the law.

The ride to the sheriff's office seemed the longest of my life. I'm sure I wasn't the only one who thought so.

After driving the few blocks from the Hastings' house to the station, Dana steered her vehicle into a parking space as if she drove on autopilot. I was sure it was more than the familiarity of parking in the sheriff's office lot every day. How terrible to be in her current situation. Her only child, arrested for killing a family member.

We got out, then Dana clutched my arm as we climbed the four front steps.

Cody was already inside. Annie sat perched on the edge of an old wooden office chair beside his desk. She had one finger to her mouth, chewing the nail until it was ragged. Poor kid. How scared she must be. True, she confessed, but saying she did something and being taken to jail for it were way different.

Rushing to Annie, Dana got almost to her, then halted. With a glance at Cody, who nodded, Dana sat next to her daughter, wrapping her arm around the girl's shoulders.

"Now," said Cody, "I've typed up a report of what you've told me, about when and how you killed your uncle. I need you to read it over, make sure it says what you want it to, then sign there at the bottom where I've put the X."

Appearing to move in slow motion, Annie reached up, taking the paper from Cody, read over it, pausing several times over certain portions, then, finally giving a single nod. As soon as she'd signed her name, something must have broken loose, because tears ran down her face. Her mom grabbed a box of nearby tissues, thrusting a handful toward her. Within a few seconds, Dana was reaching for her own. I didn't blame them. It was a terrible thing to watch.

One look at Cody told me if he wasn't careful, he might need some tissues as well.

A noise came from behind us, startling Annie. She jumped in her seat and turned, only relaxing slightly when she saw it was Bud, the deputy, who'd entered the room.

"Is it time for the..." Bud let the sentence hang, unfinished.

"What?" Dana mopped her face again. "Time for what?"

"Everyone just relax." Cody had his hand out, trying to calm her down. "Bud just wants to know if he should do the fingerprinting now."

"Oh." Dana, of course, would have known what would come next, though seeing her daughter go through it must have been surreal. She angled a glance at Annie, who nodded her assent.

Annie stood, handed the page back to Cody, and followed Bud out of the room. The sounds of their footsteps, Bud's clompy boots loud and fast, Annie's tennis shoes soft and hesitant, reached us from around the corner.

I grabbed Dana's hand. "You doing okay?" Though I knew she wasn't, I'd wanted to say something. Offer at least a little comfort. Let her know I cared.

A sigh came from somewhere deep inside, and she faced me. "Thanks for being here." It wasn't an answer to my question, but under the circumstances, seemed all she could manage to say.

We sat in silence, Cody checking over the report Annie had handed back as he entered something into his computer, and Dana and I sitting motionless on the uncomfortable chairs. A few minutes later, Annie came back in, wiping ink from her hands with a dampened cloth. When she had her hands clean, she held out the cloth to Bud, who took it and left the room.

"Now," said Cody, standing. "We have your signed confession and fingerprints. I'll need you to remove your jewelry." Bud appeared again, this time with a large, padded envelope. Annie glanced at it, then at Cody, and finally at her mom.

"Go ahead," said Dana. "It's all right." She, of course, would know the protocol for booking a prisoner, having worked here for so long. Too bad it was her own kid.

Annie's lower lip trembled when she removed two rings, a bracelet, a long chain necklace, and her gold hoop earrings. It was odd for me, too, to see her take them off. She'd worn most of those items every time I'd seen her when she worked at the greenhouse. Watching her remove them felt wrong, like she was taking part of her personality and hiding it in an official envelope.

"Normally," said Cody, "we'd keep your things here in our safe. But since your mom is who she is," He nodded his head toward Dana, giving her a sad but kind smile, "I'm sending them home with her."

Dana blinked back tears as Annie murmured her thanks.

"Oh..." Dana pressed her hand to her mouth.

"What is it?" I asked, thinking she was in some sort of physical pain.

"The next part, I'll have to do."

With a frown, I looked at Cody. "The next part?"

She took Annie's hand, leading her from the room. Cody stepped around the desk, waiting until they were gone. "Normally, Bud would assist the prisoner to change out of their street clothes into one of our jumpsuits. But when the prisoner is a female..."

"Dana has to do it."

He let out a sigh. "Right."

I stayed a while longer until Annie was in her cell. She'd had to be housed with a drunken woman who was a habitual visitor to the jail because the other two cells had men in them. Poor Annie. She scurried to a bench in the corner, huddled into the smallest size she could make herself, and stared, wide-eyed, as the drunk slumped on the cement floor and vomited up her latest binge.

Dana, who'd been standing outside the cell, hands gripped on the bars, started to cry.

With an expression of a plea for help from me, Cody gently took one of Dana's arms. I took the other. We escorted her back down the hall. Cody angled his head toward the exit.

"Come on, Dana," I said. "Why don't we go so you can get some sleep?"

I knew she wouldn't sleep. Neither would I, Cody, or Bud, for that matter. Especially not Annie. But she needed to get out of there, at least for a few hours.

Nodding, she led the way to her car. After a quiet ride to her house, I retrieved my vehicle and headed home.

# Chapter Twenty-Nine

The next day, knowing I wanted to visit Annie in jail, I kept my check-in at the café short. Everything seemed to be running smoothly. Murray was his usual grumpy self, and Evie flitted about, making sure customers had what they needed.

As I turned to leave, a flash of white caught my eye. Sitting in the corner by the door was Lorna. In a wedding veil. And she was crying. What was going on? Not wanting to poke that bear, I nevertheless couldn't in good conscience leave her there in that condition.

"Uh, Lorna?"

She blinked and wiped away tears. "Just leave me be."

"But—"

"Go away. Don't you understand English?"

Several customers turned at her loud voice. It was probably wiser on my part to do as she asked and not cause a further scene. But that woman had some serious issues going on. I had Annie and Dana on my mind right now, but I needed to keep an eye on Lorna. If what I was hearing was true and Herman Morton had dumped her at the altar, that would give Lorna a motive to have killed him. Not likely since poor Annie had confessed. Still…

When I got to the jail, Cody was inside at his desk on the phone. He glanced up when I entered. After I mouthed "Annie" and pointed toward the back, he gave me the thumbs-up sign and continued his call.

Bud was just coming out of the back area as I entered.

"Hey, Seneca. Here to see Annie?"

"Yep. Cody waved me on back."

"Sure." He lowered his voice, "Poor kid. Been crying all night."

My heart sank. Even though I'd expected her to have had a rough night, somehow, I'd hoped she'd at least gotten some sleep. I nodded to Bud, then walked down the short, dim hallway to the cells in back. An older woman was in the first cell, slumped down on the cot, snoring. From the fumes emanating from her direction, I'd guess she'd partied too hard the night before.

When I reached Annie's cell, I stopped, taking in the scene before me. There sat my assistant, red hair, normally wiry to the point of chaos, now sporting flat locks that in themselves looked despondent and depressed.

The girl's face was even more so. Downcast eyes. Drooping mouth. Cheeks damp from hour upon hour of shedding tears.

I stepped closer to the bars separating her from the rest of the world. "Annie?"

With a gasp, she startled, taking a few seconds to completely focus on my face. "Seneca?"

"I came to check on you. I won't ask how you're doing since I know, not good. Did you sleep at all?"

She shook her head, her lank hair flopping against her face.

"I'm so sorry, sweetie. I know...I mean, you confessed and all, so..."

"Yeah. I *did* confess."

Something about the way she said it made me stare at her for a few seconds. "Annie. You told me and Cody that you'd killed your uncle. You did it, didn't you?"

She didn't answer right away. Had glanced down and wouldn't meet my eye.

Oh no. What was going on?

"Annie? Honey, if there's something I should know, please tell me, okay?"

She stood, slowly, then made her way across the small, dank cell until she stood right in front of me, the only thing separating us being the cold, unforgiving metal bars. Wrapping her fingers around two of them, she finally raised her eyes to meet mine. "Seneca. I...I need help. Will you help me? Please?"

"What can I do? What's going on? "

A single tear made a rapid trail down Annie's cheek. "I wanted to protect someone."

"Protect who? From what?"

"I said I…um, I confessed…"

"Annie. Did you really kill your uncle?"

She blinked. Her answer came out so soft, I had to lean close to hear. "No. I didn't."

"Then why on earth did you confess?" My voice had come out too loud, making me cringe. "Sorry. Just…I don't understand."

"I know."

"Wait. You said you wanted to protect someone. Who?" I asked.

"My mom."

Suddenly, my earlier suspicions came back. Hearing Dana talk about the way her brother had treated her. Finding the newspaper article with the blacked-out face. As far as I knew, Cody still hadn't questioned her. Maybe he hadn't thought she was a strong enough suspect to do so. And only arrested Annie because she actually confessed. If Annie was telling the truth now, she wasn't guilty. But was her mom? Had Dana actually been the one to kill their family member?

I needed to take a deep breath and slow down. Try to get the facts. "Okay, Annie… why do you think your mom killed her brother? Do you have proof?"

The girl gave a one-shouldered shrug. "Not proof exactly. But lots of circumstantial evidence."

"I see. Go on."

"Well, my mom and I, we needed money. Really bad. Especially since I want to go to medical school."

I nodded.

"And Uncle Herman was so mean to us, especially her. Kept her from getting her rightful inheritance when my grandparents died."

"But that's not enough evidence in itself to…"

"There's more," she said.

# CHAPTER TWENTY-NINE

"Okay."

"See, my mom had been acting extra weird lately."

I wondered if kids her age figured their parents were always weird, but now her mom was more so. "What do you mean, extra weird?"

"Well, she'd started talking on the phone to someone late at night. I didn't know who it was, but I knew it was a man."

"How do you know that?"

"Because one time, I picked up our landline to call someone—mom says we can't afford for me to have my own cell right now—and some guy was yelling at her."

"But you don't know who?"

"No. I put the receiver back down, not wanting to interrupt them." She eyed me. "Yeah, Okay. I didn't want to get in trouble for listening in, so I stopped."

I let out a sigh. "Go on."

"I know for a fact the man wasn't a boyfriend or anything. My mom doesn't have one. She wishes she did, but she doesn't."

"Maybe she's seeing someone but hadn't told you?" I asked.

She shook her head. "I don't think so. He called her Daney instead of Dana. She said that's what her family used to call her when she was little. And since my grandpa isn't around anymore—"

"You assumed it was your uncle."

"Right."

I could see the logic in that. Still, to jump to her mom being the murderer? That seemed a stretch. "Is there any other evidence that you know of? Anything else you can tell me?"

"Of course. You don't really think I'd confess to murder to protect her if I wasn't sure she'd done it, do you?"

Trying to keep my expression neutral, I hoped I was successful. Because yes, that's exactly what had gone through my mind. "Go ahead and tell me what else you've got." I crossed my arms and waited.

"Okay. It's like this. See, because my mom had been acting so extra weird, I decided to try to keep an eye on her. Make sure she was all right. I wondered if maybe she had some illness that was making her do things out of the ordinary."

Annie's normally gregarious personality was making a comeback now. Trying to diagnose people with possible illnesses. I guessed that was something positive, at least. "I haven't noticed your mom looking or acting ill." But this wouldn't get us anywhere. I knew Annie, and she'd keep arguing her point until I either caved in or changed the subject. I chose option number two. "Why don't you tell me more about keeping an eye on her? How did you do that?"

"I watched her when she didn't see me. And checked her medicine cabinet to see if there were any new drugs in there. You know, for something life-threatening."

I nodded. Not in agreement, but wanting her to get on with it. Cody was going to flip when he found out about all this, but I wanted to have as much information as possible before I told him what was going on.

"And then there was that night," she said.

"Which night?"

Annie twisted a lock of her hair between her fingers. "The night my uncle died."

That got my attention. "Did you see something?"

"Yes, well, sort of. Maybe."

"Annie! Which is it? You're in jail for something you said you did and now say you didn't. Please just tell me what happened."

"Fine." Her eyebrows lowered as she frowned. "What happened was, since my mom had been acting weird and I decided to follow her, she ended up at your greenhouse."

So, it was true? She'd really killed her brother. "Did you actually see…"

"No. I followed her. I spied on her when she crouched down in the back of your greenhouse and tugged out a piece of old foundation. She crawled through!"

I nodded. At least now I knew who'd dug out around my greenhouse floor.

"I went around to the side of the greenhouse to look inside one of the windows. Mom took out her phone and did something. Sent a text or made a call? Or an email, maybe? Not sure. She'd walked to the far side of the greenhouse and had her back toward me. I couldn't see exactly what she'd done. Anyway, after a few minutes, my uncle showed up."

And Mr. Morton came in to speak to her? Why would he have done that if they hadn't spoken in years?

"But I got scared when she and my uncle started yelling at each other. Arguing. I snuck back home and went to bed. My mom never knew I'd been there. Then, the next day, I heard you found him dead in your greenhouse."

I could definitely see why Annie might have thought her mom was guilty under the circumstances. But to confess to the murder herself? "Annie, you took quite a risk, giving a false confession to killing your uncle."

"I did it for her. For Mom. I wanted to protect her."

"I know that, honey. I do. But now things are an even bigger mess than before."

Annie let out a sigh to rival one of Winifred's when she thought the whole world was against her because I'd accidentally brought home the wrong brand of cat food from the grocery.

I placed my hand over hers on the bar of the cell. "Listen, I'm going to go see Cody now. Tell him what you've told me."

"But now Cody will want to arrest my mom. No, I'd rather stay in jail than have that happen."

"But you told me you didn't do it. And you had to know I'd tell Cody."

Annie blinked back tears. "I guess I shouldn't have told you. I was just...I'm so tired and scared and...when I saw you, the words just came out."

"No. I know you confessed, and I know you did it out of love. But truth is truth, and you don't belong here. And when your mom finds out what you've done, the first thing she'll want is for you to be free of here."

As I turned to go see Cody, I didn't add what I wanted to. That once Annie was free, Cody would have to check into Dana's story next. I just hoped her ending would be as happy as Annie's would turn out to be. And that someone else had committed the murder.

Cody had ended his conversation and was turned toward the hallway to the cells. The way he watched me told me he'd been waiting to see me after speaking to Annie.

I hurried to his desk, wanting to spill all the new information in a rush. But that wouldn't help matters. He needed to know everything. As calmly as I could, I repeated everything Annie had told me. When I was done, I looked him square in the eyes. "And I believe her, Cody. Every word. I know she seemed convincing when she confessed, but you didn't see her just now. Her expression, voice, body language, it was pure, raw honesty."

Cody slumped back in his chair, then ran his hand through his short hair. "My goodness."

"Exactly," I said.

"Why didn't she tell me all this before I went ahead and arrested her? Put her in a jail cell? I feel about as small as one of your caterpillars."

"It's not your fault. I believed her, too, when she confessed. And maybe she told me just now because she knows me so well. Because we work together and..." I shrugged. "I don't know. Or maybe after spending a sleepless night in a cell, with nothing to do but think about where she was and what might happen next, she was desperate enough to blurt out the truth. Fear can make you do or say things you never thought you would."

With a decisive nod, Cody stood and headed toward the back.

I started to follow, then halted. I wasn't part of the sheriff's office staff. Just a civilian.

Cody stopped and turned. "Come ahead, Seneca. You're in this too. Thanks to you, an innocent girl won't stay in jail."

Mere minutes after Cody had called Dana to come to the sheriff's office, she was there. She'd been on her way out her door to visit Annie anyway, so made it in record time.

Dana rushed in, barreling toward Cody, barely halting before crashing into his desk. "Is Annie hurt? You said it was urgent? Can I see her? Is she—"

Cody came around the desk and placed his hands on her shoulders. "Dana. Take a breath. I need to tell you something, but I think it would be better if you sat down."

Her brow scrunched together as she eyed his chair, like she thought it might be some sort of trap. I couldn't blame her. The last twenty-four hours had been a roller coaster ride of fear, worry, and doubt. But after she looked at me and I gave her what I hoped was an encouraging expression, she finally took a seat.

Cody and I grabbed chairs as well, scooting them closer to Dana. Bud wasn't in the room, but I could hear him whistling off-key in a side office. Cody had filled him in, but maybe he'd thought it would be better to only have one law enforcement officer present when he told Dana about Annie. Probably a good choice since her face had turned white with only the two of us here.

Cody reached out and squeezed his employee's hand. "Dana, Seneca came to visit Annie this morning, and...Annie told her something surprising."

"What?" Her eyes were wide, unblinking.

"Annie said her confession was false."

"What are you saying? She didn't do it? My girl didn't commit murder?" She let out a long breath, and her shoulders slumped. I'd known Dana for many years and knew her to be honest and trustworthy. And Cody wouldn't have someone working for him he didn't trust. Her expression looked genuinely shocked that Annie was innocent. From a discussion Cody and I had had before calling Dana, that had been his first test. To see Dana's reaction. If she hadn't seemed surprised that Annie was innocent, that would have left wiggle room for the possibility that she herself had done the deed.

Next would be test number two. Cody reached behind him to his desk and retrieved the newspaper article, now covered with a see-through plastic evidence bag, about Mr. Morton. He held it out to her; she took it, and immediately, her eyebrows lowered. "What's this? Is that..." She narrowed her eyes and held the page closer. "That's Herman. What's..." Her eyes drifted lower until she found the second picture. "And me?" She shook her head.

"You've never seen this before?"

"No. Never. I must have been pretty young in that photo. Herman is— was—so much older than me. By that time, we didn't see much of him. Maybe the newspaper got our family picture somehow. I really don't know."

Cody took the photo back. "Dana, I know you'd never touched this photo.

We do have your fingerprints in our system, of course, since you work for the government."

She nodded slowly, like she was having trouble allowing all the new developments to sink in. "Then why—"

"I wanted to hear you say it. See your reaction. I know I didn't need to check it for your prints, but if what I now believe is true, I needed to do everything by the book to clear you."

"Clear…"

"Yes," he said.

"You'd suspected me?"

Cody glanced at me and then back. "From what your daughter just told Seneca, the reason she supposedly killed her uncle was to protect you."

"But why?"

"She thought you'd killed him. Because of the money," he said.

Dana let out a loud sob. I grabbed a box of tissues from the desk behind me and thrust it into her hands.

She mopped her damp face and then sighed. "Now it makes some sort of sense, I guess. Why Annie confessed. I mean, I believed her that she'd done it. I didn't want to believe her, of course, but…she confessed. So…." Dana reached for another tissue and wiped her eyes. "There's something I should tell you. Both of you."

Cody and I both leaned closer.

"You see," said Dana, "there might be a valid reason why Annie suspected me. I was desperate to speak to Herman. And he would never allow it. I got the idea to call him and pretend I was you, Seneca. That way, he might come to the greenhouse. I'm so, so sorry." She glanced down at the tissue she'd wadded in her grasp. "Also, I… I needed a way into the greenhouse without breaking in. Um…." Her face reddened. "I have to admit that I dug out in back of your greenhouse and crawled inside and—"

I edged forward on my seat, my heart aching for this woman who was so scared that she saw no other choice. "But it's over now, Dana. I'm not worried about the greenhouse. I understand how desperate you were. You've been cleared. And so is Annie."

210

Cody nodded. "Yes, Annie has been cleared. And to continue going by the book, we also tested the paper for her prints. No match."

Dana shook her head. "Then who killed my brother?"

Cody gave her a small smile. "You let me worry about that. Right now, let's go get your girl."

# Chapter Thirty

I hadn't talked to Jesse for a couple of days but needed to drop something off at his office. He'd mentioned wanting to hold a memorial for Millie somewhere in the park to honor her service to the community and her life. It was touching, especially since he hadn't known her all that long. Millie had been so sweet. I was sure she would have liked the gesture.

I had pamphlets explaining more about releasing butterflies when someone died. He'd agreed that would be a nice tribute. And that he hoped I'd do the honor of releasing them when the time came. I, of course, readily agreed. Not only had Millie been a loyal café customer, but she'd also become a friend.

When I reached the park's office, I didn't see his truck. Maybe parked out back? Or was he making his rounds to check on things in the park? And, of course, there hadn't been time to get a replacement for Millie's job yet, as painful as that thought may be, so if he was gone, chances were no one was around. Maybe I could leave the pages in the mailbox if that were the case.

As I climbed the wooden steps, one gave a loud creak. Though money must be tight on a government budget, surely Jessie or someone else could at least make some minor repairs.

*Seneca. Stop being catty.* Just because I was a stickler for taking care of most things at my farm, I couldn't assume everyone else felt the same. Cody had teased me before for being so meticulous, but I liked to think maybe the butterflies appreciated my efforts, even if Winifred ignored my attempts most of the time.

I pulled open the screen door, wincing when it squeaked. The inner door was open a few inches, so I stepped inside. The lights were on, but the place seemed dead.

Bad thought, there, with Millie and all.

Maybe Jesse was somewhere in the back part of the building? "Hello? Jesse?"

After a few seconds of hearing nothing back, it seemed obvious I was alone.

As I walked past Millie's workstation, I paused to touch her desk chair. Poor woman. To have been killed in such a violent manner. And Cody still didn't know who'd done it. Maple Junction was falling apart. Two murders. What had happened to our quaint, safe little town?

Pulling the information on the butterfly release from my purse, I continued across the room. Best to just place the pages on Jesse's work area and leave. I put them in the center of his desk where he'd be sure to see them. Better leave a note, too, asking him to call me with any questions he might have had.

I accidentally brushed against some papers sitting on the edge of the desk. Things flew right and left, some even dashing beneath the chair.

Oh, just perfect. I needed to get it all back into place so Jesse wouldn't think I'd been snooping.

Quickly, I gathered up the pages and tried to sort them into a neat pile. No way I could know the order they'd been in, but that couldn't be helped. As I set them back on the desktop, something on the top paper caught my eye.

It was a rough drawing of what appeared to be the cave at the back of the park, the area that adjoined my property. Several more pages were attached to the drawing with a couple of staples. Curious, I flipped the top page over and saw a map. It was of my property and the park. Specifically routed to the cave. What was going on? The lettering that labeled the different roads and areas looked odd. Sort of old-fashioned, with slanted letters, some taller than the others, a few with added curlicues.

I edged that one aside. The third one was a letter addressed to Mr. Archibald Gibbs. I frowned. Could that be someone related to Lonny?

*Dear Mr. Gibbs,*

*Here is the place I told you about. It's the cave where I've hidden the rubies. Since I am unable to travel at present due to poor health, I'm trusting you to retrieve the gems and bring them here to me. Once you have done so, I'll make sure you receive a generous share of the bounty. The attached map shows where you will find the cave. Once you've reached the entrance, you'll see where I've left a trail to find the gems. Scratch marks, in the form of small arrows will guide you.*

*I'm putting my trust in you to accomplish this task. Don't let me down.*

*Most sincerely,*

*Mr. Lionel Hugh*

Another paper that had stuck in between the stapled ones was a printout from the internet. It was all about Lonny Gibbs. Credentials, background, personal information. Had Jesse been doing some checking up on Lonny? Maybe, as I did, Jesse didn't believe Lonny was on the up and up.

My hand shook as I placed the page next to the map on the desktop. So, all this time, Lonny had been going after some rubies? Was he also a murderer?

My eyes widened. I needed to tell Cody. But a description of this map and letter wouldn't be enough. Reaching into my jeans pocket, I got my cell phone. What I needed was proof. And a picture of the pages would do quite nicely. Too bad Jesse wasn't around to talk to about it. But I had to get to Cody first, so he could check out Lonny.

No way was I going to let Lonny get away with theft. The more I thought about it, the more my gut told me he might very well be responsible for one murder, if not two. Because if he'd been the one to want to obtain my land so he'd have easy access to the cave, he very well might have murdered my lawyer as well.

I pushed the pages closer together, ready to snap a quick photo. As I positioned my phone over the incriminating items, a shadow darkened the desk around me. Hard and quick, something crashed down on the back of my neck.

Everything went dark.

* * *

I woke up, my vision and thoughts fuzzy. My head throbbed, especially the back, right above my neck. After reaching around, my fingers came back sticky. In the dim light, I could barely make out something dark.

Blood. Why was I bleeding?

With a gasp, I sat up, nearly losing my last meal, when a wave of nausea rolled over me from stomach to throat. A few deep, slow breaths later, I was fairly confident I wouldn't throw up.

But where was I? Why was—

A sound like pebbles dropping on rock came from my right. How had I gotten here? Where was here? Holding still, I listened in the darkness for a couple of minutes but heard nothing else. I allowed my shoulders to relax, and as my hands lowered, my fingers grazed the hard surface I sat on. Wet. A strong, musty smell. Almost as if I was in a cave.

The only one I knew of was in the park. However, I had no memory of going to the cave. Either I'd lost my memory and wandered here, or someone else had brought me. How had I—

Again, from my right came a soft sound, like a person gasping, or startled. More pebbles hitting stone. Then, footsteps, at first uncertain, like whoever it was, couldn't keep their footing, changing to a steady, determined gait.

Trying not to tremble, I held as still as I could. Who was here? And what did they want?

The sound of steps came closer, then a splat, like they'd found a puddle, followed by a muttered curse. The bright beam of a flashlight zipped across my eyes, temporarily stealing my sight. Though it was dark in the cave, at least I'd been able to see some outlines of things from distant light, maybe from the cave's opening. Now, I had to wait until the spots clouding my eyes dissipated.

"So, you've decided to wake up and join me." A man's voice. Familiar, but somehow distorted by the thick rock echoing in the cave. Was it Lonny?

My head still throbbed from whatever had caused the bleeding above my neck. I couldn't focus on who spoke, my ears feeling muffled, like they were partially covered. Was that because of the injury to the back of my head?

I shielded my eyes from the bright light. "Could you douse the light?"

Something slid across the rocks near me. Had he moved closer? The man was near now, so close that I could feel his body heat. He must have sat beside me or crouched down, because his warm breath breezed across my forehead.

I jumped when he touched me, put his fingers beneath my chin, and turned my head in his direction. Trying my best to get free, I leaned back. But his grip was tight, fingers digging into my flesh.

"Seneca, you really should have minded your own business."

I remembered finding the letter to Lonny's relative about the rubies and the computer printout about his background. Was he the one who'd brought me here?

I slowly shook my head. Wait. I knew that voice, didn't I? The person who'd recently taken such an interest in what I loved to do. Work with the monarchs. But that couldn't be right. Could it? *"Jesse?"*

I could almost hear his lips form a smile. "In the flesh."

How could I have been such a fool? So blind to be taken in by someone I hardly knew. Me, who rarely trusted anyone I hadn't known my entire life.

What would happen now? "What was the purpose of kidnapping me, carrying me to this cave? Why did you bring me here?"

"Haven't you figured it out yet?"

What had happened to the shy, scarred man who couldn't look me in the eye? Had he been a fabrication? In frustration, I clenched my jaws, nearly screaming from the pain it caused in my head. "Just tell me."

"My partners and I were trying to work out a deal. But somehow, you keep getting in the way. It would have been so much easier if you'd minded your own business from the start."

"Partners? Who do you mean? Lonny Gibbs?"

"And your neighbor Hal."

I shook my head. "Not Hal. Even he could never go that far." I let out a breath. Deep down, I knew Hal was indeed capable. Just hadn't wanted to believe it. What was the incentive he mentioned? Money? Power? So, I asked again, "Why have you brought me here?"

"To get you out of the way. Permanently."

Though some part of me had known that too, hearing the words invoked panic. Hot beads of sweat mixed with cold chills. My heart beat overtime, desperately trying to escape the confines of my ribs. It longed to flee this cave. I wanted to go with it. How would I get out of here alive?

He'd moved the flashlight beam away enough that the spots faded from my eyes. I blinked a few times, then stared at him. Where there had previously been a burn was now smooth, clear skin.

Jesse reached to touch his cheek. "Amazing what a good makeup artist can do, right? And before you ask. I don't have a limp, either."

What a liar. And I'd bought his whole act. I swallowed hard, trying to figure out a way out of this nightmare. He'd been kind to me once. Maybe he'd listen to reason. I had to try. What other option did I have? "Jesse, you don't have to do this. Let's talk about it. I'll—"

"Stop talking."

I bit my bottom lip so tight it burned. I had to figure out some way to get out of here. But how? In my present state, I couldn't physically overpower him. Not that I could have, anyway.

"I'll do the talking. Since you won't be around to tell anyone, let's clear a few things up."

Won't be around... Those had to be three of the most frightening words ever uttered.

"It was a challenge trying to find a way to get close to you. Cody was always around. The fact that he's the local sheriff made it even worse. I wracked my brain, trying to come up with some tactic to get between you. Even tried to use that story about overhearing the gossip from two women, but obviously, that didn't work. You two were still stuck together like magnets."

"Cody told me about it. He'd actually done what you'd told me about. Why would you call it a story?"

"Because I never heard it from any women in the store."

I turned my head, immediately sorry, when pain shot over the top of my scalp. "Then, how did you know? I never even heard about it until he told me. Who else would have known?"

His chuckle was low and grating, sounding not amused but pleased with his own inventiveness. "I got the information from Hal. He said he'd overheard your grandmother and Cody having a conversation one day when they'd been close to Hal's property line. Hal thought it might help me get in good with you if I could get Cody away from you."

Sorrow flooded me. Poor Gram, she would've hated knowing she'd somehow been a part of that.

"By the way, didn't you just love all the wasps that made friends with your butterflies? Imagine my delight when I researched the monarchs' predators and found it was something I could easily obtain from a contact I had at the park."

Jesse's words yanked me back to the present. "Wasps! That was you?"

"That's right. It took some doing, releasing them while you and that lunkhead sheriff were on the other side of the greenhouse. But it worked. Got the stings to prove it."

I'd never noticed any on him, even though Cody and I had kept an eye out for anyone who might be sporting some, hoping it would lead us to whoever had set the wasps loose.

He ran his forefinger around his collar, giving it a tug. "I was able to cover them with my shirt collar. Got a couple on my wrist, too, but keeping my sleeves down did the trick. Guess it came in handy to have to wear the requisite forest ranger attire. Now, the stings just itch. My dog, unfortunately, required treatment. He'd gotten hurt when I had them at the ranger station before I brought them to your place. A few wasps must have escaped the cage they were in and stung him."

How devious could one man be? He'd even endangered his own pet to obtain wasps to try to put me out of business. Even though Winifred had been injured, too, I wouldn't tell him. It would only make him happy. "Let me guess. German Shepherd?"

"Hmmm. The old veterinarian must have gabbed. Maybe I'll just pay him a visit before I leave town."

I swallowed hard. "Not Dr. Cummings. Please don't."

With a laugh, he said, "We'll see. Might not have time before this is all said and done anyhow. Time's getting away. Once my partners arrive, we'll have to divide everything up and leave town. Fast."

Something didn't add up. "Wait. When the vet described the dog's owner, the man didn't sound like you."

"That's because it was Lonny. He wore a disguise even though he was pretty sure the vet wouldn't know him. Lonny has never had a pet, so no reason to seek out the vet. Couldn't take the chance that the doctor would describe me to someone and it would get back to you that the new park ranger had a dog with wasp stings."

Jesse angled his head side to side and gave a sigh, as if he had a stiff neck. "So anyway, as I already said, I never had an interest in your butterflies. My interests run more toward the monetary kind. And not just money, but precious gems. It's a very interesting story, and since you're my captive audience, you get to hear it."

# Chapter Thirty-One

I needed to get away from this guy. Now. Where was the entrance to the cave? If I could get away somehow, I had to go in the right direction. Getting lost in here wouldn't be much better than staying with Jesse. Although, at least away from him, I might have a chance. And it would give Cody more time to hunt for me. I had no doubt he'd get worried if I was away from the greenhouse and Winifred for too long.

Jesse leaned back against the rock wall, his fingers entwined over one knee. "This goes back a long time, Seneca. Way before you and I were even thought of. You see, my great-uncle was a bit of a rebel. Loved taking risks. Was always about the big payoff. It just so happens that he was from this area. Not Maple Junction but about fifty miles away."

A noise came from another part of the cave. Had someone found out I was here? Come to help me? Or was it one of Jesse's partners? If that were the case, two, maybe three, against one didn't sound like great odds to me.

"So, way back then, when he was in his thirties, he stole a vast number of rubies. I'm not sure where he obtained them, but he ended up a rich man either way. The reason I know all of this is he left some letters explaining what he had and where he'd stashed it so he could go back later. He'd sent these letters to my great-aunt. After he hid the rubies here in this cave, he left the area for a time to try to steal something else. Unfortunately, he was killed in the process of the theft. Upon hearing of his death, my great-aunt couldn't go on. She died within weeks of him."

"Wait," I said. "The letter was addressed to someone named Gibbs, not Vance." I waited for his answer, but also stayed alert for any more noises in the cave. Who had made it? Were they headed this way? Jesse, lost in telling his story, didn't seem to have noticed the sound.

"Lonny and I are cousins. The writer of the letter is related to both of us. I happened upon those very same letters, the ones she had, in an antique desk that had been passed down to me through my father. The letters weren't in plain sight; instead, they were hidden in a secret compartment behind one drawer. Apparently, no one else had found it or even thought to look for them. That makes me the lucky one."

He'd told me not to talk, but so many questions were bursting to get out. I glared at him. "Are you even a park ranger? Was that much true?"

With a laugh, Jesse said, "Of course not. Why would anyone ever want such a boring job that pays so little?"

"How did you fake your way into the position here? Not just anyone can walk in and do the job."

"Didn't you ever wonder what happened to the last ranger?" He crossed his arms, watching with a wicked grin, like he couldn't wait to share juicy gossip.

I frowned. "Sure, but—"

"Ranger Nelson was an old coot. Too easy, really."

"What do you mean, easy?" I asked.

"Are you that stupid? I killed him, of course. Snapped his neck like a brittle twig."

A loud gasp escaped my mouth, made shriller by the ensuing echoes from the cave walls. "How could you do that? He never hurt anybody."

Jesse shrugged. "I had to. He was in my way. It was the only option to have full access to the park. I needed to play the role of ranger, so no one would wonder why I spent so much time hanging around there."

Poor Ranger Nelson. He hadn't deserved that. No one did. Did he have family somewhere who might wonder what had happened to him? "Wh-where is he? What did you do with him?"

Another shrug. "My job was only to kill him. Lonny took care of the body. I'd guess a shallow grave somewhere or dumped over the ledge along the interstate. You'd have to ask him."

"But when I saw the map and letter on your desk, I also saw something about Lonny," I said. "Like maybe you'd been checking into his background. Why would you do that for your own cousin?"

Jesse shrugged. "There's no honor among thieves. Even if it's your own family. Figured it wouldn't hurt to make sure he was on the up and up. I hadn't seen him for several years. Wanted to cover all my angles." With a frown, he glanced to his left. "And Lonny was supposed to have been here by now."

Was that who'd made the earlier noise? If so, why wasn't he here, gloating with Jesse, planning to murder me? If he didn't show up, maybe I had a better chance to escape.

Jesse tossed a small rock to his left. It clattered a few times before coming to rest. "As far as faking my way into being the ranger, I waited a couple weeks so it would appear that Ranger Nelson had just up and left. Then, I used his credentials and recreated some for me. The Internet is a great tool, isn't it? It tells you right there what a ranger should do and know, what type of education and degrees he needs. So easy. And aside from getting online to find and create information for my own ranger credentials, I used the computer to check you out."

"Why would you do that?"

"Seneca, your insistence on having that land threw a wrench into our carefully laid out plans. You were causing trouble. Right in the middle of things. In places you shouldn't have been. And your attorney, Morton, was also a problem that needed to be dealt with. You just wouldn't give up on Hal's land. Held on like some stubborn barnacle on a ship, refusing to give in."

"That's because I needed it. And he'd promised me years ago it was mine when the time was right." It wouldn't do any good to tell him that again, but I needed to say something. Keep him occupied if I were to have any chance of getting away.

"Why'd you have to get a lawyer involved anyway?" he asked. "Just one more problem I had to deal with."

"Because Hal and I had a signed contract for me to get the land. I needed

Mr. Morton's help to get things straightened out."

"What you did was get the man killed. You left me no choice. I followed Morton to your greenhouse one night. Someone at the door let him in. I thought it was you. I waited while they yelled at each other for a while, then after that Hastings woman left, I walked right in. He was old, so it was easy to do him in." Jesse didn't glance to the side as he had when I first met him. Now he glared, his eyes boring right into mine.

I shook my head, which caused the throb from the injury to start up again. "But I didn't know. How could I have...?"

As Jesse rolled his eyes, the beam from the flashlight reflected from the white portions of them. "This subject is dead. Like you'll soon be. Anyway, I needed an excuse to get to know you that would seem plausible." He watched me and waited.

Closing my eyes, I blew out a breath. Of course. How could I have been so stupid? "The monarchs."

"That's right. From what I'd read online about your work with them and what people around here had said, those butterflies are pretty much your whole life. Once I found the documentation that the previous ranger had left about the butterflies, it was easy to get your attention. I figured that was the best way to gain your trust."

I checked in the direction from where I'd heard the sound earlier. Was Lonny on his way right now? How long before he showed up, maybe Hal too, and I'd be history? If I could somehow distract Jesse, or harm him in some way to give me a few minutes head start, would I have a chance?

Jesse grunted something I couldn't make out and flung his arm out to his right. "Where are they?"

"Maybe they changed their minds, are leaving you alone with me." Too bad I couldn't take advantage of the fact before the others arrived. But what could I do to overpower him?

As if he'd forgotten I was even there, he startled, then watched me. "No. They'll be here. That is, if they want their share of the rubies."

Should I keep Jesse talking? Was there a chance someone would figure out where I was and come to find me? Maybe I could distract him long enough for Cody to get concerned that I wasn't at the farm. If my truck was still parked at the ranger's station and I was nowhere around, Cody's big-brother instinct would be on high alert. He'd figure out what happened and try to find me no matter what.

I shifted a little to ease a cramp in my leg. How long had I been here in the damp, dark place? "How did you and Lonny come up with this scheme?"

With a glare, he said, "Why do you care?"

Giving a shrug, I said, "You gotta wait for them, right? Might pass the time. To talk. Like you said, I'm a captive audience and have to listen to you."

The way he glared at me said, *not sure if I can trust you.* After a few seconds, he said, "Yeah. Why not? We've got some time. As kids, Lonny and I were closer. Even went to the same school."

"Let me guess. This isn't the first crime you've planned and committed together?"

His harsh laugh bounced around in the enclosed area. "Good guess. We started out with petty stuff as teenagers, mainly purse-snatching. Moved up from there."

"Your mother must be so proud."

His head whipped around, his eyes hard, the dim light making them appear demented or evil. "You've got a smart mouth on you, ya know that?"

Trying not to show my fear, I said, "I've been told that once or twice." Maybe showing bravado would be to my advantage. Throw him off center a bit.

He pointed his finger at me, though in the dim light, I couldn't tell exactly how close it came to my face. "Keep it up, see what happens."

"You already told me you plan to kill me. What's the harm in making you mad?"

He lunged at me so fast, I crashed against the rock, hitting the sore spot on the back of my head again. Though I tried to keep it inside, a moan of pain escaped.

"Seneca." He grabbed both of my wrists easily in one hand and squeezed. It was all I could do not to cry out. Tears ran down my cheeks, though. Nothing I could do to stop those. "Don't push me. You don't want to find out exactly what I'm capable of."

Hadn't I already heard the terrible things he'd done? To hear anything worse might not be tolerable. I swallowed hard, afraid to move. He'd been a great actor. Now I'd met the real man. One I wished I didn't know.

Instead of loosening his hold, he clamped his fingers down harder. "Remember when you found Millie in the pines?"

"Yes," I whispered, nearly unable to breathe.

"She'd gotten too nosy, just like you. Had followed me to the cave one day, demanding answers. Seems she'd found the same letter you did. I couldn't let her live after that and take the chance she might spout off her theories to someone else. I killed her without a second thought. So, you might want to rethink provoking me."

What had I done? I'd only wanted to distract him, maybe get him talking about something, thinking about someone besides me and what he'd planned to do to me. Then I went too far. Would he now inflict the same horrible death on me that he'd used on Millie? Yes, he'd planned to do me in regardless, but a big part of me knew it might be more painful now. And I'd brought that on myself.

# Chapter Thirty-Two

Loud footsteps approached. "Jesse? You in here?"

Hearing another voice jolted Jesse out of his present rage. He shoved me roughly away and stood. "Back here," he called.

I couldn't decide between rubbing my numbing wrists or checking the back of my head for more bleeding. Wrists first. If there was a chance, any at all, of me slipping out of here alive, I'd need the use of my hands to help navigate my way to the mouth of the cave. Who was coming? I couldn't tell. Somebody who knew that Jesse would be here. It had to be one of two people.

Hal stepped into the faint light. First, he gave Jesse a nod, then, his eyes wandered toward the wall, to where I sat pressed up as tight against the cold, wet stone as I could. He pointed his thumb toward me. "Why'd you bring her here?"

"Thought it'd be more convenient. This way, no one will find her body."

Find her body. With each passing second, it became more real. The very seconds I was running out of. Only so many more breaths to take before...

Hal's eyes widened. "What? You never said anything about killing her!"

Jessie glared at him. "You're getting the money you wanted. Why do you care?"

With an expression of sudden remorse, Hal said, "No. You can't do it. I didn't want you to kill any of the others either."

"You're a lightweight, Hal. Don't have the stomach for this."

"Maybe I don't," said Hal. "I just wanted enough money to get out of the deep debt I'm in."

I gasped. Hal was in debt? Why hadn't he ever said anything? "Hal?"

"Look, Seneca," he said. "I've had a gambling addiction for a very long time. Didn't even let on about it. Not to you. Or your grandmother. But I was in deep trouble. Getting the rubies from this cave seemed a quick way out."

"But you nearly ruined my farm. My livelihood."

He rubbed the back of his neck. "My plan was to get away someplace safe. Away from the goons who want to break my legs since I couldn't pay them. I was planning to help you out with deeding you my farm once the danger was past and no one could find me."

"But you put me through so much!" I yelled, causing my whole head to ache.

"It had to be convincing that you and I had no relationship anymore. I needed to leave here with no contact with anyone here. I didn't want the people after me to think I had any dealing with you."

"Are you trying to say you did it to protect me?" I asked.

He avoided eye contact with me. "That's right."

I shook my head. There had to have been some other way than his skewed thinking to get that accomplished.

Jesse stood. "Enough of this. Sorry to say, Hal, I don't need you now. Your part is done."

Hal frowned. "What're you talking about? How can you say—"

The blast from the gun nearly blinded and deafened me. It took a few seconds for me to focus clearly. But when I did, Hal lay lifeless on the stone floor, arms flung out to the sides, blood oozing from a hole in his chest.

"No!" I got on my knees, prepared to stand, then Jesse turned the gun on me.

"Don't move. You can't help him now anyway."

"Why?" I asked. "Why did you kill him? What had he done to make you do that?" Jesse Vance had a black heart. How had I ever thought he was someone I could trust?

He waved the gun back and forth in front of me, making me unable to take my eyes from it, the horrible anticipation of when it would go off next, and that it would be at me. "Don't be stupid, Seneca. Do you really think if I could get out of sharing the rubies with your ignorant neighbor, I wouldn't do it?"

I slumped back down, shivering. Not from the cold this time. From witnessing a murder right in front of me. Discovering two dead bodies had been bad enough. But this... I'd never get that sound or vision out of my head. Ever. Eyeing the gun still aimed at me, I swallowed hard. Hal and I would soon be sharing this cave as our crypt, our final resting place. Even Arnold, the mortician, wouldn't be able to find us here.

Slowly, Jesse lowered his weapon and sat back down. He set the gun next to him, close enough to grab if needed. Maybe he didn't see me as any kind of a threat. Yet. How long before he turned the gun on me?

My ears rang, my eyes sported dancing spots, and the smell from the fired gun gave off an acrid stench that hovered in the stale air all around me. If he hadn't killed me yet, was there a reason? Would I have a chance to get away? But with that gun right there, within his reach, how could I?

A sound came from far away, like before. Pebbles kicked, or someone lost their footing. Jesse, on high alert, turned his head. "Ah, must be Lonny. Finally. Time to get this thing finished once and for all."

Did he mean take all the rubies and leave, or kill Lonny as he had Hal? Or murder me?

Someone's shoe slid on wet rock, close by. My mouth went dry, and my heart hammered. Was this it? My final moments before death?

A man edged around the corner of rock to my right, his long shadow preceding him into the small area where Jesse had taken me. Was this it for me? Had my time run out? Jesse wouldn't keep me around once Lonny showed up, and they divided the spoils.

The man stepped farther into the faint light. I inhaled sharply, my mouth gaping open.

Cody!

At my reaction, Jesse whipped his head toward me, then behind him. Startled, he jumped up. *"You?"*

Cody stepped out farther. "That's right. Sorry to disappoint." With a glance at me, he said, "Okay, not sorry."

I cried. Couldn't help it. Hot tears coursed down my face, off my chin. Cody had searched for me. Figured out what had happened. He'd come to get me. Maybe we had a chance of getting out of here alive.

Scrambling for his gun, Jesse grabbed it from the ground and aimed at Cody. I let out a scream which echoed from the walls and ceiling.

But Cody had his own gun. And it was pointed right at Jesse's chest. "Drop. Your. Weapon."

"I don't think so." Jesse's aim never wavered from his newest intended victim. I watched, paralyzed, as his finger edged toward the trigger, ever slowly, like he wanted to relish the experience, enjoy this particular murder.

My heart nearly stopped. "No!" With all my strength, I lunged forward, wrapping my arms around Jesse's knees. He went down with a thud, crushing my hands beneath him. But I didn't care. Not only because the feeling was muted from my numb fingers, but because I might have given my best friend the opportunity to save himself from being shot.

Cody raced forward, gun still held on Jesse, and with his foot, punted Jesse's gun several feet away. It clattered across the uneven rock floor, spinning in place before coming to rest in a slight depression of wet stone.

Jesse rolled out of my grip, then kicked, hard, smacking me square in the jaw. He crawled away from me, toward his gun. Pain from his well-placed boot shot from my chin to my right eye, arching out toward my ear. I groaned and curled sideways, just wanting the pain to subside, wishing the pounding at my temples would leave, so I could take a deep breath without fearing I'd throw up.

"Not gonna happen, Jesse." Cody's voice was steady, strong.

I forced my head up, watching Cody as he kept his weapon trained on the criminal, who was now standing halfway between me and his gun. Slowly, Cody approached him, hand rock-steady, eyes narrowed, jaw set in determination. "Stay where you are."

Instead, Jesse ran forward, head lowered like a battering ram. Straight for Cody. They collided, and for the second time, a gun went off in the close confines of the cave.

I gasped. Who'd been shot when they fell? "Cody? Are you…."

Nobody moved. My heart nearly stopped. Was he okay? I stood, nearly passing out from dizziness, but finally made my way to them. Jesse was sprawled across him. When I reached them, I watched closely. Still, neither man budged. Were they breathing? Or both…dead?

Kneeling beside them, I touched my friend's face? "C-Cody? Cody!" Warm air hit my hand from his nostrils. I breathed hard, like I'd run a few miles. He was alive!

His eyes fluttered open, and he blinked, finally focusing on me. "Seneca. Are you okay?"

I nearly laughed. It was so like Cody to ask about me at that moment.

Not wanting to worry him about my painful jaw, I said. "I'm fine. But are you… The gun went off and…"

"Not hit. Must have been…" He lowered his gaze to Jesse, who still hadn't moved. That's when I noticed a stream of blood coming from between the two men.

Trying to ignore the way it jarred me, caused new jolts of pain down my jaw, I grabbed Jesse and rolled him off Cody.

Cody took a deep breath, maybe something he'd not been able to do with the other man crushing his chest. Then, he tried to sit up, but faltered. I took his hand to help him.

As soon as he was able, Cody leaned over Jesse to feel for a pulse. "Dead."

I shook my head. So many deaths. So senseless. And all for monetary gain. What a waste.

When I turned back to Cody, he'd fished out his phone. "No reception in here. Let's get you outside, and I can call someone to come get Jesse out of here."

My head still throbbed, and everything swirled. Closing my eyes briefly only made it worse.

"Hey." He grabbed my shoulders and studied me closely. "You've got a large welt on your chin. That happened in here? You're not okay, are you?"

Swallowing hard, hoping not to embarrass myself by throwing up right here, I shook my head.

# CHAPTER THIRTY-TWO

"Why didn't you say something?"

I tried hard not to move my jaw too much as I said, "Didn't want to worry you."

"Seneca, don't you think I was already worried when I got here?" He half carried me out, which seemed to take forever since I wasn't much help.

Finally, we emerged into the daylight. The sun, though hidden partially behind a cloud, was so bright, it seared into my eyes.

Within a few seconds, Cody had helped me to sit down beneath a large shade tree just outside the mouth of the cave. "You stay there."

"No problem." I leaned back against the tree, grateful to feel its rough bark, to hear a wren calling from a few yards away, to breathe fresh air.

To be alive.

I must have dozed off, because when I opened my eyes, Cody was shaking my shoulder gently. "Hey. Hangin' in there?"

I gave a shrug. No use pretending I was fine since he knew I wasn't.

"The rescue team is here to get Jesse from the cave, and Bud's going to supervise them."

"Okay." I closed my eyes, wanting nothing more than to sleep the rest of the week.

"I'm taking you to the hospital."

"No, you're..." My eyes popped open, which hurt.

"Stop arguing. Besides, you're so weak, how're you going to stop me?"

My shoulders went up and down in another shrug. What could I say? He bent down. "Can you put your arms around my shoulders?"

Though every muscle hurt, I did it. That was the only way I was getting away from the cave. All my strength had been used up tackling Jesse when he'd tried to shoot Cody. But it had been worth it. Effortlessly, my friend picked me up, holding me close to his chest. The warmth of him, right next to me, helped curb my trembling. I was safe. Cocooned.

Cocooned.

My mouth lifted in a small smile. Guess I'd spent too much time around butterflies.

# Chapter Thirty-Three

He took me to his car, which was parked nearby, and gently settled me on his back seat. After shutting the door softly, thank goodness—I didn't think I could take another loud noise just now—he drove me the short distance to the small community hospital close to the park. The builders must have figured they'd get lots of business from people doing stupid stunts when they visited Pines Park.

When we got to the hospital, Cody parked right in front. Someone came out with a wheelchair, but Cody would have none of that. He hurried to the back seat and scooped me up, treating me as gently as I treated the monarchs, all fragile and vulnerable.

Before long, I was in a curtained cubicle, being checked out by an emergency physician. Cody, irritated, stood just outside, having been informed by a bossy, scary nurse that he'd have to leave. I could hear his boots pacing a few feet away. Ten steps left, a squeak when he pivoted around, ten steps back.

Until Scary Nurse scolded him. Then came an argument. And Cody was relegated down the hall to a small waiting room.

I could only imagine what he said after they'd stuck him in there. After a thorough—ouch—exam of my whole face and neck, they took some X-rays. All of that wore me out. Once again, I woke later to Cody standing beside me.

I squinted one eye open. "Thought they kicked your sorry self out."

He smirked. "I got the last laugh. Told her I'd arrest her for harassing an officer of the law. She gave in, so I came back. But you've been asleep the whole time. Probably the real reason she gave in and let back here again."

"No, I'm guessing she saw through to your soft inner core."

"I am not a jelly-filled doughnut."

"Think about it. Cops. Doughnuts."

He scowled, but I could tell he was trying hard not to laugh. "Enough of that."

I rubbed my jaw, glad to have some painkillers for the time being, but knowing that soon, when they wore off, it would hurt like crazy. I thought back to the cave. Getting kicked. Cody and Jesse, fighting. The gun going off. Then, I caught Cody's attention. "Hey, when I was in the cave before you got there, Jesse killed Hal."

"Yeah, saw the body. Figured that's what happened. I'm sure the state police will want to question you about what happened in there."

I groaned. "Not them again."

"At least you're not a suspect this time."

"True. Jesse was waiting for his partners. Hal and Lonny." I shook my head, the movement reminding me I'd have to be careful not to do that after the meds wore off.

"Let's spring you outta here."

"I like the way you think, sheriff." Time to move on. Get away from the filth and dishonesty that had been my world for the past few weeks. He helped me sit up and twist around, so my legs hung over the edge. "Wait. Did they get the X-rays back?"

"Nothing broken. Just badly bruised. And somehow, you even managed to miss getting a concussion."

"Then why does it feel like I was kicked by a horse?" I rubbed my chin, then sighed. "Such a waste. So many people dead."

"Yeah." He ran his hand down his face, glanced over his shoulder and back. "Hey, let's get you out of here, and we can talk, okay?"

I nodded and started to stand.

The curtain was flung open with enough force to rip it from the ceiling. The nurse stood, frowning, standing behind a wheelchair. "You'll leave the building in this or nothing." Then, she made a noise in Cody's direction.

Pretty sure it was a growl.

Even better than Winifred's, though I wouldn't tell the nurse that. Or my cat.

Once I was settled in Cody's car, the front seat this time, we headed out. I glanced around, surprised that it was already dusk. "I feel like I've lost a day somewhere. Jesse must have knocked me out cold before taking me to that dark, wretched cave." Angling a glance toward Cody, I said, "I'm assuming it's still Tuesday?"

"Yep."

I attempted to make conversation on the way to my house, but that doesn't work if the other person opts out. Maybe everything was just now hitting Cody, like it was me. The difference was when I was upset, I chattered even more than usual, trying to burn off some nervous energy. But Cody... his clenched jaw, death grip on the steering wheel, and lowered eyebrows showed his opposite reaction. He was still in full-out Papa Bear mode. And for that, I was so grateful.

The ride to my house only took a few minutes, but every bump in Cody's vehicle sent a jolt of pain right through me. I'd be glad to get home and lie down. Maybe let more painkillers do their thing and get some sleep.

Cody had his arm around me as we walked to my front door. I tried to open it, but it was locked. I frowned.

Cody reached into his pocket and retrieved a set of keys. Mine. He glanced down at his hand, then back up. "Found these still in your truck."

A sudden wail, mournful, primal, and deep, caused the skin on my arms to ripple. "Winifred? Cody, hurry and open the door."

He must have been flustered, because it took two tries before he got the key in the lock. He swung the door open. An orange apparition leaped straight up and landed in my arms. Winifred kept patting my face with her paws until I had to make her stop.

"Kitty, I love you too. But maybe you could show your love without smacking my sore face."

Ignoring my request, she rubbed her face against my chin, time and time again. It must have been something she felt strongly about, so I let her do it for a minute more.

"All right," said Cody, taking Winifred and setting her on the floor. She glared at him and growled.

"Impressive noise quality," I said, "but the nurse still has her beat." Winifred's next snarl was aimed at me. She ran to the cabinet where I kept her food. "If I don't feed her, and right now, one or both of us will be missing some body parts because she'll take bites out of us and come back for seconds."

Finally placated, Winifred dove into her bowl of food, swishing her tail back and forth across the kitchen floor.

"I'd better sit down." I sighed. "Suddenly, I'm exhausted."

"I would think so." He wrapped his arm around my waist and helped me to the couch in the living room. Then, he left the room.

"Hey, where're—"

"Just a second." His voice floated in from the kitchen. Had he decided he needed a snack? Now? Maybe watching Winifred chow down had made him think he needed something, too.

I stuck a pillow behind my back and angled around so my feet were propped up on the other end. My eyes got heavy, and I nearly fell asleep, until Cody came back carrying a plate and a glass. "What-cha got there, Sheriff?"

He set them down on the coffee table. "Thought you might want to eat something."

Three peanut butter sandwiches sat on the plate. "Um, thank you. I must look starved."

His mouth curved up in a smile. "Well, one's for me."

I stared up at him and waited.

"Okay, two."

After taking a bite of the sandwich, then a sip of milk, I sighed. "It's so good to be home. I thought I might never…." I blinked, trying not to cry. It was like all the bad thoughts, fears, and emotions had been held back until right now. My throat and eyes burned.

Without a word, Cody jumped up and grabbed a box of tissues from a nearby end table. He thrust them toward me. "Here."

Nodding my thanks, I took one and dabbed my eyes. "Sorry. I—"

"Why are you sorry? You didn't do anything wrong." He picked up my feet and sat down, then placed my legs on his lap.

"Cody, you nearly got killed, trying to protect me."

"And you tackling Jesse and knocking him down helped a little. All right, a lot."

"Just glad we're both here. Safe. Relatively unscathed."

"Me too."

I took another drink of milk, then set down the glass. "Everything about this is confusing, especially since I pretty much blacked out for a good part of the day. How did you ever find me in the cave? How did you know?"

"I got a phone call from Ranger Nelson's sister. She'd been trying to reach him but had no luck. His family, who all live in Oregon, were getting very worried that they hadn't heard from him. I started to suspect Jesse might be involved somehow."

"But why would that make you suspect Jesse?"

He let out a long sigh. "Because right after the call from Ranger Nelson's sister, I got another call."

"From—"

"A couple of teenagers. They'd found Ranger Nelson. Dead. Buried in the wilderness of the park where hardly anyone ventures anymore.

I gasped, making my jaw throb again. "Oh no."

He shook his head. "I know. So awful."

"You never said anything about your thoughts on Jesse," I said.

"I wasn't one hundred percent sure. I kept an eye on him and mainly gave him the benefit of the doubt. At first. When Ranger Nelson's body was discovered, and since Millie was killed, I decided to check Jesse out. It suddenly seemed too convenient that Ranger Nelson disappeared, Jesse showed up, then Millie was killed. Something didn't add up."

I waited for him to continue, afraid of what further atrocities Jesse may have committed.

"I couldn't find any info on him being a ranger," said Cody. "Nothing.

There should have been an online footprint somewhere mentioning his name and a connection to a park or at least to the occupation. And then, a sheriff from the next county over gave me a call. He'd arrested Lonny Gibbs for drunken driving and harassing some people in a bar. Once he was behind bars, he began to talk about Jesse."

That explained why Lonny never showed up at the cave.

Cody shook his head. "I see now I should have checked Jesse out when he first arrived. But with Morton's body found in your greenhouse and dealing with that, and with Hal's accusations against you, I dropped the ball."

"It wasn't your fault, Cody."

"I will always believe I could have handled it better. But thank you for saying that." He sighed. "After hearing what Lonny had said about Jesse, I wanted to check him out further. Got a warrant to search the ranger station house. Jesse was nowhere around, which was another red flag. His truck was gone, and his desk was messy, like he'd left in a rush. One of the papers stuck near the top of the pile was a letter."

"From someone named Gibbs. I found it, too. I ended up doing some sleuthing on my own," I said.

Cody lowered his eyebrows.

"I know, that's how I nearly got myself killed."

"But thank goodness, you're okay," he said.

"Yeah, what went on in the cave was bad enough for months' worth of nightmares. But how did you know I was at the cave?"

"After I read the letter, I figured out what Jesse might be up to, then saw what looked like a struggle near the desk and your truck, keys in the ignition, parked out back. I put two and two together."

"Amazing. Maple Junction is lucky to have you as our sheriff. And I'm lucky to have you as my best friend." I fidgeted with the sandwich on my plate, wanting to change the subject to something a little cheerier. It was then I realized that Cody hadn't had anything thing to eat yet. "Gonna have a sandwich? They're pretty good. The chef did a great job." I smiled.

Cody glanced down at the food but didn't bother grabbing a sandwich for himself. So unlike him.

"Cody? Are you—"

"It's surreal."

"What is? The cave and everything that happened there?" I asked.

"That and…." He leveled his eyes right at mine. "Seneca, that's the first time I've ever actually killed someone."

How terrible. I couldn't imagine having to do that to anyone, ever. "Oh, honey, I didn't even think of that." Reaching out, I clasped his hand.

"Don't get me wrong. I'm not sorry. I mean, I had no choice. And I'd do it again."

My eyes teared up. "You saved my life."

He squeezed my hand back. I could see a sheen of tears in his eyes, as well. "What are friends for?"

# Chapter Thirty-Four

The day of the auction for Hal's property was sunny and bright. Monarchs swirled around me as if giving me their good thoughts, wishing me the best. What were my chances of getting Hal's land? Since Hal had died and hadn't left a will, the state had the property and buildings up for sale.

I checked on the caterpillars in the greenhouse while I still had a little time before the auction began. A thud, like something had fallen against the outside of the greenhouse, caught my attention. Had someone from the auction wandered over to my property by mistake?

I hurried outside and jogged around the building. When I rounded the corner to the back, I saw Lorna. As Evie had described her before, Lorna was crouched down on the ground a few feet away from the building.

"Lorna? What are you doing?"

She gasped and turned, then awkwardly stood. "Um...Seneca...I...."

I walked closer. Now that I knew she hadn't killed Mr. Morton, I wasn't afraid she was violent, or that she'd try to do something to me. But my cat-like curiosity had to know why she was hanging around back here. "Can I help you, Lorna? Have you lost something?"

She swallowed, then grabbed a tissue from her pants pocket. "Oh yes. I've lost something, all right. But it's nothing you can help me find."

As I stepped closer, I saw tears shimmering in her eyes. "Are you hurt?"

She pressed her hand against her chest. "Just inside."

Knowing of her feelings for Mr. Morton, I was sure it had something to do with him. "This is where Mr. Morton was killed."

"Yes." She hung her head.

"And you... cared for him?"

She blinked and stared at me. "How did you know?"

I held up my hand. "Nothing bad. I just heard someone say you had feelings for him."

"It was more than that. I dearly loved Herman Morton. He said he'd only dated me because his parents insisted it was time he got married and that he'd never actually cared for me. Even though he ended it between us and broke my heart, I couldn't stop loving him."

I pointed to the ground at her feet. "And you came here to pay your respects?"

She dabbed her eyes with the tissue. "That's right." Her eyes grew large. "Oh, I never... I mean, I guess I should have asked your permission to be back here."

Taking a chance that her normally catty behavior was on hold for the time being, I touched her arm lightly. "Don't give it another thought. You can come back here to pay your respects any time you like. All right?"

A tiny smile tugged at her lips. "All right. Thank you, Seneca."

I smiled back. "You're welcome." I pointed behind me. "I need to head to Hal's now. For the auction."

"Oh, that's right. I hear you'd like to buy his property."

"Yes. Very much."

"Then I wish you luck," she said.

With a wave goodbye, I left Lorna to her mourning and headed toward Hal's.

There were quite a few people at the auction. I wasn't sure if the others were hopeful buyers or just nosy. Most likely, the latter. Couldn't really blame them. The events of the last few weeks had been more eye-opening and exciting than anything since Philly's romp in the fountain.

And no one had wanted their eyes opened for that.

It warmed my heart that several of my friends had shown up for support. Evie, Murray, Betty, and Linda smiled at me from a grouping of lawn chairs. Even Sid and Norman stood a few yards away, waving happily at me as if they'd never thought I was some sort of serial killer. Annie wanted to be here but was at the moment signing papers to attend medical school. A court had awarded Dana her rightful inheritance after Herman's death. Annie could now afford to attend.

A pang struck my chest. Millie should have been here, too. How terrible for her friends that she was gone. I would miss her. We'd gone ahead and had a butterfly release ceremony for her after all. I think she would have liked that.

I recognized the auctioneer as someone from the next county. She was around sixty, tall and lean, with a ferocious, take-no-prisoners expression. However, the few times I'd spoken with her, I'd found her to be friendly and approachable. Maybe, being a woman in a male-dominated field, she felt the need to overcompensate her toughness.

Several neighbors had called this morning, asking if they could park in my drive since I lived right next to Hal's land. Though I'd agreed, I secretly hoped they were only here out of curiosity. Because I really needed that land.

Hal's vehicles, plus the contents of his garage and outbuildings, were auctioned off first. Then, the furniture and contents of the inside of his house. I had no interest in any of that. No, my eye was on the prize at the end.

The land. The milkweed. Security for the growth of the monarchs. My future.

Auctioning off the preceding items took longer than I expected. Tired of standing near the front, waiting for what I'd come for, I wandered back to stand closer to Hal's barn.

"Anything happen yet?"

I turned and smiled at Cody. "Not yet. Good grief, these things are slow."

He checked his watch. "It only started an hour ago. You're just impatient."

Opening my mouth to disagree, I reconsidered, then closed it. He was right. But didn't I have cause? For years, I'd assumed the land would be sold directly to me, because Hal had promised. Then Hal had gone off the deep end, trying to destroy my milkweed and butterflies. Four murders later, things were still uncertain. Add to that being considered a suspect, getting kidnapped and almost killed, Cody risking his life to save mine, and I still didn't have the property I'd assumed would be a slam dunk to purchase.

"I'm sure it will be soon," he said. "Looks like they're coming to the end of the house's contents."

I watched as several people raised their hands, bidding on various items the auctioneer pointed out. Betty bid on a dresser and Linda on a table lamp. Barely able to contain myself, I said, "If I get Hal's property, the first thing I'm going to do is increase the milkweed."

With a frown, Cody said, "Seems like there's already a lot there. You need more?"

"I need tons more. Haven't you been listening to me all this time?" I elbowed him in the ribs, but not hard.

"Oh yeah. I've heard it all." He rolled his eyes. "Over and over."

"Be nice," I said, but I couldn't keep the excited smile from my face. "Anyway, the more milkweed for the caterpillars, the more of them will turn into monarchs, and I'll have a bigger operation and make more profit from the ones I sell, and then there's always—"

"Take a breath, will ya?" He angled left to look over my head. "I don't see a doctor around anywhere if you pass out."

"Like you don't know CPR as a sheriff. Don't you have to take refresher courses? Besides, you've taught the class before. I took it once." It was so good to be kidding around with him again. After all the recent events, I'd missed that. Missed just hanging out with him.

He shrugged. "Sure. And I'd have every intention of giving you mouth-to-mouth to save you…"

"But?" I raised my eyebrows nearly to my hairline.

He darted his eyes away and down, like he was embarrassed to even be seen talking to me. "I'm afraid people might think I was just making a pass at you, trying to kiss you. Wouldn't that give the gossips lots of ammunition for something else to spread around? Don't they have enough fodder already?"

"I can't believe you used the word fodder in a sentence. Correctly." I clapped. "Yay for you."

"So, as you can see, Seneca, saving you if you lost consciousness might not be the best idea."

My mouth dropped open in mock horror. "You would sacrifice me, your friend, let me perish because of what someone might think?"

Cody pursed his lips and lowered his eyebrows. "Now that you say it that way…"

Again, I aimed my elbow at his ribs. This time, not gently.

"Ow."

"Be nice, and I won't have to do it again," I warned.

"Hey." He caught my hand, nodding his head toward the group of people. "Look. I think the auctioneer is ready to do the land. Come on." He yanked me nearly from my feet and propelled me to a spot right in front of the live-action. With slight pressure, he gave me a little push, encouraging me to get as close as I could.

The auctioneer saw me and gave me a little wave. I smiled back. "Now," she said, "the sales are final for the contents of the house, of the garage, of the outbuildings, and the vehicles. On to the acreage and buildings."

Standing on my toes, as if I could see better though I was in the front row, excitement quivered through me.

The starting price was stated by the auctioneer. It was much lower than what Hal and I had originally agreed the selling price would be. I quickly stuck my hand in the air, waving my small, numbered sign on a stick.

"We have one bid," she said. "Anyone else?" The woman frowned, like she was disappointed, but I'd told her how important it was to me to buy the land. She'd said she hoped I got it. "No other bidders?"

Though I was afraid of what I might see, that someone, or several someones, might have decided to bid, lift their signs in the air, when I got brave enough to check, there was no one. No signs. No waving hands. No excited chatter that one of them planned to get in on the action. Just smiles from Murray and Evie.

"Well, Seneca James," said the auctioneer. "You are now the proud owner of the land adjacent to your own. Congratulations."

People behind me clapped. I turned, seeing all the smiling faces, the well wishes, the neighbors I'd known all my life. Without thinking, I gave a happy yelp and leaped in the air, putting my arms around Cody's neck. With a loud *oof*, he caught me, wrapping his arms around my waist. We were eye to eye, our lips so close I could feel his warm breath caress mine.

Several people clapped again, some chuckled.

I let out a gasp. What was I doing? Jumping on my best friend like that with half the town gawking at us?

As I slid down to the ground, I glanced at Cody, whose face had gone a deep red. Mine heated in response. The last time my lips had been that close to a man's, I'd been married. Part of me felt like I'd nearly smooched my brother. But another part? Definitely not a brotherly feeling. So confusing.

Talk about more fodder for the local gossips.

I gave Cody a smile and shrug as I took a step back. Maybe if I didn't make a big deal of it, he wouldn't either. He still seemed to be in shock. Eyes wide and unblinking.

Footsteps came from my right, and I turned.

"Seneca." The auctioneer handed me an envelope. "At your convenience—" she gave a glance to Cody and back to me "—go see Mrs. Ames seated up near the barn to make your payment arrangements."

"Thanks." I took the envelope, hoping my face wasn't red. Cody's had lessened to an attractive pink, though I wouldn't tell him that.

Maybe he was still embarrassed at my reaction to buying the land. I'd caught him off guard. Surprised myself, too, by jumping in his arms. Or had the stress from the past few weeks, combined with the elation of getting something I'd wanted for so long, given way to me doing something out of character?

Finally, he blinked and seemed to relax. His one-sided smile told me he would recover from the shock of me nearly kissing him. "Guess it's good I didn't have to give you mouth-to-mouth after all."

Leave it to my best friend to make me laugh. "Yeah, the bystanders wouldn't be able to handle the fodder."

Relieved he and I seemed to be okay, I turned and accepted hugs and congratulations from friends who crowded around us. Evie eyed me, then

Cody, then me again. With her eyebrows raised, she made the call me sign with her hand. Uh oh. She thought there was more to the situation than there was.

I must have been with my friends too long because the auctioneer came over, giving me a tap on the shoulder, smiling, and tilting her head toward where the treasurer was set up. I rushed over to settle up my purchase. Before I knew it, papers were signed, bank information traded, and a future meeting to finalize payments was made.

As I headed back toward the group, I watched as Cody chatted with Murray and the women. For some reason, Cody looked different today. Even more handsome than before. Was it because of what had just happened? Or maybe it was more?

Maybe it was nearly losing him in that cave. As if he knew my thoughts, he glanced at me and smiled. Truth was, we'd nearly lost each other that day. Would that change our relationship? Time would tell. Throughout the rest of the day, I found myself thinking about our near kiss. What would have happened if I'd really kissed him? I'd always said I didn't want to mess up our friendship by making our relationship more, but part of me, a really big part, would love to find out.

# About the Author

Ruth J. Hartman spends her days herding cats and her nights spinning mysterious tales. She, her husband, and their cats love to spend time curled up in their recliners watching old Cary Grant movies. Well, the cats sit in the people's recliners. Not that the cats couldn't get their own furniture. They just choose to shed on someone else's.

Ruth, a left-handed, cat-herding, farmhouse-dwelling writer uses her sense of humor as she writes tales of lovable, klutzy women who seem to find trouble without even trying.

Ruth's husband and best friend, Garry, reads her manuscripts, rolls his eyes at her weird story ideas, and loves her despite her insistence all of her books have at least one cat in them. See updates about her cozy mysteries at Ruthjhartman.com.

SOCIAL MEDIA HANDLES:
   https://www.facebook.com/ruth.j.hartman
   https://www.facebook.com/profile.php?id=100063631596817
   https://www.bookbub.com/profile/ruth-j-hartman

AUTHOR WEBSITE:

www.ruthjhartman.com

# Also by Ruth J. Hartman

The Kitty Beret Café Mystery Series

*Dial M for Meow* (Book 1 of the Bookshop Kitties Mysteries)

*Brushed Up on Murder* (Book 1 of the Mobile Cat Groomer Mysteries)

*Ring of Death* (A Dorey Cameron Mystery)

Printed in the USA
CPSIA information can be obtained
at www.ICGtesting.com
LVHW042338241123
764834LV00007B/58